"Why did y[...]

Dave snorted. "[...] to stay." His brows pushed down over his forehead as he stared at her chest. "Is that my T-shirt you're wearing?" he asked, his voice low, gravelly.

Nicole tipped her head back. "I found it in a drawer."

"Give it back."

"Fine." She reached for the hem and dragged it up over her head and tossed it into his face. She moved past him, naked, her head held high.

His eyes widened, the dark brown turning almost black. He reached out and grasped her arms. "Put the damn shirt on," he said through gritted teeth.

Nicole attempted to pull her arm free, her jaw tight, her body cool in the night air. She was beginning to regret her rash decision to strip in front of the man. He held her steady, refusing to release his grip.

The heat his body gave off did nothing to smooth the chill bumps rising on her skin, which had nothing to do with the cold and everything to do with the animal attraction this man exuded....

Dear Reader,

I love coming back to Cape Churn and revisiting my characters from previous books. In *Deadly Allure* we get to see Nicole "Tazer" Steele's story unfold. I looked around for a man for her in Cape Churn and almost didn't find him. Then off-the-fishing-dock Dave Logsdon appeared from an earlier book, *Deadly Engagement*.

In my mind he reminded me of Captain Ron from an old movie I'd watched—a reprobate who could care less about what anyone else had to say. It was great getting into his head and learning what had caused him to leave the military and have such a jaundiced view of the world and people. Pairing him with the ultra-intense Nicole "Tazer" Steele, I knew sparks would fly.

In *Deadly Allure*, we have all the excitement and danger of the first three Devil's Shroud books and more. We follow Dave and Tazer on a dangerous mission that leads all the way to treachery in the White House.

Here's another tidbit for you. Nicole "Tazer" Steele can be found in other books I've written. Look for her in the following Harlequin Intrigue titles: *Nick of Time*, *Alaskan Fantasy* and *Blown Away*.

Enjoy the journey!

Elle James

DEADLY ALLURE

Elle James

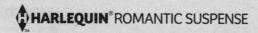

HARLEQUIN® ROMANTIC SUSPENSE

Recycling programs
for this product may
not exist in your area.

ISBN-13: 978-0-373-27882-4

DEADLY ALLURE

Copyright © 2014 by Mary Jernigan

Printed in U.S.A.

www.Harlequin.com

Books by Elle James

Harlequin Romantic Suspense

Deadly Reckoning #1698
Deadly Engagement #1785
Deadly Liaisons #1797
**Secret Service Rescue* #1808
Deadly Allure #1812

*Triggered #1433
*Taking Aim #1439
*Bodyguard Under Fire #1446
*Cowboy Resurrected #1451

*Covert Cowboys, Inc.
**The Adair Legacy

Harlequin Intrigue

Dakota Meltdown #938
Lakota Baby #961
Cowboy Sanctuary #987
Blown Away #1014
Alaskan Fantasy #1033
Texas-Sized Secrets #1052
Under Suspicion, With Child #1080
Nick of Time #1100
Baby Bling #1127
An Unexpected Clue #1156
Operation XOXO #1172
Killer Body #1191
Bundle of Trouble #1226
Hostage to Thunder Horse #1244
Cowboy Brigade #1281
Engaged with the Boss #1306
Thunder Horse Heritage #1357
Thunder Horse Redemption #1382

ELLE JAMES

A Golden Heart Award winner for Best Paranormal Romance in 2004, Elle James started writing when her sister issued a Y2K challenge to write a romance novel. She has managed a full-time job and raised three wonderful children, and she and her husband even tried their hands at ranching exotic birds (ostriches, emus and rheas) in the Texas Hill Country. Ask her, and she'll tell you what it's like to go toe-to-toe with an angry 350-pound bird! After leaving her successful career in information technology management, Elle is now pursuing her writing full-time. Elle loves to hear from fans. You can contact her at ellejames@earthlink.net, or visit her website, at www.ellejames.com.

This book is dedicated to my editor,
Dana Hamilton, who has been with me for most
of this series, dotting my i's, crossing my t's, fixing
my grammatical errors and encouraging me to
be a better writer through her gentle editing and
suggestions. She's my cheerleader and coach,
and a joy to work with. Thank you, Dana,
for being there for me!

(Now could you please perform your magic on
this dedication to make sure I didn't make a
grammatical faux pas?) Hugs!

Chapter 1

Nicole Steele, "Tazer" to those who knew how lethal she could be, slipped through the loading docks entry of the corporate headquarters of Ryan Technologies. Dressed in the white coverall and cap of the Acme Cleaning Services' staff, she blended in with others coming on to the night shift to clean the multistoried building.

Once inside, she claimed a cleaning cart and followed the other janitors to the service elevators. At 2200 hours she didn't expect many of the executives to be in their offices, most having gone home or out for drinks by now.

The three other contracted cleaners who entered the elevator car with her talked about their kids, sports and the price of gasoline. Nicole kept her head down, aware of the camera located in the upper corner, above the control panel.

A rounded woman with brassy orange hair, her gray roots showing, smacked her gum. "New at Acme?"

"Yeah." Nicole kept her answer short, abrupt, not inviting further conversation.

Undaunted, the woman prompted, "Got kids?"

"No."

"Guess that's why you can still find your hips."

Nicole shrugged without responding.

"I used to have a figure. Four brats ago." The woman snorted. "Now I figure life's too short to pass up a piece of apple pie and ice cream."

The others laughed and the car stopped on the seventh floor.

"Well, this is my floor. Have a good night." The brassy-haired janitor left the elevator and Nicole breathed a sigh.

Another stop on the tenth floor and again on the twelfth left Nicole blissfully alone. She rode the elevator up to the twentieth floor, two floors short of her target, Brandon Ryan's office. She'd take the stairs the rest of the way.

Having studied the building schematics and the security system camera points, she was prepared. As soon as she left the elevator, she rolled her cart to the door nearest the east stairwell, closest to the security camera for the floor. Digging her hand into her pocket, she unearthed the miniature can of black spray paint, ducked under the camera and sprayed the lens until it was completely covered in one short burst of paint, then checked her watch.

Ten after ten. She had exactly fifteen minutes to get into Ryan's office, download the data and get out. Another five minutes to leave the building and this operation would be complete. Short, sweet, uneventful. That's the way she liked it.

Nicole stepped into the stairwell, raised her hand to spray the camera in the corner and climbed the steps two at a time to the floor above. She blacked out the camera there and moved up to the next floor. Once on the top floor, she disabled the security camera and hurried to Brandon Ryan's spacious office, paid for by taxpayer dollars meant to be used to supply guns to the military. It was the potential other deals he was making with the opposing forces in the Middle East that had landed her there.

As a member of the Stealth Operations Specialists, Nicole was part of a very small force of secret agents called on by the President of the United States to handle situations neither the FBI nor the CIA could handle. Sensitive cases that only a handful of people knew about.

Her boss, Royce Fontaine, had prepared her for this mission; given her the equipment and knowledge that would get her inside and to the computer Ryan used to store the top secret data concerning his organization's dealings.

Intel from SOS operatives in the Middle East had informed Royce the Taliban had new guns that looked suspiciously like those supplied to the U.S. military.

Nicole's job was to ferret out the information necessary to determine whether the Taliban had stolen the weapons or if Brandon Ryan was supplying them to the opium-rich leaders of the terrorist organization.

She'd spent the past two weeks schmoozing with Ryan, playing the pampered debutante to get closer to the renowned womanizer so that she could get a tour of his office and see the security layout in person. She'd gotten that and more—a copy of his key card and a viable fingerprint she'd had imprinted on the thumb glove. Now she was putting her groundwork to use.

With security disabled, she moved quickly toward Brandon Ryan's office where she paused to slip a rubber glove over her thumb, the glove imprinted with Ryan's thumbprint. She ran the key card Geek had supplied her with and touched her gloved thumb on the scanner.

For a long moment she held her breath. Either the door would unlock or alarms would go off, alerting the security guards on duty to the presence of an intruder in the boss's office.

A soft click sounded. Nicole twisted the door handle and the door opened into a lushly appointed outer office with a beautiful mahogany desk blocking entrance to Ryan's inner office. His executive assistant, having long since gone home for the night, had been a pretty but determined young woman with a glare that could sear scars into a person's skin. Nicole hadn't given her more than a cursory glance down the straight length of her nose. Being a socialite had meant disregarding the peons surrounding Ryan.

Though she'd pretended to ignore the executive assistant, she'd been very aware of the woman and her position as the last line of defense against intruders into the great Brandon Ryan's inner sanctum.

Once inside his office, she pulled the door shut, leaving it cracked open enough so she could hear movement in the outer office. Then she eased into the plush leather chair behind Ryan's massive mahogany desk. As big as the expensive piece of furniture was, it didn't begin to fill the roomy office with the floor-to-ceiling windows overlooking the sparkling lights of the Los Angeles skyline. Armed with a flashlight, she pulled out the sliding keyboard tray, stuck a flash drive in the side of the sleek combined video display monitor and CPU and went to work decoding the encrypted password. Geek, back at SOS headquarters, had been adamant. "All you have to do is plug it in. It'll crack the password within minutes."

As soon as she plugged in the flash drive, the monitor blinked to life, lighting the room. She pressed the button on the side to turn off the display, returning the room to near darkness, her vision taking a moment to adjust.

Nicole worried she might not have minutes. If the regularly scheduled cleaning lady happened by the office, she'd either be caught red-handed or have to find a place to hide until she left.

While the password hacking module worked its magic, Nicole pulled the drawers open, searching for anything that looked like evidence Ryan was sleeping with the enemy. His desk was clean, the drawers only containing designer pens and extra golf balls.

She rose from the seat, the leather so soft it barely made a sound. A bar in one corner had a cabinet below it. She checked the contents, finding only additional bottles of the best booze money could buy. The man was cocky and insanely rich. Too bad he was a lying bastard who betrayed his country. If he was selling guns to the enemy, Ryan was personally responsible for the deaths of American soldiers. His own countrymen, fighting for *his* freedom. He was just the kind of high-powered sleazebag Nicole liked to bring down.

Just like Rodney, her former lover who'd pilfered her access card, broken into the FBI data center, stolen secrets he'd had no right to take and ruined her reputation with the Bureau. She'd been placed on administrative leave during the investigation, but had resigned before they could fire her.

Young and naive, she'd believed Rodney loved her, when all the time he'd been using her to get to FBI data that would potentially compromise hundreds of undercover agents.

The horror of what she'd done stuck with her and would never go away. Since then, she'd refused to believe any man, no matter how true he might appear. She even kept her teammates at arm's length, preferring to distance herself than to trust her instincts, which had proved faulty in the worst possible way.

Nicole straightened and ran her hand over the beautiful crystal decanters containing alcohol Ryan had served her on her last visit. She'd pretended to drink, letting him run his hands over her silk dress. To a point. Then she'd laughed and stepped away, flirting with him enough to gain a moderate level of trust.

She snorted softly. Men could be so pathetically predictable.

A sound from the front office alerted her to someone else's presence.

Nicole shot a glance at the video monitor, still dark, the soft whir of the building's central air the only sound in an otherwise quiet office.

The outer office door closed with a sharp click.

Nicole dove for a closet, sliding in behind one of Ryan's spare suits hanging beside a crisply starched white shirt.

Lights blinked on, filtering through the gap she'd left in the door to allow her to peer out. Her hand went to the lipstick tube of pepper spray she'd placed in her pocket before starting out on her mission.

The carpet muffled any footsteps as Nicole strained to hear or to see the progress of the person in Ryan's office. Then she saw a man in a suit pass by. *Crap.* If he noticed the miniature flash drive poking out of the side of his monitor, he could disrupt the password hacking module and the download. That would make him aware that he might not be alone in the room.

Nicole held her breath, waiting for any indication of discovery.

The buzzing sound of a cell phone rang out in the silence.

"Ryan," he answered. After a moment he said, "I know. I'm here to download the data now. Yes, I understand how important it is."

While Ryan talked on the phone, Nicole eased the zipper down on her coveralls and slipped the garment over her shoulders, letting it drop around her ankles. She stepped out of it and smoothed her hands over the snug-fitting, black leather pants that molded to her body and the low-cut leather corset she'd worn beneath the coveralls. Pushing the hat from her head, she fluffed her hair and peered around the closet door at the man seated at his desk, his back to the monitor, and staring out the windows.

"Nobody will trace back to you. I guarantee it." He paused again. "I know the consequences," he said, his voice tight, strained.

Nicole eased out of the closet and crossed the floor. The man glanced up at that moment, catching her movement reflected off the darkened windows. Her gaze met Ryan's and she gave him a sensual smile and a wink.

Ryan spun in his chair, his hand still holding the phone to his ear. "Look, I have to go." He hit the end button and pushed to his feet. "What the hell are you doing in here? This room is off-limits."

Nicole shrugged, her breasts pushed higher in the corset, the effect almost working on Ryan. For a moment his gaze shifted to the rounded swells, then his jaw tightened and he glared at her. "How the hell did you get in here?"

She crossed the room to him. "The door was unlocked." Her brows rose, begging him to argue the point. "I'd hoped to find you here." Her hand curled around the lipstick tube of pepper spray. All she had to do was to get close enough to spray him in the eyes. He'd be effectively incapacitated.

"You shouldn't be here." He reached for the phone on his desk at the same time she raised the pepper spray and shot him dead on in the face.

Ryan screamed and grabbed for his eyes. "You bitch!" He staggered backward, tripped over his chair and landed on his back.

Nicole pulled a zip tie out of her back pocket, planted a foot on his side, rolled him onto his belly, and yanked his wrist behind his back, pushing it up between his shoulder blades.

"You won't get away with this. Argh! Why'd you have to use pepper spray? It's burning my eyes."

"Don't worry. It won't leave a scar on your lying, cheating face." With her knee in his back, she dragged his other arm up and secured the wrists together behind his back. Then with smooth precision, she secured his ankles with another zip tie. A soft ping indicated the password hacker had done its duty and the download had begun.

"What are you doing?" he demanded. "You're trespassing in my office. I could have you arrested and thrown in jail."

"Yeah, if you could get up." She sat behind his desk, switched on the monitor and checked the status of the downloading software. The status bar indicated already 40 percent complete. Just a little longer.

"You don't know what you're doing."

"Oh, I think I do," she said.

"The people I work for won't let you get away with this."

"They won't have a choice, now, will they?"

"They'll come after you. Kill you." He struggled against the bindings. "Damn, this is burning my eyes!"

"It'll only last a couple hours."

"You can't leave me like this."

"Oh, I think I can."

"You'll never get out of the building."

"Wanna bet?" The progress bar indicated 88 percent complete. *Hurry, damn it.*

"Any data on that computer is proprietary and fully encrypted. It'll do you no good."

"We'll see."

"Help!" Ryan yelled.

Great. With a calm she wasn't exactly feeling, she pulled the tight roll of duct tape from her pocket, unrolled it and bent to slap it over Ryan's mouth. "There, now. Let's not disturb the cleaning staff. They have enough filth to clean."

He grunted and jerked, trying to tear into her.

Nicole glanced at the monitor. The status bar filled

and disappeared, displaying the message Download Complete.

Now the fun began. With Ryan trussed up like the pig he was, it wouldn't be long before the security staff got smart.

Tucking the flash drive in the pocket of her black pants, she nudged Ryan with her toe. "I'll be seeing you in court."

The man grunted and rolled toward her in an attempt to stop her.

She grabbed the white coverall, slipped her legs inside, crammed her hair into a messy bun and shoved it into the cap. She grabbed a straight-back chair from the front office and dragged it into Ryan's office. Leaning it against the back of the door, she then exited the outer door of Ryan's office, the chair leaning against the back of the door dropping to the floor behind it. She tried to open the door, but the chair legs dug into the carpet on the other side, jamming it. It would take time to get to Brandon Ryan. The time she'd need to get out of the building.

As she stepped into the hallway, the elevator car dinged. Before the door could slide open, Nicole ran for the fire alarm and jerked the handle down, setting off a screeching alarm and blinking lights marking the exits.

Two security guards leaped out of the elevator car and pulled guns on her. "Halt!"

"Oh, thank God!" She dropped to her knees on the hallway floor. "Mr. Ryan is in his office. There's something wrong with him. I didn't know what to do. Please help him. Please. And hurry."

The two guards ran past her and through the open outer office door. As soon as they were through, Nicole rose to her feet, pulled a pocketknife out of her pocket, closed the outer door and stabbed the keyboard. Wires shorted out and sparks flew.

Wasting no more time, she ran to the stairwell and down all twenty-two floors of the building to the ground level and exited into the service area.

The night shift evacuated the building, all talking at once about the fire alarm. Nicole blended in with the Acme Cleaning Services' staff and left through the rear dock entrance. Once she cleared the building, she broke off from the rest, ducked behind a large trash container and waited until the others moved far enough away that they wouldn't notice when she headed the opposite direction.

A block away, she'd stashed a motorcycle behind a stack of empty pallets. Stripping out of the coveralls, she tossed them to the side, climbed on the motorcycle and drove away.

Three fire engines and a ladder truck passed her on their way toward Ryan Technologies.

Nicole kept going all the way out of the city, past the high-rises and big business of L.A., the six-lane freeways less crowded now than during the daytime. Eventually she passed through the suburbs, continuing north to Santa Clarita where she would rendezvous with the SOS plane and settle back for the long flight to D.C.

As she neared the small airport, a police car pulled in behind her, lights flashing. A cold feeling washed over her. She hadn't been speeding and she'd followed all the rules of the highway, determined to fly under the radar of local police. No one but the folks at SOS knew where she'd go after the heist at Ryan Technologies.

Slowing, she debated pulling over and going through

the motions of a routine traffic stop, but instinct told her, as late as it was, and after breaking and entering a building in L.A., there was nothing routine about this stop.

As she neared the turn to the airport, she noted at least a half dozen police cars, lights strobing the night sky. Nicole revved the engine and peeled out, taking the motorcycle across a median, down into a ditch and onto another road that would lead her out of town. As soon as she lost the police car, she pulled around to the back of a deserted storage building, heart racing and dread filling her gut like poison.

She fished out her cell phone and dialed Royce Fontaine's number. It rang five times before voice mail picked up.

Nicole frowned. Fontaine should have picked up on the first ring. Hell, he was expecting her report as soon as she reached the airport. He wouldn't have deserted her when they stood a chance of nailing Ryan.

She dialed Geek, who should have been in the computer lab following her every move via the GPS. Again, no answer.

Sirens blared on the road behind her. Three police cars converged on her from two different directions. She gunned the engine, hopped over a sidewalk and sped down a quiet residential street to burst out on the main road. How had they found her so soon?

For a moment she thought she'd shaken them. Then at the end of the alley another police car appeared. It was as if they knew where she'd be before she got there, as if they were tracking her.

Nicole left the road, drove down a steep embankment and up to the other side, crossed a wide-open field and headed into a wooded area. She didn't slow until she was completely surrounded by trees.

As close as the police had come, they had to be tracking her. Nicole stopped long enough to ditch her cell phone, the only tracking device she had on her. Somehow her position had been compromised. With Fontaine and Geek offline, the entire operation could have been compromised. Her best bet was to get as far away from L.A. and her cell phone as possible and lay low until things died down and she could contact her boss.

She knew of only one place far enough off the grid she could hide where she could keep in contact with other members of the close-knit SOS team.

Having ditched her cell phone, she drove out of Santa Clarita and headed north toward Oregon and Cape Churn. The legendary Devil's Shroud that could hide the rocks jutting out of the ocean from view of passing ships would be a great place to disappear to until she could decrypt the data she'd stolen from Ryan Technologies. Now all she had to do was to survive the more than nine-hundred-mile trip and avoid all members of the law-enforcement community.

Chapter 2

Dave Logsdon slowed for a four-way stop. The fog had drifted in off the sea, blanketing the shoreline, homes and roads of Cape Churn, discouraging the residents from getting out. They called it the Devil's Shroud. When it settled over the town, everyone hunkered down and waited until it cleared. Only the naive or desperate went out on nights such as this.

Unfortunately, Dave had been in Portland to purchase additional supplies for the old yacht he'd been refurbishing. He rarely took a day off from his fishing and dive boat business until the end of the summer season when business slacked off. Today had been the first day in a month he hadn't had a booking. If he hadn't had to wait in line for the guy behind the paint counter to get to him, he'd have been back at least an hour earlier, before the fog settled in over the coast. Instead he'd been stuck in Portland rush hour, behind thousands of other motorists trying to get home from their day jobs.

No sooner had he crossed the mountains, he'd run into the first signs of fog formed by warm air over the cool Pacific Ocean, the resulting formation of ground-hugging clouds pushed inland by a slight breeze.

About the time he pulled into the intersection, he received a text from Sal and Olie. The marina owners asked him to pick up a loaf of bread on his way through town.

He smiled and increased his speed, his thoughts on the only grocery in Cape Churn, hoping it was still open. He didn't mind stopping for the Olanders. They were a nice, older husband and wife who'd taken him in as though he was the son they'd never had. He got a chuckle out of their nicknames. Olie, he understood, was short for Olaf. But how you got Sal out of Gladys was a mystery. But they loved each other and were very special to him.

Out of the corner of his eye, something moved in the mist. The next thing he knew a speeding motor-cyclist burst through the fog, turned sharply in an attempt to avoid hitting him, slammed into the truck and lost control.

Dave hit his brakes.

The motorcycle slid in front of the truck and the rider tumbled into the ditch.

Dave shoved the shift into Park and left the truck in the middle of the intersection, hoping to keep other traffic from running over the cycle or the rider. He dropped down and ran to the ditch.

A black-clad body lay facedown, groaning in his helmet.

"Hey, buddy, are you all right?" Dave asked, kneeling and touching a hand to his shoulder.

In a flash of movement the biker rolled onto his back, grabbed Dave's wrist, planted a foot in his chest and launched him into the air.

Performing a perfect head over heels, Dave landed flat on his back, the wind knocked from his lungs.

The helmeted rider stood over him, a lipstick tube held out in front of him.

"What the hell?" Dave tried to get up, but the cyclist planted a booted foot on top of his gut.

Anger surged and, with it, all the combat training he'd acquired while serving in the Army Special Forces.

His arm shot out, grabbed the ankle of his leather-clad attacker and yanked him off his feet.

He landed beside Dave on his back, the helmet bouncing off the dirt.

Dave rolled over and pinned the rider to the ground, arms trapped at his sides. "I should have left you in the ditch," he grumbled.

"Then why didn't you?"

The voice coming from behind the helmet's face shield didn't sound much like a man's voice, though he was tall and slight. "Damn."

With his knees clamping his assailant's arms against his body, Dave unbuckled the helmet and shoved it up and off.

Long, straight, silky blond hair spilled out onto the ground and angry blue eyes flashed up at him, sparkling in the beam from his truck's headlights. He'd been bested by a woman. His buddies back on active duty would have gotten a good laugh out of that.

Dave glared down at her, recognizing something familiar about her, something to do with her and two of her teammates nabbing a bad guy a couple months' back right there in Cape Churn.

"Don't I know you? Nicole Steele, right? Your friends call you Tazer." If he remembered correctly, she had the body and face of a runway model.

"Give the guy a prize. And you're the fish boy from the Cape Churn Marina. Sorry if I don't recall your name." She rocked beneath him, wrinkling her nose, looking not in the least sorry about forgetting his name. She arched her back, pressing her breasts against him. "Get off me."

"I will." He couldn't help his body's natural reaction to this beautiful woman's breasts rubbing against his chest or the way her pelvis rose with each attempt to unseat him. "I'll let you up as soon as you promise not to throw me again."

She seemed to think about it, finally saying, "I promise. Now move." Her words were strained, tight and insolent.

To Dave, her whole attitude proved to be more of a red cape flung in the face of a bull.

Her last visit to Cape Churn she had been aloof, distant to everyone and completely unruffled by the terrorist threatening the small town.

She'd also given him one brief glance and then treated him as if he were a pesky fly to be shooed away. Her whole attitude had rubbed him the wrong way. He'd blown it off, knowing she wouldn't be around long. But here she was, back in *his* town. Lying beneath *his* body.

Interesting.

Now that he knew she wasn't a threat, he wasn't as eager to let her go. Especially since he wasn't entirely sure she'd keep her promise. Dave smiled down into her angry face.

"I promised," she reminded him. "You can move."

He chuckled. "I don't know. I'm thinking I need to check you over…for injuries, of course."

"I can take care of myself," she insisted.

He eased to the side, his hands sliding across her arms. "You could have a broken bone."

She slapped his hand away. "I think I could tell if I had a broken bone. I'd feel the pain. And right now the only pain I'm feeling is the pain in my neck. And that's you." She shoved him back and tried to stand.

As soon as she did, her face blanched. She swayed and would have fallen had Dave not risen with her and grabbed her on her way down.

He scooped her up in his arms. "All kidding aside, you need to see a doctor."

"No!" She fought, her feet kicking out. She almost kneed him in the face.

Dave grunted, struggling to keep his grip. "Really, you took a pretty significant spill. You might have a concussion."

"No hospitals, no police… Can't trust…" Her eyes rolled back and she passed out. From a wiggling, spitting she-cat to a deadweight, she lay in his arms, her body completely limp.

Great. Now what was he supposed to do with her?

He loaded her into the passenger seat of his truck and went to stash her motorcycle behind a bush on the side of the road until he could get back to pick it up. First, he had to get Nicole Steele some medical attention. He punched a number on his cell phone and waited.

"Emma?"

"Dave, is that you?" Emma's voice sounded concerned. "Everything okay?"

"I don't know. Where are you?"

"At the Seaside Café with friends. What do you need?"

"Meet me at my boat at the marina ASAP."

"Dave, what's going on?" she asked.

"Just meet me there and I'll explain." He clicked the phone off, shifted his truck into Drive and hurried to the marina, his safe haven. The one place he felt at home. Hopefully, once Emma got there, she'd talk sense into this woman and get her to see a doctor.

He glanced down at her still body, sprawled out across the bench seat of his old truck. For the first time since he'd known her, she appeared vulnerable, not the kick-ass female that looked like a model but could knock the stuffing out of any guy who thought she was a cream puff. Hadn't she just kicked his butt?

Then why was every protective instinct in him coming to life? The woman obviously didn't want his help, though she needed it, considering she was out cold. Wasn't she?

Dave pressed two fingers to the base of her throat and held his breath, waiting for the thump of blood passing through her veins. He let out a long-held breath when he felt the steady thrum of life. So she wasn't dead. The fact she was unconscious couldn't be good.

Hopefully, Emma could get her to go to the emergency room. An ambulance could pick her up and she'd be off his hands and out of his truck. He didn't particularly want to be saddled with her, but having hit her with his truck, he figured he at least owed her the courtesy of getting her medical attention, even if the accident had been her fault. She'd run the stop sign.

Dave knew Steele and her teammates were some kind of government special agents, he just wasn't sure which branch—FBI, CIA or something else. She'd arrived a few months ago to help stop a terrorist plot going down in Cape Churn. She'd worked with two other men: Creed Thomas and Casanova Valdez.

Whoever they were, they were on their game, something Dave could appreciate. When he'd been a member of the U.S. Army Special Forces, he'd been equally dedicated to his country and his commanding officers. Until his unit had been fed faulty intel and bad orders.

It was while he'd served in Afghanistan he'd learned that getting too close to someone, male or female, left you vulnerable to the devastating pain of loss. He was better off keeping his distance.

When he pulled into the parking lot of the marina, three other vehicles were already there. A Jeep and two other SUVs.

Emma was the first to greet him, stepping up to his door as he climbed down from his truck. "Where's the fire? Why the secretive call?"

He moved aside.

The overhead light shone down on Tazer's light blond hair.

"Nicole." Emma's eyes rounded. "Is she…?"

"She's alive, just passed out."

Emma rounded to the other side of the truck and opened the door, climbing up on the running board. "What happened?"

He told her about almost running her over and that she'd taken a spill from her motorcycle.

Casanova Valdez stood behind Emma, holding Molly McGregor's hand. "What the hell was she doing here anyway? I thought she was on assignment."

"Nicole." Emma tapped her arm gently. When she didn't respond, she lightly slapped her face. "Nicole," she said sharply.

"Let me." Valdez switched places with Emma and said in a stern voice, "Tazer, quit foolin' around. It's time to go to work."

Dave's fists clenched and he stepped forward, ready to punch Valdez's lights out for being so forceful when the woman wasn't capable of holding her head up, much less going to work.

"Nova?" Nicole blinked her eyes open and stared up into her fellow agent's face.

"Yeah, it's me. You look like hell." Valdez held out his hand and she grabbed it, letting him pull her into a sitting position.

"Way to make a girl self-conscious," she grumbled.

He snorted, giving her a derisive grin. "Like you've ever been that." His lips turned downward. "What the hell happened? I didn't know you were scheduled to be here."

She pressed a hand to the back of her neck. "I wasn't."

Creed Thomas stepped up behind Valdez. "Tazer, what's going on?"

"I was hoping you could tell me." Her voice was stronger, clipped and, if Dave wasn't mistaken, strained. "I need your help," she admitted. "Is there somewhere we can meet that's not so out in the open?"

Valdez and Thomas converged and helped her down from the truck.

Emma glanced at Dave. "Can we meet on your dive boat?"

He shook his head. "Better take her to the *Freedom's Price*," he said, immediately regretting getting involved, but leading the way to the far end of the marina where the yacht was tied to the end of the dock. Everything about Nicole Steele spelled trouble, from her slim figure to the swell of her breasts and hips beneath the black leather.

When she set her feet on the ground, her knees buckled. Her teammates caught her before she hit the ground.

She laughed shakily. "I've been on that bike for two days just to get here."

"Two days?" Thomas asked. "I thought you were back in D.C.?"

"No. I was on assignment in L.A." She straightened, her brows forming a tight V over her nose. "Tell me, what's going on at headquarters? Why aren't Royce or Geek answering their phones? I couldn't get them to answer calls or texts."

"Nothing that I know of. I heard from Royce three days ago." Thomas frowned. "Come to think of it, he was going to contact me today with my next assignment." He glanced at his watch and cell phone. "I've gotten nothing."

Valdez scrolled down through the contact list on his phone. "I just returned from a short assignment two days ago and had requested a week off. I didn't expect to hear from anyone back at HQ." He hit the send button on his phone and pressed it to his ear. After a moment his gaze met Tazer's in the light from the post hanging over the dock. "Nothing."

"Let me get in touch with Sam. I think he and his

wife, Kat, were supposed to be in D.C. this week."
Thomas scrolled through his phone contacts, selected
the one he wanted and pressed Send, then put the phone
on speaker.

After a moment a gravelly voice answered. "Yeah."

"Sam, it's Creed."

"Thank God. Kat and I contacted as many people on
the team as I dared to let them know what went down,
but couldn't get them all. One minute it was business
as usual, the next, FBI was raiding headquarters. Then
all hell broke loose. They nabbed Royce and Geek and
all of the SOS computers, and took them to an undis-
closed location."

"Damn," Thomas said. "What's going on?"

"We're not sure. Look, I don't want to stay on this
phone long, in case someone's somehow monitoring
this call. I suggest you ditch all your SOS phones, now.
Contact me on Kat's personal phone, if you need us.
Out here."

Dave's fists clenched. He wasn't sure what Thomas
and Valdez did, but his gut told him they were the good
guys. He had yet another reason not to trust the government or those who considered themselves "in charge."

Valdez swore softly. "We need to get back to D.C. to
find out what happened." He started for the parking lot.

"Wait." Nicole stuck out an arm. "I have a bad feeling it has something to do with my last assignment."
She glanced toward Dave.

Dave shrugged. "Don't worry about me. I have better
things to do than listen to conspiracy theories."

Emma backhanded him in the belly. "Don't mind
Dave, he can be grumpy in his best mood." She winked
at him and leaned into the conversation. "Want me to

leave so you three can talk all the supersecret stuff you do so well?"

Nicole glanced from Thomas to Emma and back to Thomas.

"We can trust her," Creed said.

"And Molly," Valdez confirmed.

"I'm just a mere mortal small-town cop, maybe Kayla and I should bug out." Gabe McGregor glanced at his watch. "Dakota should be ready to climb the walls babysitting Tonya."

"He's so good with her, I know I take advantage of him," Kayla said softly, pushing a strand of her curls behind her ear. "We can leave."

"No." Nicole put out her hand and touched Kayla's arm as she and Gabe turned to leave. "Now that you know I'm here, you need to know what I'm up against." She glanced at Dave. "You, too."

Dave snorted. "No, thanks. I have to secure the boat for the night."

"Yeah, right," Emma said. "Stay and hear what Tazer has to say."

"Could we take it inside?" Nicole asked, glancing over her shoulder again as if she expected the boogeyman to pop out of the shadows.

Not really wanting to be dragged into the drama of special agents, Dave motioned toward the dilapidated yacht. "Take her inside. There should be enough room for all of us below."

They followed him aboard his yacht fixer-upper and descended the steps into the living area, crowding around the tiny dining table. Dave had been in the process of repairing the teak wood paneling. Some of the doors were missing and the cushions had seen better days.

"If someone's following you, perhaps we should take you directly to the police," Kayla said as they settled on the worn cushions.

"No." Nicole held up her hand. "I don't know who to trust. I barely got away from L.A. and though I might have lost my tail, something tells me they'll find me soon enough."

"Tazer, slow down. Who's following you? And why?" Valdez reached out and gripped her hands. "Good God, woman, you're shaking."

Dave stared at the beautiful blonde. "You've been on the road for more than two days straight? On that motorcycle?"

She nodded, the shadows beneath her eyes appearing even darker in the cabin's limited lighting.

"Have you eaten?" he asked.

She shook her head. "I had a couple candy bars from rest-area vending machines. I didn't want to stop long enough for anyone to catch up to me."

Dave reached into the fridge and pulled out sandwich meat and cheese slices. In less than a minute he'd slapped them on bread and handed it to her. "Eat this."

Nicole took it, glancing up at him with a tired smile. "Thanks."

"Start from the beginning," Creed Thomas said. "Don't leave anything out."

Dave hated to admit it, but he was glad they hadn't excluded him from Tazer's story. He hadn't heard a story that good since the last action movie he'd seen at the theater in Portland.

He glanced at the model-thin woman with the glorious mane of blond hair and shook his head. He found it hard to believe she was some undercover secret agent. Not when she looked weak enough to be broken in two with his bare hands. After she'd thrown him, however, he'd known how deceiving her looks could be.

When she finished her story, he was even more amazed. "So what you're telling us is that you have some data someone's willing to move heaven and earth to retrieve?"

"Looks that way." She shoved a hand through her hair, her face pale with exhaustion.

"I'd call that breaking and entering, which constitutes a felony." Dave shook his head. "Which means I'm harboring a felon. Nice."

Nicole stared at him with narrowed eyes. "We do what has to be done to protect our country from criminals."

"By becoming criminals yourselves?" Dave snorted. "I'm sure cults and fundamental extremists believe the same. What makes you any different?"

She gave him a cold, hard stare. "We aren't out for ourselves."

"Dave, we're the good guys, even if we're breaking and entering. The guy she went after could be selling weapons to our military and our enemies. Guns for the people killing our troops." Thomas tapped his fingers on the table. "And it sounds like he's in bed with someone in D.C., especially considering they've taken hostage Royce, Geek and our entire operating system, probably holding them until Tazer gives back what she's taken."

Nicole swore softly. "We can't let them get away with it."

Valdez's leg bounced with nervous energy. "Sam said it was the FBI and CIA that stormed headquarters."

Thomas picked up from there. "Which means someone with clout in the government has a stake in that data and probably doesn't want it exposed."

"So we can't just turn it over," Nicole concluded.

"We have to decrypt the data." Thomas glanced across at Valdez then back at Steele. "I'm not an IT guy."

Valdez held up his hands in surrender. "I know my way around hardware, but Geek's the one I go to for software. The guy's a wizard at hacking passwords, data encryption and decryption."

Nicole sighed. "That leaves it to me. I had some training in military intel, but it's been a while. So many things have changed, gotten more complicated and semifoolproof."

"If you can break the code, it might reveal who in the government is determined to see the data deep-sixed."

Nicole pinched the bridge of her nose. "It'll take time."

"You'll need a place to hide out," Valdez said.

Her hand dropped to her lap and she gave a wan smile. "That's why I'm here. Cape Churn is like falling off the map."

Kayla McGregor laughed softly. "Then why do we manage to attract serial killers, terrorists and relatives of drug lords?"

"I don't know. It seems like such a nice little town," Emma added.

Valdez squeezed Nicole's hand reassuringly. "The main thing is to lie low while you're working the data."

"First things first." Nicole ran a hand through her hair. "I could use a shower and a bed. If I could, I'd sleep until the problem went away."

"Sorry, we need you on it." Thomas glanced across at Valdez then back at the woman they called Tazer. "We'll run interference the best we can, but you'll have to break the code so that we can take the information to the right people and possibly get Royce and Geek out of hot water."

Thomas nodded toward Molly. "You can stay in a room at the B and B."

Molly's lips twisted. "Except I have a group coming in for a wedding. It'll be anything but private and there will be too many people around. Not to mention all the rooms will be full."

"You could stay at our little bungalow, but the renovations on the spare bedroom aren't complete and you'd have to sleep on the couch."

"All my bedrooms are full at the lighthouse cottage," Kayla offered. "It would be a couch there, too, and it's exposed to the windows."

"I'd sleep anywhere with a pillow." Nicole leaned against the wall.

Emma grinned. "I know the perfect place. It's quiet, secluded and no one would think to look for you there."

With frown, Dave braced himself, intuition telling him he wasn't going to like what Emma had to say next. "Where did you have in mind?"

"The answer to the perfect place to hide." She turned to face him. "Why doesn't she stay here? What do you say, Dave?"

All gazes turned toward Dave. "Why can't she stay at one of the hotels in town?"

Valdez shook his head. "Too public."

"She could rent a vacation cottage," he offered.

"They're all full," Molly said. "The wedding guests took over a lot of them and most of the hotel rooms."

Dave crossed his arms. "She's not staying here."

"But it makes sense. If she needs to get out of town, why not go by boat?" Emma continued to grin, making Dave's teeth grind.

"No." He shook his head. "Besides, haven't you heard of sitting ducks? A boat is easy to spot in the water."

Nicole glanced around, her brows rising. "I seriously doubt this old boat's engines even work."

Dave glared at Tazer. "The engines work great. I refurbished them first, now I'm working on the cosmetics."

Valdez chuckled. "Sorry, Dave, but it is a good solution. If the people who are looking for her get close, you can head out to sea at night."

"She's not staying," Dave insisted.

"I can't sleep on Kayla's couch. I won't put the baby and your son at risk." Nicole laid her head on the table. "Frankly, I'm ready to climb into a cardboard box and sleep on the street."

The room went silent as she laid still. Her eyes were closed, the dark circles more pronounced in the soft glow of light from overhead.

A knot of guilt churned in Dave's gut until finally he said, "Fine. She can stay here." He didn't know what came over him to open his big fat mouth and offer her a place to stay. But now that it was out there, he couldn't take it back. And as much as he valued his privacy, he didn't *want* to take it back.

The woman could barely stand on her own two feet.

If she didn't get some rest, she'd fall flat on her face. That and the fact he'd nearly killed her.

"One night. She can stay one night. Tomorrow you have to come up with another plan."

Emma's brows crooked upward. "That's really noble of you, Dave. You sure it won't put you out too much? I mean, this being the lap of luxury and all." She winked.

"Don't push it, Emma." Dave glared at his friend. "This place looks like hell on the outside for the sole purpose of keeping people from dropping by."

"Oh, honey." Emma laughed. "It's working."

"Which is perfect." Valdez clapped his hands together. "If possible, it's the ugliest boat at the marina."

"I wouldn't say ugly," Dave defended. It was his home, after all. "It's my boat and I like it the way it is."

Emma's lips twitched. "Trust me, Dave, it's ugly."

He shrugged and glanced at Tazer. "Suit yourself."

Nicole's head came up. "Does it have electricity?"

He nodded. "And running water."

"Hot?" she asked hopefully.

Again he nodded.

"Sounds like heaven." She sucked in a deep breath. "I'll stay. Tomorrow I'll retrieve my motorcycle. I need to be able to bug out if I'm discovered."

Now that he was committed to putting her up for the night, Dave said, "I'll take care of it for you."

"Where's the shower?" Nicole yawned, covering her mouth.

"The head's through that door." Dave motioned toward a narrow wood-paneled door.

Emma clucked her tongue. "You could be a little more hospitable. You shouldn't be such a loner. No man's an island."

"I like being a loner. I'm a freakin' island and love it that way."

"Everyone needs a friend." Emma patted his arm. "And right now, Tazer needs you to be her friend."

"I've committed to one night. That's it."

Nicole fought a smile. "Have pity on poor Dave. The man's being railroaded."

Dave's eyes narrowed. The woman looked as if she was actually enjoying watching him squirm. *Damned woman.*

Valdez handed Steele his cell phone. "Tazer, take my cell phone."

Nicole held up her hands. "No way. And I suggest you all ditch your SOS cells, like Sam said. If someone has our database, we're all at risk."

Valdez nodded. "I knew that." He dropped his phone on the floor of the boat and stepped on it.

Thomas followed suit.

"In the meantime, you know where to find me," Nicole said.

Valdez laughed. "I think we can find you. We just have to look for the ugliest boat on the dock."

The two agents laughed and joked as they exited Dave's yacht, reminding him of how close he and his squad had been, making light of difficult situations and being there for each other when the going got tough. His chest tightened as he recalled Mike's ultimate sacrifice. He'd have given everything for his brothers in arms, and ultimately he had.

Molly, Kayla and Gabe followed Valdez. Emma was last to climb out of the boat, leaving Dave stuck with his guest.

Nicole pushed to her feet, swayed and steadied. Then she headed for the shower.

He grabbed a towel from the storage cabinet and handed it to her as she ducked around him. For a moment she paused and looked over her shoulder. "Dave?"

"Yeah."

She stood tall, her blue eyes almost gray in the shadows. "Thanks for pulling me out of the ditch."

For a moment he didn't react, then his gut clenched, remembering. "Don't mention it."

Dave climbed the stairs out of *Freedom's Price* and strode across the dock to the parking lot, determined to put some distance between him and the woman occupying his yacht. Now would be as good a time as any to retrieve her motorcycle and hide it, under the cover of darkness and the Devil's Shroud.

Later he'd come up with a cover story for the woman living with him on his boat.

Great, he'd just broken the three rules he'd imposed on himself since leaving the Special Forces.

Don't get involved. Don't get involved. Don't get involved.

He was now up to his neck in involvement.

Chapter 3

Nicole climbed into the tiny shower, trying not to imagine the bulky, well-muscled man who'd carried her to his truck when she'd been out cold as she fit herself into the confined space. It was hard enough for her to turn and rinse, how did a guy that big manage?

Her body heated at the thought of Dave standing naked in the shower. She dropped the soap and bent to retrieve the bar, thinking how it was too bad the unit was too small for two.

As soon as the idea entered her mind, Nicole jerked upright, banging her head on the shower nozzle. "Damn!" Already dizzy from lack of sleep, she didn't need to knock herself unconscious again. Dave would have to fish her off the shower floor, naked and wet.

Molten hot blood thrummed through her veins at the thought of Dave's rough hands on her naked thighs, possibly skimming the sides of her breasts. She was weak from pushing too long, too far and on too little food. That had to be the reason for the ache building deep in her core.

Dave Logsdon was nothing to her. So what that he'd pulled her out of a ditch? His truck had put her there.

You ran the stop sign.

Arguing with herself only made her angrier and she was entirely too exhausted to care. Her whole world had been ripped apart. She hadn't felt this off balance since she'd been shamed out of the FBI. Now the only person she truly trusted, Royce Fontaine, had been apprehended and was being held by some government entity.

What the hell was in that data she'd stolen from Ryan Technologies?

The water turned cold, forcing her out of her musings and the shower. The old yacht probably only had a five-gallon water heater. She finished rinsing the soap out of her hair and turned off the water. The towel Dave had given her was thick and fluffy and completely covered her. She stepped out onto a bath mat and dried off, her gaze shooting to the door, half expecting it to open while she stood naked, half disappointed when it didn't.

Her leather pants and jacket lay on the floor, too dirty from road grime for her to want to put them back on. She ducked her head out the bathroom door, her hair dripping on the wooden floor. "Logsdon?" she called out.

No answer.

She ventured out farther, poking around the other doors leading off the small cabin. Dave was gone.

Well, at least she had privacy. She rummaged through a drawer and found a T-shirt that smelled a lot like Dave. He must leave clothing onboard for when he took the yacht out to sea.

When Nicole put it on, the shirt covered her from shoulders to midthigh.

Perfect for a nightshirt.

A yawn struck her. Too tired to think past at least four hours' sleep, she went in search of a mattress and pillow, finding them in the forward berth. A queen-size bed covered in a clean, white, down comforter took up the entire space.

Nicole crawled across the top and dropped face-first onto a pillow. Less than a minute later she was sound asleep.

Minutes, or maybe hours later, a noise disturbed her, dragging her out of a nightmare about running through a large building with no doors to escape.

Nicole rolled over and tried to drop off the side of the bed, but there were no sides to roll off of. She scooted to the end of the bed instead and slid down, crouching low in the oversize T-shirt, blinking the sleep from her eyes and the fog from her brain. She was so tired she found it hard to keep her eyes open.

Another sound forced her eyelids upward.

When a large figure appeared in the doorway to the forward berth, a rush of adrenaline hit Nicole's body and she launched herself at the intruder, knocking him backward and flat on his back.

He landed with a grunt, taking her down with him.

Too late. Nicole realized the man she now lay on top of was the same one who'd rescued her and given her a place to sleep.

Dave grasped her arms in his big hands and demanded, "What the hell?"

"I thought you were an intruder." When she tried to move, his grip kept her in place, long enough to recognize the hard ridge of his denim fly pressing into her belly. Wearing nothing but a soft, old T-shirt, there wasn't much between them, leaving her vulnerable to him and her own traitorous desires.

Tazer had learned long ago, when in doubt, go on the offensive.

"What are you doing here?" she demanded with as much control as she could muster, considering she was naked under the shirt.

"I live here." He sat up, pushing her to the side.

"Live here?" She glanced around the cramped interior of the boat. "All the time? Or just when this old tub is out to sea?"

"All the time." Dave rose, leaving her on the floor to get up by herself. Anger burned off him like steam.

Nicole couldn't fathom why he'd be so mad and ready to pick a fight. She scrambled to her feet, still tired but not one to back down from an argument. "Then why did you let me stay?"

He snorted. "If you recall, I didn't want you to stay."

She stood, straightened the shirt hem to cover her bare bottom, feeling more exposed than if she'd been completely naked. "I understand. The couch at Creed and Emma's will have to do."

When Nicole made to pass Dave, she had to squeeze between his solid body and the wall. He didn't make it easy. No, he didn't allow her to pass at all.

His brows pushed down low as he stared at her chest. "Is that my T-shirt you're wearing?" he asked, his voice low, gravelly.

Nicole tipped her head back. "I found it in a drawer."

"Give it back."

"Fine." She reached for the hem, dragged it up over her head and tossed the shirt into his face. "It was too long anyway." She moved past him, naked, her head held high.

His eyes widened, the dark brown turning almost black. He reached out and grasped her arms. "Put the damn shirt on," he said through gritted teeth.

Nicole attempted to pull her arm free, her jaw tight, her body cool in the night air. "I'll wear what I rode in with." She was beginning to regret her rash decision to strip in front of the man. He held her steady, refusing to release his grip. The heat his body gave off did nothing to smooth the chill bumps rising on her skin, which had nothing to do with the cold and everything to do with the animalistic attraction this man exuded.

"Don't you have anything else?" He practically bit the words out.

"In case you didn't hear the part of the story that specifically stated I drove straight here with nothing but the clothes on my back, let me remind you." She threw back her shoulders. "I don't have a change of clothes."

His nostrils flaring, Dave shoved his T-shirt at her. "Put the damned thing on," he growled, turning his back to give her privacy.

Nicole hesitated, ready to throw the shirt back in his face. But knowing battles with this man would be better fought fully clothed not buck naked, she pulled the shirt over her head and gathered all her righteous anger.

When Dave turned back, she stared straight into his eyes, daring him to say one derogatory thing about her body. When he didn't, her chin lifted. "Now, if you'll excuse me…" With a flip of her damp hair, she headed for the stairs leading out of the boat, snatching her clothes off the hook on the bathroom door as she went.

"How do you plan to get to Emma's?" Dave asked. "Your motorcycle won't start. I tried it. Until I have time to check all the wiring and the battery cables in the daylight, you're without transportation."

With her hand on the rail, she paused. "I'll walk."

"It's over three miles...uphill, most of the way."

She shrugged, though the effort seemed huge at that point. Three miles seemed like forever after straddling a motorcycle for so long. "It'll be a good stretch of the legs." The legs that were shaking at the thought of climbing out of the cabin, much less climbing a hill up to Emma's.

A loud sigh behind her made her stop with only one foot on the bottom step. "I said you could stay the night. But you'll sleep on the couch. The bed is mine." He grabbed a pillow and tossed it her way.

She caught it but wasn't in time to catch the blanket he threw right behind it. It landed over her head, blocking her view of the smirking man.

Humph!

Not stupid enough to set out in the fog on foot in the dead of night, Nicole lay on the worn cushions of the built-in couch that doubled as seats for the dining area. Tucking the blanket around her bare legs, she rested her head on the pillow and closed her eyes.

Sounds of Dave rustling around in the forward cabin kept her from falling right to sleep. Having him so close disturbed her in a way she hadn't been in a long time. Why, when she was so tired, was she so drawn to this infuriating man? He was nothing like the kind of man she usually found interesting. Pigheaded, grumpy and unshaven... What did he have going for him?

Broad shoulders, rich brown hair and eyes so dark a woman could fall into them. With his muscles and trim figure, he could have been so much more than the captain of a dive boat. So why was her body humming at his every movement? And why was she wondering if he slept in the nude?

"I'm not changing the way I live just because you're here."

"So?" She lifted her head, staring into the darkness of the forward cabin.

"It's just a fair warning," he said. "I sleep in the nude."

Nicole's mouth fell open, and then she snapped it shut. Not only was he infuriating, he was a freakin' mind reader.

She'd hoped to sleep, but his final comment left her wide awake and angry. At him, absolutely. But more at herself for imagining him in his bed, sprawled out, naked and gorgeous.

Damn him.

Her body thrummed with white-hot desire that refused to fade.

Not until the clock over the galley stove blinked past two o'clock did she finally calm down and drift into sleep.

Less than an hour later thrashing sounds brought her wide awake. She lay still, listening, wondering what had been loud enough to drag her out of the sleep of the dead, her nerves on edge in case the men who'd been chasing her had found her.

A moan from the other room made her swing her legs off the side of the couch and sit up.

"No!" Dave's shout sent her to her feet. She grabbed the small fire extinguisher from the clamp on the wall and edged toward the forward cabin. Who could have snuck past her?

Another moan and more thrashing, the thud of something hitting the wall made her jump and move faster until she stood at the end of the bed, extinguisher raised, ready to clobber whoever was hurting Dave.

Only he was alone, asleep and having one heck of a nightmare.

Setting the extinguisher aside, Nicole hesitated. Should she wake him or let him keep dreaming?

The moan turned to a soft keening sound like that of a wounded animal or a heartbroken person. Nicole climbed up over the end of the bed and spoke softly. "Hey, Logsdon."

His body went still.

Convinced she'd shaken him out of his bad dream, she eased backward toward the foot of the bed, realizing he'd been truthful about sleeping in the nude. He lay there, bathed in the soft green glow of an alarm clock, his body sculpted as beautifully as a Greek statue. Before she could think through her actions, she reached out to touch the rippled, hard plane of his abdomen.

His belly sank in as his hand reached out, grabbed her wrist and yanked her onto her back. Then his body covered hers as he straddled her, his hands circling her neck.

"Why did you do it?" he growled.

She clawed at his fingers, gasping for breath.

"Why did you kill him?"

She wanted to scream at him, tell him she wasn't who he was dreaming about, but no air could make it past her vocal cords. She pounded his shoulder with the heel of her palm and tore at the fingers wrapped around her throat. The fog of unconsciousness crept in around her vision.

In a final effort she rolled to the side, forcing him to hit his head against a low-hanging storage cabinet.

When he did, his grip loosened and Nicole was able to breathe long enough to say, "Wake up, Dave!"

His fingers tightened around her neck again and squeezed, his weight effectively pinning her beneath him.

Please, she begged with her eyes.

Dave shook his head, his eyes widening as he stared down at his hands around her neck.

Nicole could tell when he finally woke up. His glazed eyes cleared and he jerked his hands back. "What have I done?" he asked.

"Almost choked the living daylights out of me." Nicole coughed, her voice rough, gravelly. "Remind me to never wake you up from a bad dream again."

His brows pulled down low over his eyes. "What are you doing in my bed?"

"You were having a nightmare. I would have let you continue, but you were keeping me awake." She rubbed her neck. "Next time, I'll bury my ears in my pillow. At least I'd live to see another day."

He raised his hands as if they were foreign to him and then closed his eyes, his face etched in pain.

Nicole's heart slowed, absorbing some of the horrible emotion he must have been feeling. "What was it about?"

"What?" He looked up, his gaze far away.

"Your dream?"

He shook his head. "Nothing." He lay back, pulling the sheet up over his lower half, covering the evidence of his arousal. "Get out."

"On my way." She scooted to the end of the bed and was about to get up when she paused. "Were you ever in the military, Dave?"

"Yeah," he said, his voice harsh. In a softer tone he added, "A million years ago."

"Ever consider that you might have PTSD?"

"So?"

"They have therapy available for soldiers with PTSD."

"Do they have therapy for those who died to save the rest of their unit?" He snorted. "Show me the therapy that'll bring them back." Raising his head, he glared at her. "I said get out."

Nicole raised her brows. "Touchy, aren't we?"

She slid off the bed and padded barefoot back to the couch, where she lay, her thoughts revolving, not around her own predicament but around what Dave had said.

He must have seen his buddy killed in battle, trying to save his life. How did someone get over something like that?

She raised her fingers to the tender skin around her neck. Obviously, Dave hadn't.

Not that it mattered to Nicole, but perhaps there was more to the slovenly dive boat captain than she'd first surmised.

"Dave?"

"What?" he said, his tone flat, hard and uninviting.

"Who was he?"

"Who was who?"

"The guy who took the bullet for you?"

For a long moment he didn't respond.

Nicole assumed he wouldn't and settled in, curious, but understanding the subject was a difficult one for the man.

"Bradley. Tom Bradley. And it was a grenade."

"May he rest in peace," she said softly. She sent a silent prayer to the heavens that Tom Bradley truly did rest in peace, and by doing so would give Dave Logsdon permission to also live in peace, free of his demons.

With Dave in the room nearby, his strength and loyalty to a fallen comrade radiating through his dreams, Nicole rolled onto her side, closed her eyes and slept the sleep of a dead woman. Tomorrow was certain to bring plenty of challenges and, if her pursuers caught up to her, maybe even the opportunity for someone to pray for her eternal rest.

Chapter 4

Dave laid awake the rest of the night, thoughts roiling around his mind like a propeller spinning out of control. As the sun rose over Cape Churn, he climbed out of his bed, slipped into a pair of jeans, a T-shirt and boat shoes. He did no more than run his hand through his hair, splash water on his face and pass on shaving.

Who did he have to impress? Not his uninvited guest. That was certain. When he passed through the main cabin, he moved quietly, not ready to face the woman, not without a gallon of coffee in his system.

She lay stretched out on the couch cushions, her long blond hair splayed across her cheek. Dressed in his oversize T-shirt, sleeping peacefully, she appeared to be more innocent than the kick-ass woman who'd fought him in her black leather the night before. Who was she? Other than a member of the supersecret organization

Creed Thomas and Casanova Valdez belonged to, Dave didn't have a clue. They'd called it the SOS. He wondered what SOS stood for.

Dave reached out and brushed the strand of hair off her cheek, tucking it behind her ear, her skin warm to his touch.

She stirred, blinked open her eyes, realized it was him and closed them again without uttering a word. Bunching the pillow beneath her, she slept on. Two days on a motorcycle, after a stressful operation, and being followed had to have taken its toll. A long, slender, naked leg slipped from beneath the blanket, bumping up his heartbeat.

Dave struggled with himself to keep from reaching out to adjust the blanket over her, instead admiring the leg, the shape, definition and smooth silkiness of her skin.

When he realized how long he'd stood there, studying her, he turned abruptly and climbed the steps up onto the deck.

"Good morning, Dave." Olie Olander waved at him from farther along the dock where he handed a Styrofoam ice chest to a couple of men in a fishing boat. After they thanked him and settled the chest into the boat, they started the engine and took off.

Dave came to a stop beside Olie. "Morning."

Olie studied him. "Good or bad?"

"Just morning." Since coming to Cape Churn, Dave hadn't let himself get excited about much. Whenever something good happened, something bad came along to counteract it. By keeping an even keel, he avoided rollercoaster emotions. Neither too happy nor too sad. He refused to let himself dwell for long in either emotion. Deep down, he carried the memory of his friend, Tom. That was enough to remind him that the world was full of terrible tragedies.

"Sal's got a fresh pot of coffee in the marina."

"That's where I'm headed."

Olie joined him, walking alongside across the wooden planks of the dock. "Have some friends over last night?"

Dave shrugged. "A couple." Sal and Olie lived in the apartment above the marina's bait shop. They saw just about everything. If it happened at the waterfront, they knew about it.

Not sure of how much he could share about who'd been to his boat the night before, Dave opted for as little as possible. He'd trust Sal and Olie with his life. They treated him like the son they'd never been fortunate enough to have. And he loved them. If any of what Tazer had told him was true, just by being on the same dock as her could put them in danger. The less they knew, the less they would inadvertently spill to passing strangers.

Olie opened the door to the bait shop. "Does one of them belong to that motorcycle you stored in the shed?"

Dave paused on the threshold. He couldn't get much past the Olanders. "Belongs to a…friend."

"The one you carried onto the *Freedom's Price?*" Sal asked softly.

He couldn't get much by these two older people. "She had too much to drink."

Olie nodded, still holding the door open for him to proceed into the marina's store and bait shop. "Sal, you got any of that coffee left?"

"Fresh pot." The little woman with the care-worn

face and hair dyed a rich brown to cover all of the gray ran a washrag over the counter. "Good morning, Dave. No charters today?"

"Not until later." He helped himself to a cup of coffee and sat on the stool on the other side of the counter from Sal to sip the steaming brew. As the hot coffee traveled down his throat, the warm rich aroma swirling around him, Dave could almost pretend all was right in his world.

"I made some fresh biscuits for breakfast. Care for some?"

Sal always made more than she and Olie could eat, and, as with every morning, Dave accepted her hospitality. "You know I love your biscuits. Please."

She lifted a basket covered in a bright red-checkered cloth from behind the counter. When he reached for a biscuit, she pushed the basket toward him. "Oh, please. Take all of them. Your guest might like some."

Dave stared across at Sal. "Thank you."

"Oh, give up, Sal. You know you're dying to ask who she is."

Sal's face reddened. "I wasn't going to ask, but since Olie opened his big mouth… Who is she? Someone we know?"

"No. She's an old friend I knew from back in my service days. She was here a couple months' back." Dave took one of the biscuits and jammed it in his mouth, hoping the inquisition stopped there.

Sal stared at him a moment, giving him a chance to elaborate.

Making a big show of chewing, he didn't.

After a moment she nodded. "Well, I'm glad to see

you interested. I was beginning to think you had sworn off women."

Having just taken a sip of the hot coffee, Dave practically spewed. "Wait a minute. Who said I was interested?"

Sal smiled like the proverbial cat that had swallowed the canary. "Honey, when a man carries a woman into his yacht and she doesn't leave all night…" Her face reddened again. "Just because Olie and I are old, doesn't mean we're naive. Please."

Olie slapped him on the back. "Me and Sal figured it was about time you got back in the dating scene."

Dave stood, a little angry and a lot disconcerted to be having this conversation with the two people he'd come to care for like surrogate parents. "Anything else you two deciding on my behalf? It might help me to be forewarned."

Olie scratched his chin. "Well, Sal thinks I need to talk to you about protection—"

Heat radiated up his neck. "I'm out of here." Grabbing the basket of biscuits and his cup of coffee, Dave headed for the door. "Next thing I know you'll be telling me all about the birds and the bees."

"Oh, no, honey." Sal rested her hands on her hips. "We figure you know all about that. But sometimes a man needs reminding about other things."

"I'm not hearing this. Please stop talking." He ran for the door, sloshing hot coffee on his hand.

"Have a nice day with your lady friend," Sal called.

The echo of Olie's chuckles followed Dave out the door.

What had gotten into those two meddling, well-meaning old people? He was happy as a confirmed bachelor.

His footsteps slowed as he approached the battered yacht that had seen better days a couple of decades before.

What did he care what his home looked like? The engine had never run smoother and he was working on the exterior as he got time. Now that the summer season was waning, he'd have more time to work on his special project. As soon as his guest moved out.

Biscuits, coffee and the boot. She couldn't stay. He liked his peace and quiet and certainly didn't want to get caught up in a felony looking for some people to arrest.

He still couldn't get over the fact Gabe hadn't arrested her, knowing she'd broken into a business and stolen confidential information.

Still shaking his head, he stepped onto the boat and descended the steps into the living area.

The couch was empty. Had she gone? His pulse quickened as he glanced around the cabin. Then he heard the water running in the bathroom and he let go of the breath he'd been holding, annoyed that he'd been strangely disappointed thinking she'd gone without saying goodbye.

As he set about the task of plugging in the coffeepot and measuring out coffee, the door to the bathroom opened.

Still wearing the shirt she'd borrowed, she now had on the black leather pants and boots and she'd pulled her hair back into a neat ponytail. Somehow, in the makeshift outfit with no makeup on her face and nothing fancy about her hairstyle, the woman still managed to look gorgeous.

He dragged his gaze away. "Coffee will be ready in a minute."

"Don't make any for me."

Good, more for him, since he hadn't slept worth a damn and Tazer would soon be leaving. Dave poured water into the device and set it on brew.

"I don't drink coffee, but I'd love a Coke if you have one."

"There's one in the refrigerator, help yourself." And, it was a can and could be taken with her. "Is there somewhere I can drop you off today?"

"I could use some clothes and a few personal items and a good computer."

"I'm sure your friends will help you out."

"I can't be seen in the daylight with them. Someone could be watching them."

He crossed his arms. "Do I look like a chauffeur?"

"No, of course not. But I can't be seen too much in public." Nicole smiled, her face lighting the room, her lips twisting into a wry grin as she handed him a list of items and five one-hundred-dollar bills. "I need you to pick up these items for me."

Dave stared for a moment, clamping his jaw tight to keep his mouth from dropping. "Do you always carry that kind of money around?"

She smiled. "A girl has to have her mad money."

"I thought mad money was limited to cab fare home."

"Not when you're in my business."

"No, thanks. I'm not your gofer." He tried to hand her the list and the money, but she backed away.

"I'm not any happier than you are, but it seems my options are limited. I'm staying here." She glanced around the tight confines of the cabin, refusing to look him in the eye. "Surely you have a computer I can use until Thomas or Valdez can get me a faster one."

"Why would I need a computer? I captain a charter boat."

Her face fell and she redirected her attention to him. "You don't have a computer?"

He fought to keep from yelling. How had he gotten roped into harboring a fugitive? He crossed to a cabinet, removed a fairly new laptop and handed it to her. "I should have run you over."

"Actually you did."

"You were only supposed to stay one night."

Nicole sighed. "Didn't you say my motorcycle was damaged?"

"I tried to start it, but it wouldn't turn over. I think some of the wiring got messed up when you decided to run that stop sign."

"When you hit me."

Dave shook his head. "I'm not feeling sorry for you, if that's your plan. Women don't get far trying to manipulate me."

"No? I had you pegged for a pushover." She plopped onto the couch cushion and gave him a challenging look. "You know, the sooner I get a computer and decrypt the data, the sooner I'm out of your hair. You can either work with me or you're stuck with me." She shrugged. "It's up to you. Oh, and could you leave your cell phone? I need to make some calls."

Fifteen minutes later Dave stumbled through the door of Brigit's Ladies Apparel store on Main Street in Cape Churn, clutching Tazer's list in his fist. "Damned woman. I'm a confirmed bachelor, not a glorified baby-sitter."

"Hi, Dave," Brigit Summers called out from behind the counter. "What can I help you with?" She walked around and met him halfway across the small store.

He wanted to tell her he needed help getting a squatter out of his yacht. Instead he handed her the list. "I need these items in the sizes and colors listed."

Brigit scanned the list, her brows rising. "That's quite a list." She relieved him of it and moved around the store, gathering panties, bras, shirts and trousers. "She must be someone special."

"It's for my mother," he lied, frowning hard enough to scare an enemy fighter.

Not Brigit. She laughed. "Right. You don't have a mother."

"And how would you know that?"

She rolled her eyes. "Sal and Olie have been trying to set me up with you since you arrived in Cape Churn. I know your height, weight, that you like coffee and biscuits for breakfast and your favorite food is seafood chowder. Your parents live in Arizona, but you never visit. You were in the Special Forces and you got out of the army after eight years." She stared across at him. "Did I leave anything out?"

"Just the reason why you didn't go out with me."

She snorted. "You never asked." With a pointed look at the clothes in her arms, she sighed. "I suppose I should have known you had someone special already. Nice, eligible men are very hard to find."

He wanted to tell her the clothes weren't for his lover, damn it. "I'm eligible. The nice part could be debatable."

Her face brightened. "Are you asking me out?"

He frowned and backed toward the door. "Look, if you could bag those things, I'll be back in fifteen minutes to square up."

Her face fell and she gave him a sad smile. "See? Hard to find." She pasted a smile on her face. "At least I'll make my sales quota for the day. I'll have these things ready."

Dave ducked out of the store, feeling as though he'd escaped a spider's web. What was wrong with women? All he wanted was to be left alone.

When he got back to the boat, he'd hand over the clothing and show Tazer the door. The yacht, no matter how ratty, was his home, not hers.

Nicole spent the better part of an hour cyber-poking at the flash drive, hoping the encryption on the data was a simple fix. After trying everything she'd learned from Zip, her super-geek informant she'd met while undercover with the FBI, she knew she had to do more.

Fortunately, Dave wasn't such a Neanderthal that he didn't have internet service. In fact, he had a pretty good setup for the captain of a fishing charter business. Beneath the scruffy unshaved face, shaggy hair and sloppy clothes, she suspected there was more to Dave Logsdon than he let on.

Too bad she didn't have time to figure him out. Then again, he'd probably end up being just as untrustworthy as most males she'd encountered, and not worth the effort to learn more about.

The image of Dave's face when he'd been deep in the nightmare and choking the breath out of her flashed through Nicole's memory. He must have seen some pretty serious stuff to be that traumatized.

Her hand rose to her throat. She'd remember to stand way back if she had to wake him from one of those night terrors again. Not that she would be venturing into his bedroom. If he had a bad dream, he'd have to tough it out.

As quickly as his enraged countenance came to mind, it faded and left her with the image of him lying on the bed naked. The man had muscles. Yes, sir. Not a spare ounce of flesh on that fisherman.

Nicole's body heated; a strange ache building low in her belly. Since Rodney's betrayal and her subsequent leaving the FBI, she hadn't let a man past her bedroom door.

After what she'd witnessed in Dave's nautical bedroom, she might have to reconsider. If only for some recreational sex. As much as she'd like to deny her baser instincts, she had physical needs.

Needs be damned, she'd need more firepower to crack the encryption on the data she'd downloaded. Normally she'd go to Geek for this kind of stuff. Thank goodness she knew a hacker outside of SOS. He went by Zip. If she could contact him, perhaps he'd pass her some code that she could use to hack into the files.

She'd have to wait for Dave's return with her clothing and the disposable cell phone she'd asked him to pick up while in Cape Churn. It was too risky to use Dave's phone to call a known criminal. Not only did it expose Dave, it might expose Zip.

Cooped up in the boat, she didn't dare get out until Dave brought her clothes. She couldn't risk being seen in the black leather pants and jacket. What she'd really like was a chance to go for a run. She could probably scrounge some oversize sweats and she could wear the shirt she'd borrowed from Dave, but without tennis shoes, a run was a no-go. Too conspicuous in black boots and sweats.

At a standstill on cracking through the data on the flash drive, she rose from the couch cushions and wandered around the living area, inspecting drawers and cabinets. For a man who needed a haircut and a shave, the items in his drawers were neat, orderly and folded or rolled in the fashion of a footlocker kept up by a top-notch soldier. This soldier hadn't forgotten his training.

In one cabinet, a faded, crumpled picture hung on the inside of the door. In the photograph two men in desert camouflage uniforms, Kevlar vests and helmets, carrying Colt M-4 carbines stood grinning at the camera. At first, Nicole didn't recognize either one until she looked closer. The taller one was Dave. Not the surly, scroungy man who wanted to kick her off his boat. This was a happier man with a clean-shaved face and unguarded eyes.

What had happened to make him so mad at the world?

The date on the photo was two years ago.

Footsteps on the deck above made Nicole jump. Unable to see who was coming, she ducked around the corner into Dave's sleeping quarters. If anyone but the boat's owner was there to pay a visit, she'd be ready.

Bags dropped down the steps, landing with a paper-crunching whomp on the floor. "Your clothes are here," Dave called out. "I got a charter gig in thirty minutes. See ya later."

"Wait." Nicole darted out of the bedroom and nearly

tripped over the bags getting to the steps. "When will you be back?"

He smirked from the halfway up the stairs. "Miss me already?"

She tried to play off her boredom. "No, I just like to know who and what to expect. Helps me to know if it's a good guy or a bad guy."

Dave snorted. "Honey, I'm bad to the bone. What's the difference?"

She didn't respond, maintaining eye contact until he gave in.

"I'll be back around dark."

"Thanks."

"You got everything you need for now?"

She nodded. "Now that I have clothes, I can get around. I won't need you to run my errands."

"If you need a vehicle, the keys to my truck are—"

"Hanging inside the cabinet by the fridge. I know."

"Snooping around?"

"I was bored."

"You don't have to stay here, you know," he said, his brows raised. "You have clothes."

"That reminds me. Did you get the hair dye?" she asked.

His lips pressed together for a moment, his gaze sweeping over her head. "No."

"Why not?"

"I gotta go." He started up the stairs, refusing to answer.

"Well, I appreciate what you did get. I can pick up the dye at the store later."

He paused, almost out of the cabin, and then turned back. "Don't."

She glanced up from the packages. "Don't what?"

"Don't dye your hair."

Nicole studied the frown on his face. "Why not?"

"I like your hair the way it is." Then he left.

Shaking her head, Nicole went to work sorting through the clothes he'd purchased, imagining how uncomfortable he must have been asking for a ladies bra and panties. She could have gone without the bra, but she'd wanted him to be a little uncomfortable. As opposed as he'd been to her staying on his boat, he deserved a little embarrassment.

She glanced out the window on the port side facing the dock. Dave strode away in his boat shoes, worn jeans and T-shirt, a fishing cap pulled down over his shaggy hair. He carried himself like a soldier, with all the pride and dignity drilled into him. And beneath the sloppy outfit was the body of a warrior.

Nicole had seen it. And damn if she didn't want to see it again.

As she tore through the bags, arranging the items, she set herself straight.

Messing with Dave Logsdon would be a big mistake.

Chapter 5

Nicole dressed in a pair of jeans, new tennis shoes and a white button-up blouse. Then she carefully braided and wound her hair up on top of her head and jammed one of Dave's baseball caps over it to keep it from being too noticeable. She wouldn't have to worry as much if Dave had gotten the brown dye that she'd put on her list.

Warmth stole over her again at his parting words. He liked her long blond hair just the way it was.

Nicole knew she was blessed with a good body and beautiful hair. If anything, it was her one vanity she hated to disguise. She'd done it before and probably would do it again if she had to. If she could keep it hidden beneath a hat, she might not have to sacrifice the natural color yet.

Once dressed, she pocketed the flash drive and climbed up onto the deck of the boat for the first time since Dave had carried her aboard. She blinked in the brightness of daylight, letting the sun warm her head and shoulders. She didn't like staying hidden, preferring open spaces to tight quarters. As many tense situations as she'd been in, she liked it better when she could actually see her escape route.

Having been in Cape Churn only a couple of months before, she remembered the layout of the town. It wasn't difficult; the town was small with only two major highways leading into and out of the city limits. With the throwaway cell phone in her grip, she set out to get as far away as possible from the boat and the marina before she placed her call. If anyone was monitoring Zip's calls, she didn't want to be traced back to her hiding place on Dave's yacht.

After walking a full mile along the coast, she climbed down a rocky path to the narrow strip of beach far below. The tide was out, exposing the rocky shore that normally would have been under water. She found a dry boulder and sat on it, then entered Zip's number and hit Talk.

After three rings she hung up, waited a minute and then dialed again, letting it ring two times before she hung up. It was the contact method they'd established when she'd worked with him before. She keyed in a text message: 9-1-1. Need help.

While she waited for a response, she gazed out across the water, wondering which way Dave had gone. With the sun warming her back and a breeze cooling her cheeks, she could almost believe she was just another tourist enjoying the beauty of the Oregon coast.

The cell phone pinged.

Who? Good. Zip was in. Nicole keyed TG X-26, her

call sign modeled after the Taser X26 CPW. Only she and Zip knew what it stood for and that it identified her to him.

In Zip's nefarious line of business, he couldn't be too careful. Though he was an expert hacker himself, he had enough enemies determined to hack him and bring him down, from mafia and drug lords to government entities he'd hacked into just because he could. He had to be careful.

Sup? he texted.

Call me.

A moment later her cell phone rang and she pressed the talk button, holding it to her ear.

"Wha'cha need, Sugar Baby?" Zip's familiar voice crackled through the air.

"Need to decrypt some data."

"Can you send it to me?"

"No. Too dangerous. Have to do it myself."

"Heard through the grapevine something's going down in D.C. Feds are scrambling to contain some of your buddies. You part of that?"

"Could be. Can you loan me some code?"

"What's in it for me?"

"Maybe a clean slate."

"Not interested. I make more on the dark side."

"Can you help me?"

He sighed before he responded. "I wouldn't if I didn't like you so much."

"Thanks, Zip."

The sound of fingers hitting a keyboard filled the

silence and then Zip said, "Sending it to our usual location."

"Thanks."

"Got the tech guts to run it with?" he asked.

"No," she responded. "I'm going primitive."

"Hmm. Might take time."

"How much?"

"Depends on the complexity. Hours, maybe days."

Nicole's stomach sank. "I might not have days."

"I could do it faster," Zip offered.

She wished she could hand it over and let someone with better hacking chops do the work. "Not an option."

"Sorry, TG. Unless you got some major firepower, you're stuck with a slower decryption speed."

"Understood." She stared out at the ocean, wondering how the hell she'd stay hidden long enough to decode the file and get her friends out of hot water.

"And, TG, if anyone asks…"

"I don't know you." She smiled. "But I still like you."

"And the same to ya." He paused. "Be careful."

"Will do." Nicole clicked the off button and sat for a long moment, contemplating the waves, wishing she could join the whales on their migration path. How simple life would be if all you had to do was swim and eat, eat and swim.

Not one to dwell on her troubles, Nicole rose from her perch on the rock and climbed the rocky path to the road above. If the laptop Dave had loaned her couldn't handle the volume of hits against the encrypted code, she'd have to bring in more capacity.

With a vague memory of the streets, Nicole headed back into town and turned onto the street where Emma lived. Perhaps Creed or Emma could loan her a computer. And they might have an update on the rest of their team back in D.C.

Rather than walk right up to the little cottage where Emma lived, Nicole ducked around the building, knocked on the back door and braced herself.

A dog's loud woof echoed inside the kitchen.

Not long afterward, the curtain over the door's window flicked to the side and a familiar face peered out. A second later the door opened.

Creed grabbed her arm and yanked her into the kitchen. "Get in here. The less people who see you, the safer you'll be."

"You think I don't know that?"

"Yeah, you do. I'm just a little spooked by all that's happening back in the capital."

A large golden retriever nosed her crotch, its tail sweeping the floor.

Nicole bent to scratch the dog's ears. "Hey, Moby. They treating you all right here?"

Creed laughed. "That dog rules this house."

"I used to have a dog." Nicole patted Moby. She'd had a yellow lab named Biscuit. She hadn't thought of that dog in a long time. Now the memory of him came back in a flood she'd be better off not recalling. It brought back thoughts of her childhood, of how her father had walked out on them and her mother had been forced to take Biscuit to the pound because she could barely put food on the table, much less in the dog's bowl.

That had been her first experience with a man disappointing her. She sat at the cute little dinette with its speckled Formica-top-and-chrome-rim, fifties-style table and matching shiny red-vinyl-and-chrome cushioned seats. "What have you heard about the situation in D.C.?"

Creed took the chair across from her. "Not much."

"Have you heard from Royce?" Nicole asked.

"Nothing. Not a peep. Sam and Kat are on the run, keeping a low profile to avoid being arrested while they try to figure out what's going on."

"Have they found where they're keeping Royce and Geek?"

"They think they're being held in one of the bunkers under the Capitol. The security is so tight they haven't been able to make heads or tails of what's going on."

"How are they staying out of trouble?"

"They've gone underground, moving only at night and staying clear of anything to do with SOS."

"Damn." Nicole shook her head. "Why is this happening?"

"I have a feeling the data on your flash drive will tell us everything we need to know."

Nicole pushed the hat back off her head and ran her hand through her hair. "I wasn't getting anywhere on the decryption."

"What are you going to do?"

"I should be getting a little help soon enough."

"Good to know."

"I need another computer. I don't have sufficient CPU storage and random access memory for the program to run fast enough. It could take days to decrypt depending on the complexity of the encryption."

Creed tapped his fingers on the tabletop. "What do you need?"

"I need an additional laptop. I'm going to link the

two computers to give the one running the decryption code enough power to speed up the process."

"You can have mine."

"I'm afraid to use it. If the feds have the SOS operatives under surveillance, your cell phone, computer or anything else SOS provided could be compromised."

"Maybe Emma or someone she knows will have a computer you can use. If not, I'll make a run to Portland."

"I figure it's only a matter of time before they figure out I'm here. If they know you and Valdez are here in Cape Churn, they might put two and two together. Where one SOS agent is, you're likely to find more."

"Then we don't have much time. Would it be better if Valdez and I got the heck out of town?"

"At this point, I need to know you two have my back."

Creed draped an arm around her shoulders. "You got it."

"Thanks." Not one who usually needed the reassuring hug of a friend, Nicole appreciated her teammate's show of affection. But not for long. She stepped out of his hold and got serious again. "If you can get me another computer, even better. I could also use a solar-powered battery charger in case I'm forced to go deep undercover."

"I have one among my equipment. I'll bring it by later."

"Good. I also need access to the internet that won't lead anyone monitoring for me back to the yacht."

"There's a library in town with computers. Patrons are allowed to access the internet from there."

Nicole chewed on her bottom lip. "I might be too exposed in the library."

"I could get Emma to do whatever you need her to do when she gets off work." He glanced at his watch. "She'll be off her shift in an hour. Should be enough time for her to stop by the library and look up anything you might need."

Emma was a nurse at the local hospital. She'd helped Creed and the team stop a terrorist plot. He wouldn't offer her assistance if he didn't trust her implicitly.

Nicole nodded. If Creed trusted Emma, she could trust her. "She'll need a clean flash drive."

"I'll get one to her before she leaves work."

"Got a pen and paper?"

Creed dug in a kitchen drawer and pulled out a pad of paper and a pen and handed them to her.

Nicole jotted down the internet address and password to the shared file Zip had set up and where he'd send the decryption code. She handed the sheet of paper to Creed. "Don't let anyone get hold of this information."

"I won't."

"And once Emma downloads the file, have her delete it from the shared file."

"Will do."

"And, Creed?"

"Yeah, Tazer?"

"It would be best if you didn't go with her."

He nodded. "Understood."

"Wouldn't hurt to watch her, though."

"Don't worry." He grinned. "I'll be close by."

"Thanks."

"Want me to bring the flash drive and computer equipment by the marina?"

"No. If I recall, there's a scenic overlook. You and Emma can pretend to be going out for dinner at the McGregor B and B. Stash everything in a backpack, wrap the backpack in a trash bag and stop at the overlook. Leave everything in the trash can there. I'll hide close by. Once you've left, I'll retrieve it."

"Do you really think whoever is targeting the SOS is already in Cape Churn?"

She raised her brows. "I don't know, but I'm not willing to risk exposure to find out."

"Agreed."

Nicole pushed back from the table and stood. "I need to go. No use putting you and Emma in the line of fire any more than I have to."

"Granted, I don't want Emma to suffer any repercussions of my career choice, but she's proved she's tough."

Nicole nodded. "Anyone who can fight in scuba gear and take down a terrorist bent on destroying the entire West Coast is okay in my books."

Creed's chest swelled and a grin spread across his face. "I'm gonna ask her to marry me."

Nicole's heart tightened at the happiness shining from Creed's eyes. He deserved to be happy and Emma had done that for him. "You should make an honest woman out of her."

Moby gave a low *woof.*

With a laugh, Nicole scratched the dog's ears. "Moby agrees. So when are you going to ask her?"

"When this mess is straightened out."

Nicole shook her head. "It's always one crazy case after another."

"Yeah, but the agency isn't usually the one being

targeted. I need to know I'll have a job when this is all over."

"Don't wait too long," Nicole advised. "She might get away."

Creed's smile faded. "Can't let that happen. She's everything I ever wanted. I love her."

"My point exactly. And there's never a perfect moment." Nicole snorted. "Like I'm one to give advice. Don't listen to me. But if I were you, I'd make it official before something stupid happens."

"Yeah. You have a point."

"I'm out of here."

"What are you going to do now?"

"I'm headed back to the dock to wait until sundown. It was risky enough getting out in the daylight, but I needed the exercise."

"Stay low, Tazer."

Nicole left through the back door and slipped around the side of the house and onto the street behind Emma's house. She hoped whoever was after her wouldn't find the tiny town of Cape Churn before she had a chance to run the decryption software Zip would provide.

As she moved through the streets, her thoughts ran the gamut of scenarios, each more devastating than the last. Amid all the images of her being cornered and forced to hand over the flash drive, two thoughts kept surfacing.

One of Creed down on one knee proposing to Emma.

The other of a naked boat captain, lying across the sheets.

Her pulse quickened the closer she came to the marina, a sense of anticipation building when she caught a glimpse of the dilapidated old yacht.

* * *

The sun was setting as Dave steered the *Reel Dive* toward the Cape Churn marina.

The seven businessmen who'd driven over from Portland to charter his boat for a team-building fishing trip had been good sports and easy to deal with, managing to bait their own hooks and take the fish off their lines by themselves.

Unfortunately that had left Dave with too much time to think about the woman who'd moved into his yacht despite his arguments to the contrary.

He'd given the businessmen an extra hour of fishing, no charge, just to stay out on the ocean longer. All in an effort to avoid his new roommate. The longer he stayed away from his yacht, the angrier he became. At Tazer, at the SOS team and mostly at himself for letting her disrupt his life so much. He shouldn't have to give up anything just because she'd insinuated herself into his home and life.

While he'd been filleting the catch and stowing it in coolers, images of Nicole's long, silky legs had his insides tied in knots. That damned bulky T-shirt she'd borrowed from his drawers had done nothing to hide her figure, the soft cotton draping over her curves only calling attention to those long, sexy legs. When she'd ripped the shirt over her head to prove a point, he'd almost lost it. Wow. Just wow. She had a killer figure.

Too deep in his thoughts about Nicole and her sexy body, Dave approached the marina faster than normal. When he realized it, he jammed the engine into reverse to slow it enough to avoid driving the boat up onto the dock.

Damn. There he went again. The woman was an unwanted distraction.

The businessmen finished off the last of their beer and stowed the fish in the ice chest now empty of drinks. One by one, they shook Dave's hand and thanked him for a great day, the last man handing him a wad of bills as a tip.

"We'll be sure to recommend you to our friends back in Portland," one guy said.

"Thanks. If you take that fish by the Seaside Café, Nora will cook it for you."

"Good idea. We'll do that now."

Dave pocketed the money and finished cleaning the boat as the last rays of the sun disappeared below the waters of the Pacific Ocean.

He'd been careful not to allow his gaze to cross to the rumbling yacht at the end of the marina until he had all his work done and the *Reel Dive* locked down for the night.

With nothing more to do, he considered heading to the Seaside Café for dinner, but he smelled too fishy and needed a shower and change of clothing before he went anywhere. Normally he'd drop his clothes on the deck of his boat and enter the cabin naked, thus not smelling up the yacht with his fishy clothing.

With Tazer aboard, he couldn't exactly be himself.

She was messing up his routine and he didn't like it.

About to step off the *Reel Dive* onto the dock, movement at the end of the marina caught his attention.

Someone dressed in dark pants, a black jacket and a dark baseball cap left his yacht and moved toward the end of the pier and stepped out into the parking lot.

Not a light shone from the windows of his yacht. Had someone already found Nicole?

He studied the way the shadowy figure moved, hips swaying, stepping out like a ballerina.

Female.

And by the model smoothness of her gait, it had to be his guest.

Still smelling fishy, and not really giving a damn, Dave waited a moment or two, letting Tazer get a good hundred-yard lead on him.

Why he followed, he didn't know. The stealthy way she slipped in and out of the darker areas had his hunter instincts on alert. His training as a Special Forces soldier kicked in and he moved softly over the wooden planks of the dock, stepping out onto the gravel of the parking lot.

Tazer had already moved up to the road leading down into the marina.

His exhaustion from a day at sea disappeared as he slid in and out of shadows along the road, following the woman who'd turned his quiet little corner of the world upside down.

What was she up to? Who was she meeting and why was she dressed like a burglar?

Even more to the point, why was he following her?

Dave barely kept up with her. Several times she disappeared.

He'd waited patiently in the dark until he spotted her again. Her general direction was toward the southern edge of town.

Was she going to meet someone who would take her away from Cape Churn? If so, why didn't he feel a huge sense of relief? Instead he found himself a bit disappointed that his unwanted guest would be leaving so soon. And without saying goodbye.

If he were honest with himself, he would admit that, despite delaying the inevitable, he'd actually been looking forward to seeing her again. Maybe even exchanging barbed comments and sharp retorts. She was an intelligent agent. One with the ability to take care of herself. He could appreciate that in any woman.

On the edge of town there weren't as many buildings to hide behind and the trees were fewer and farther between. The coastal highway ran along the shoreline, rising steeper away from the sea.

Tazer moved along the roadside, in the shadows of the trees as much as possible, on the shoulder when it wasn't possible, hurrying to keep out of sight. When a vehicle passed, she dropped to the earth, pressing her body as close to the ground as she could to avoid being spotted in the headlights.

At one point the terrain dropped sharply over the side, giving her no cover or concealment. If a vehicle passed at exactly that moment, she'd be spotted.

Headlights swung around the curve.

Dave stepped behind a tree and watched as Tazer dropped over the edge of the road.

His heart in his throat, he nearly jumped out and yelled for her. Willing himself to stay put, he waited for the vehicle to pass and for Tazer to rise from the rugged drop.

A minute passed and she didn't appear. After two minutes Dave pushed out from the cover of the trees and jogged along the road. To hell with keeping his cover and concealment. If Tazer had fallen over the edge of a cliff, she might be injured and need help.

As he neared the last spot he'd seen her, he peered over the edge of the road at a sheer drop, his heart hammering against his chest. Had she—?

Something grabbed his wrist and yanked it behind him up between his shoulder blades. Pain ripped through him, forcing him forward, to teeter on the edge of the cliff.

He let his assailant manipulate him to a point before he jerked his head back and smacked his skull against his attacker's head. The grip on his wrist loosened momentarily, allowing him to pull free, spin and sweep his leg out, knocking over the person behind him.

Dave threw himself down on the jeans-clad, black-jacketed figure who was kicking and twisting so hard he almost fell over the edge of the cliff. He took a punch in the face until he could control the flailing hands and feet. "Be still, damn it!" He grunted and held on.

"Dave?" The struggles ceased. The hat tipped back off his captive's head and glorious long blond hair splayed out on the roadside. "What the hell? Why are you following me?"

"Not to get beat up, that's for sure." Still pinning her wrists above her head, he straddled her hips, securing Nicole to the hard ground.

Her breasts rose and fell with every breath and the stars overhead sparkled in her eyes.

All Dave could think of was how beautiful she was and how much he wanted to bend down and kiss those full, lush lips.

Then her nose wrinkled. "You stink like fish."

Nothing like a woman telling it like it was to bring a guy back to earth and the reality of the situation. She was an unwanted guest with a whole lot of trouble following her. He was a bachelor who wanted his privacy back. Still he didn't move, didn't rise from where he straddled her.

"You didn't answer me." Nicole lay still staring up at him. "Why are you following me?"

"Curiosity."

"Well, can you get your curiosity off me before we're seen or, worse, run over?"

"I don't know, I kind of like it here." A smile pulled at the edges of his lips. For once he had her at a disadvantage. And he liked it.

The glow of headlights rounding the curve ahead of them made him move. Wrapping his arms around her, he rolled to the side, taking her with him. When he stopped, he landed with her on top of him. He raised his hands to cover her bright hair, pushing her face down on the other side of his head to hide the only bright spot on her.

They teetered on the edge of the cliff, Dave holding his breath until the vehicle passed without slowing.

Once it had disappeared around the next corner, Tazer pushed against his chest. "We need to move. We're too exposed here."

His arms clamped around her middle, refusing to let her all the way up. "Not until you tell me what you're up to."

"Oh, good grief. Creed's dropping off equipment I need at the scenic overlook. He should be there any moment. The longer you delay me, the more chance of someone finding it before I get there. Let go of me."

"Anyone ever tell you that your eyes flash when you're angry?" They were sparkling, and she was even more beautiful with fire in her eyes.

"No. And I wouldn't care if they did. I've told you what you wanted to know." Her voice faded, her gaze sliding lower to his lips. "Will you please let go of me?" she whispered, " before…"

"Before what?" he lowered his head. "Before I kiss you?"

"You don't want to kiss me," she said so softly he could barely hear the words.

"Oh, but I do."

"Please…" she begged.

"I won't let you go. Not until you kiss me." He didn't know why he'd demanded the kiss, but once he had, he wasn't letting go until she met his demand.

Chapter 6

For one crazy moment, she considered the kiss. "Are you insane?" She pushed against him, wiggling, but not too much that they'd end up flying over the edge of the steep drop-off. Her pulse pounded in her chest so hard she was sure he'd feel it through the thick material of the black leather jacket she'd borrowed from his closet. "We're going to get run over or discovered. Is that what you want?"

"Nope. All I want is a kiss. It's a small price to pay for letting you use my yacht as a base of your operations."

Fire built in the lower regions of her body. "What if I don't want to kiss you?" she asked, her voice breathless, not firm as she'd intended.

"Guess we'll stay here a little longer."

Another set of headlights shone around the corner.

"Damn." She ducked her head, her cheek pressed against his, his breath warming her neck.

A kiss? Really? They were perched on the edge of a cliff, in danger of falling off, and the fishing boat captain wanted a kiss.

A thrill of something zinged through her.

When the vehicle passed, Nicole lifted her head. "Fine. You can have your kiss. Anything to get this operation moving."

She lowered her lips, aiming for his cheek.

Dave turned in time for her lips to meet his. One hand slid up her back to her head, his fingers burying themselves in the thickness of her silky hair.

The pressure of his lips on hers deepened. When she should have jerked her head away, the tension in her body melted and the kiss stretched on.

Not until another flash of headlights illuminated the roadside did she break the kiss and hide her head beside his again.

When the car had gone, she lay against him, her heart slamming against her ribs, the entire length of her body burning where it touched his.

His hands held her, but not tight enough to trap her. She could have gotten up at any time.

But she didn't.

Nicole raised her head and stared down into his dark-as-sin eyes. "Why?"

"Why what?"

"Why did you kiss me like that?"

He smiled and sat her on the ground beside him. "Damned if I know."

For a moment her head spun, her thoughts tangled around the feel of his lips still lingering on hers. Then she pulled herself together once she reminded herself of the severity of her situation. "Well, don't do it again." The steel she normally put behind a rejection just wasn't there. What was wrong with her? Had she gone soft? Where was the Nicole who'd earned her nickname of Tazer?

She stood, brushing gravel and dust from her jeans. "Now, if you'll excuse me, I need to be in place before Creed makes the drop." Without looking down at him, she took off at a jog, racing around the corner before he could get up from the ground.

Footsteps pounding the ground behind her made her pick up the pace until she was running full-out. Thankfully, not another car came along the highway at that time. She'd abandoned stealth operations in her desire to get away from her nemesis, the hot-lipped kisser who'd stirred her passion and made her want more.

Hell. How had he done it? The man smelled like fish and could use a shave and a haircut. He wasn't the usual type she found attractive. Then why did she want to turn around, fling herself into his arms and go for round two on that kiss?

The road was uphill all the way. By the time she reached the pullout for the scenic overlook, she was huffing and puffing like a new recruit at Quantico. She barely had time to throw herself behind a large boulder before headlights knifed through the darkness.

Dave dove behind the boulder with her.

"Find your own hiding place," she snapped.

"Why, when it's much cozier here with you? Besides, how can I protect you if I'm not anywhere near you?" He pressed against her in an attempt to get his entire big frame behind the boulder.

"I don't need your protection," she said.

A truck pulled into the overlook and the driver's door opened long enough for Nicole to see Emma's silhouette in the passenger seat and Creed's outline as he stepped out from the driver's side, closing the door behind him. He carried a trash bag to the courtesy trash receptacle at one end of the overlook and laid it gently inside.

Nicole tensed her muscles and started to rise.

A hand on her arm stopped her. "Wait," Dave whispered.

Another set of headlights shone in the night, rising up the hill toward the overlook.

She strained against Dave's grip. "I need to get to that package."

"Not now," Dave insisted.

Creed climbed into the truck and slammed the door shut. He leaned across the seat and kissed Emma in a long, slow lip-lock. The headlights coming up the road behind them silhouetted the couple, making it look as though they were there to make out.

Creed broke off the kiss, shifted the truck into gear and eased out onto the highway, headed toward the Mc-Gregor B and B, another two miles down the road.

A dark SUV slowed and pulled into the overlook, headlights shining briefly out over the ocean before they blinked out. With the engine still running, two men dropped down from the back of the SUV, the interior light remaining dark, not illuminating the inside of the vehicle or the people within. One man walked to the edge of the overlook, close to the boulder behind which Nicole and Dave hid.

Nicole eased back out of view of the overlook.

The crunch of gravel indicated the man was getting closer.

Holding her breath, Nicole waited until the crunching sounds moved away from them. Her head low to the ground, her body flattened against the earth, she stole a look around the boulder.

When the man turned to the side, he held out his hand in front of him, the shape of a pistol outlined by moonlight.

Dave's fingers tightened on Nicole's arm.

She didn't need the warning.

These men had come to find her. Why else would they be armed and following Creed?

The other man stopped at the trash receptacle and glanced down into the can.

Nicole braced herself. If they took the trash bag, she'd have to go after them. Zip's decryption code in the wrong hands could be dangerous, if not downright disastrous.

The man reached into the can and poked at the trash with the nose of his weapon.

"Nothin' here. Come on. We can catch up to Thomas. If she made it to Cape Churn, he'll meet up with her sooner or later."

Not until the two men climbed into the SUV and left, disappearing around the next bend in the road, did Nicole take a full, deep breath. Then she launched herself out of her hiding place and grabbed the trash bag out of the can. In two seconds she had the plastic ripped away and the backpack removed.

When Nicole started to slip the straps over her shoulders, Dave stopped her. "Let me carry it."

"No way. I can and will."

"I have more upper body strength." He stared into her eyes, his face lit by the starlight. "We can stand here and argue or get back to *Freedom's Price* and get started decoding that data before the goons figure out where you are."

She knew he was right. The "she" those men had been referring to had to be her. "Fine. But I'm not letting you out of my sight."

He grinned as he slipped the backpack over his broad shoulders. "You just needed an excuse to appreciate my fine butt."

"Shut up, Fish Boy, and move." She gave him a nudge toward Cape Churn.

Dave set off at a steady jog, his stride eating up the distance between the overlook and town.

Though she prided herself in staying in top physical shape, Nicole struggled to keep up with the man. She'd complain at his pace, but he was carrying the weight of a computer and solar battery charger and she wasn't. Besides, following him did give her a chance to appreciate the way his jeans hugged his tight buttocks.

So he'd been right about her admiring his backside. Big deal. It didn't mean anything.

As soon as they reached town, Dave moved into the shadows and eased his way toward the marina, keeping low every time a vehicle passed or he sensed movement.

All the duck-and-cover maneuvers he'd learned in the Special Forces came back to him. He could almost feel the tension of searching through an Afghani town for hidden members of the Taliban.

A loud crash sounded nearby. He spun toward the continued rattle of metal on pavement. A cat raced away from a trash-can lid it had knocked off the overloaded container next to a cottage.

His heart racing, Dave had to remind himself to remain calm. He was in Cape Churn, a quiet little town on the coast of Oregon, not the war-torn streets of an enemy-infested village.

A soft hand on his arm jerked him back from the edge. "Are you okay?" Nicole asked.

"I'm fine," he seethed out between tight lips. By the time he reached the marina, he was ready to dive into *Freedom's Price* and down a six-pack of beer.

When he reached the end of the pier, Tazer slammed her arm across his chest. "Let me clear it first."

"No. I'll clear it." He handed her the backpack, climbed aboard the boat and eased down the steps. The cabin door was locked. Which didn't mean it was safe.

Slipping the key into the lock, he turned it quietly and pushed the door open as he pressed his back against the wall beside him.

Nothing stirred inside.

He entered and gave the cramped interior a quick once-over to make sure no one had been there. "Clear," he called out softly.

A moment later Tazer descended into the cabin and set the backpack on the table. "We might have a problem."

"Yeah. I have no doubt in my mind—" he started.

"—they're looking for me," Tazer finished.

Much as he hadn't wanted her to live on the boat with him, Dave didn't want anything bad to happen to her. The woman had guts. "Think you should hit the road?"

Before the kiss, he'd have been happy if she'd said yes. Now...

"I'd have to borrow a vehicle and it would cut into my time for decrypting. Maybe following Thomas and Valdez will keep them busy for a while."

"I think you need to leave."

"You heard them. They don't know I'm here. They're playing on a hunch. If I stay buried in this junk heap for a couple days, they won't see me. Who would think to look for me here?"

He could see her point, but he didn't feel comfortable about the situation. "It's not safe."

"And driving around the countryside on a busted-up motorcycle is any better?"

"No."

"Unless you know someone who wants to sell a motorcycle?" she asked.

He shook his head. "Not off the top of my head."

She shrugged. "Wouldn't help me, anyway. I need to be in one place to run the computers, and I'll need electricity to keep the computers charged, or the solar-powered battery in a place with sunlight. Not in a back-pack while I'm riding across the country."

"Okay, I get your point." His eyes narrowed. "But you can't venture outside the boat."

"And I can't contact my friends anymore. It puts them in danger as well as me."

"One other thing…"

Nicole frowned. "As if there wasn't enough?"

"The marina owners know you're staying here."

She blew out a long stream of air. "What do they know?"

"That I carried you in last night."

"What did you tell them?"

"That you'd had a little too much to drink."

"And did you tell them who I was?"

"I told them you were an old girlfriend from my service days." He could feel the heat rising up his neck again. "They even offered advice on protection."

"Old girlfriend, huh?" A smile tugged at her lips.

He glared. "Hey, they're nice people, concerned for my welfare."

"I didn't say anything."

"Yeah," he muttered. "You didn't have to."

"Look, I'm going to set this equipment up and get started." Tazer wrinkled her nose. "You might consider a shower."

"Would have had it a lot sooner if you hadn't gone wandering out to the overlook." He ripped his shirt over his head and reached for the buttons on his jeans. "I usually hang my fishy clothes outside on the deck so that they don't stink up the cabin. Fair warning. If you don't want to watch, you might turn around."

"You don't have anything different than the last time I saw you, do you?" Her lips quirked.

Their sparring had driven away any fatigue he'd been feeling from being out on the ocean most of the day, and jogging through town had gotten his blood pumping. Having a woman in the close confines of his cabin had made him more aware of her than if she'd been out walking on the street. He could smell the light scent of his shampoo in her hair and he remembered the way she'd bucked beneath him when he'd straddled her along the side of the road.

Yeah, things were different than the last time she'd seen him naked. With a quick yank, he unbuttoned his fly and dropped the jeans down around his ankles and stepped out of them.

She gasped and spun away. "You could have warned me you go commando. And what's with…that…that… Oh, hell, you know."

"That's what you get for assuming nothing's changed."

Chuckling at her discomfort, he climbed the steps to the deck above and tossed his smelly clothes, then descended.

She had her back to him as much as she could, but he caught her sneaking a peek as he slid behind her, forced to touch her to get around her.

Nicole pulled in a sharp breath and stiffened.

All that sassy confidence was wound up tighter than a rattlesnake with a new button on his tail. He bet if he spun her around and kissed her, she'd come unglued.

The thought of kissing her made him so hot he wondered how he'd ever relax. There wasn't enough cold water in his boat's holding tank to douse the flame burning in his groin.

After he washed the fish smell off his body in ice-cold water, he stayed in the tiny bathroom as long as he could. Finally the smell of hamburger frying drove him from his hiding place, his stomach rumbling. He emerged in a clean pair of jeans he'd had to zip carefully not to hurt himself.

Nicole had the equipment set up, the computers connected to each other, their fans humming.

"Get the decoder running?" he asked.

"Yup." Having removed the black leather jacket she'd borrowed from his closet, she stood at the stove, stirring hamburger meat in a skillet. "I don't have to do much but let it run. Spaghetti sound okay?"

"Sounds great." He started to pull a shirt over his

head, thinking to disguise the fact he was still aroused by her. On second thought, he tossed it over the back of the couch. The woman intrigued him and made him hot. Let her stew a little.

Her gaze followed the shirt and she nearly missed the pan as she poured a jar of sauce over the meat. She cleared her throat and nodded toward the pan of boiling water. "Think you can handle the noodles?"

"Got it." He grabbed the package of noodles and tore it open with a little more force than was necessary. The bag came apart, the noodles spilling over the stove and floor.

They bent at the same time, trying to catch them, and knocked heads.

Nicole staggered backward.

Dave caught her arm and steadied her, pushing her hair back from her forehead where a red spot appeared. He gently brushed his thumb over the mark. They stood so close he could see the pulse pounding at the base of her throat. Her chest rose and fell, the shirt he'd purchased for her tight over her breasts.

"Sorry about that," he said. "I'm not used to sharing my kitchen with someone else." Rather than withdraw his hand, he skimmed it along the side of her cheek and down the long line of her throat to where the skin moved to the beat of her heart.

Her eyes rounded, her tongue swiping across her lower lip. "What are you doing?"

"I can't seem to resist."

"Then why bother?" she whispered.

"From your lips to God's ears." He bent to claim her soft, full lips.

She opened to him, her teeth parting to allow his

tongue to slide along the length of hers, the delicate dance growing wilder by the moment.

The noodles remained on the floor as he explored her mouth, tasted her warmth.

Her hands circled the back of his head and she deepened their connection, pressing her breasts against his chest.

They didn't come up for air until the water bubbled over and the sauce popped and splattered, spitting thick red tomato puree across the stovetop.

Nicole pulled away first, turned the heat down on the stove and moved the sauce from the burner. "I can clean up the mess. I'm sure you have something else to do."

Not wanting to end it there, he stepped up behind her and brushed the hair back from her ear. "Nothing that can't wait."

When he bent to take her earlobe between his teeth, she closed her eyes. "This is crazy."

"You're telling me. I can't seem to get you out of my system."

"Those thugs could come crawling aboard this boat at any moment." She leaned her head to the side, giving him better access to her throat.

He trailed another kiss along the back of her neck. "Anytime," he repeated, his concentration on her not the threat lurking in Cape Churn.

"Taking this any further would be foolish." She turned in his arms, resting her hands on his naked chest.

"I've been called a fool on more than one occasion." His arms swept around her waist and pulled her against his hard erection. "But I'd be a bigger fool to walk away."

She skimmed her hands up his chest and circled them around his neck. "You sure you aren't hungry?"

"Starving," he said, taking her mouth in a ravenous kiss, his hands slipping low to cup her bottom, lifting her to wrap her strong, supple legs around his waist.

She met his mouth with as much passion and force as he did, her tongue lashing out, thrusting and pulsing against his. Her fingers laced through his hair, dragging him closer until her breasts smashed against him.

Spaghetti and sauce forgotten, he staggered blindly to the sleeping cabin. Setting her feet on the floor, he worked the buttons on her shirt, his fingers fumbling.

She brushed his hands away and freed the buttons in quick and efficient moves. As she'd reached the bottom, he shoved the shirt over her shoulders and it fell to the ground around her ankles.

He fumbled with her bra catch and flicked it free, dragging the straps over her arms and down to free the beautiful mounds of her breasts. He stopped long enough to feast his eyes on their beauty and fullness. Then he lifted her and set her in the middle of the bed, hooking his fingers in the elastic of her panties and stripping them off her.

Seconds later his jeans joined her clothing on the floor and he was climbing across the mattress.

Nicole let her knees fall to the side, her fingers slipping down between her folds to stroke herself.

"Mine," he growled, shoving her hand to the side.

She chuckled. "Are you always this much of an animal in bed?"

"Only with you, babe." He kissed a path from the back of her knee along the inside of her thigh to that center point where her entrance glistened.

He wanted to taste her, to feel the warmth of her on his lips, to bring her to the brink of insanity and launch her over the edge.

Parting her folds, he flicked the pulsing strip of flesh with the tip of his tongue.

She dug her heels into the mattress and cried out, her back arching off the bed. "Holy hell."

He backed away from her. "Want me to stop?"

"No!" Threading her fingers in his hair, she urged him back to the task.

Dave lapped, flicked, teased and sucked on her until she cried out, pulling his hair so hard he thought it would come out.

When he finally let up, she remained tensed as he reached over the side of the bed to dig in a drawer built into the wall.

She grabbed the foil packet from him, pushed him onto his back, and tore it open. With shaking hands, she smoothed the condom over his thick, hard erection and straddled him, lowering herself over him.

Dave surged upward, filling her as she fully sheathed him deep inside her.

"You feel so good."

"Shut up and move," she said through gritted teeth and leaned forward, planting her hands on either side of him. Then she set the pace, rising up on her knees and lowering back down over him.

After a while, Dave flipped her onto her back and went after it for real, sliding into her again and again.

She met him thrust for thrust, her fingers bunching in the sheets beneath her, her head flung back, her eyes squeezed closed. "Yes!" she cried.

A surge of sensations hit him like a tidal wave, engulfing him and then raising him higher until he shot over the top. He dropped down over her and pumped into her one last time, holding steady, deep and pulsing with the walls of her channel gripping him. When he could think to breathe, he dragged in a long, steadying breath and let it go, easing down beside her on the bed, pulling her with him to keep from severing their connection.

She laid in his arms, breathing hard, a thin coat of perspiration coating her soft skin. "Wow."

"Yeah. Wow." Dave lay against the pillow, staring up at the ceiling and wondering what the hell had just happened. "I feel like I should say something profound. But all I can come up with is 'wow.'"

Her hand drifted over his chest, swirling around one of his nipples. "Don't get too worked up about the afterglow wording." Her fingers stopped moving and her hand lay warm over his heart. "When it's all said and done, it was just sex."

Chapter 7

Nicole had purposely made the comment to minimize the impact he'd had on her. She wasn't there to start something with him. Not that she was any good at relationships…but… Who was she kidding? She *wasn't* any good at relationships.

"Just sex? Are you crazy? That's like saying walking on the moon was just another stroll in the park." He captured the fingers tweaking his nipple and brought them to his lips. "Just sex… I must be losing my touch." With deliberate attention to detail, he kissed one finger after another, her palm and then went to work on that sensitive place just below her ear.

She closed her eyes, trying not to respond when her body was screaming "Hallelujah!"

"That wasn't a challenge, you know," she said breathlessly, the heat rising as if someone had cranked up the thermostat.

"Maybe not to you." He rolled over her, leaning up on his elbows while his lips trailed across her cheeks and up to brush across her eyelids, her nose, her chin and lower.

Her back arched when he found one of her nipples and sucked it into his mouth.

"No, you're definitely not losing your touch! Do the other one." She gasped. "Please."

"That's more like it." He worked her body, teasing her along, letting her think she could relax, then he'd touch her just so and have her tensing all over again. When his fingers parted her folds this time, she was so close to losing it already, all he had to do was touch her with the very tip of his tongue and she breached the surface, launching into the sky, shattering into a million sparkling pieces of sunlight.

"Holy hell, let me die now," she cried, her fingernails digging into his shoulders as he devoured her in an unrelenting assault, bringing her aboard with the best orgasm she'd ever had.

When she finally fell back into the sea of rippling sensations, she gathered in a deep breath and said, "Give the fish boy a prize. You were right. That wasn't *just sex*."

Dave lay for a long time with Nicole nestled in his arms, slightly dazed and loving the feel of her naked skin against his. She'd been the most passionate lover he'd ever experienced or ever wanted to experience again.

Before long her breathing became steady and deep as

she slipped into sleep. Tempted to join her in slumber, he reminded himself of what had happened the night before. He couldn't go to sleep, not when his dreams ruled his actions. Having almost choked Nicole before, he refused to tempt fate.

Far from sleepy, Dave rose, nervous energy making him want to be up and moving, working out the adrenaline rush brought on by making love to Nicole. Once in the living area of the cabin, he cleaned up the spilled spaghetti noodles, finished cooking and set the food aside for when she woke, starving from all the running, hiding and mattress gymnastics. He didn't know how she'd lasted as long as she had. The previous night's sleep could only have put a small dent in her exhaustion after being up for two days, dodging those who wanted what she'd stolen.

When Dave thought about it, he wondered how she would get out of this mess. If the government wanted to get technical, they could arrest her and throw her in jail for breaking and entering and stealing. Felony and felony.

He checked the computers to make sure they were still running and that the decoding executable was humming along, racing through as many permutations as it took to decrypt the data on the flash drive. Staring at the screen wouldn't will the program to work any faster. He had to trust in the code and hope it would get the job done sooner rather than later.

Nicole didn't have much time. Not with an SUV full of agents in town looking for her.

Dave slipped on his black leather jacket, which now smelled like Nicole, pushed his feet into his deck shoes and climbed the steps to the deck. The clear sky allowed the heat to rise and the cool air to settle over the coast. He shivered as he stretched out on the deck, lacing his fingers together behind his head. Staring up at the sky, he could almost believe he was alone in the world, with no worries, no demons threatening to beat down his door. The sky didn't care that he'd watched his friend die, didn't care if the bad guys got away or if Nicole Steele or Dave Logsdon lived or died. The universe continued on as always, quiet, steady, forever.

Most nights the quiet and the stars had the effect of settling his PTSD-fractured nerves. Not tonight.

Dave rose from the deck, locked the cabin door and then left the boat, the dock and the marina. He strode up from the parking lot and into Cape Churn, the town that rolled up the sidewalks after the sun went down. He'd roamed the streets like this before when he couldn't sleep or his dreams woke him, and he didn't want to go back to relive them.

Cape Churn slept. Lights glowed from the streetlights and from some of the porches of homes and businesses. Nothing moved but a stray cat and one vehicle slowly patrolling the streets.

Cape Churn's nightly police patrol car pulled up beside Dave and the window slipped down. "Hey, Dave. Can't sleep?" Gabe McGregor leaned out.

"Nah."

Gabe glanced toward the marina, now out of sight. "Has she made any progress on decoding the data?"

"Not yet." Dave dug his hands into his pockets. "I'm glad you're the one out tonight. I'm worried."

"What about?"

He told Gabe about the handoff at the overlook. "You might want to check out a black SUV if it happens to pass through town. I'd bet money they're looking for Nicole."

McGregor blew out a breath. "Sounds like it."

"Also, it would be a good idea to warn the others that we won't be in contact with them. It would be too easy for them to trace back to me and Nicole."

"Gotcha." Gabe stared off into the distance. "I wonder if she shouldn't get the heck out of town."

"That was only one SUV. We don't know if there are more out there."

"There's an off-season golf tournament going on, which means lots of strange people and vehicles in town to muddy the works."

"I'll keep that in mind. For now, Nicole's agreed to lie low and out of the public eye. Hopefully the decoder will finish before they find her."

"If not, you two better have a backup plan."

Dave started to argue that he wasn't part of any "you two" or in need of any backup plan. Since she'd arrived, Nicole had gone from an unwanted visitor to someone Dave couldn't seem to let go of. "I'd better get back."

"I'll wait a few minutes and then do a drive-by to make sure no one's lurking."

"I thought you were working days?"

"One of the guys called in sick." He gave a wry smile. "I'm pulling a double, much to Kayla's disappointment. I'd rather be with her and the kids."

"How's that going? You went from being a bachelor to a man with a teen and a baby. That has to be hard."

"I think being a parent is the hardest job you'll ever love."

Not a job he considered himself fit for, Dave had to take Gabe's word for it. "I gotta get back."

The police officer nodded. "Let me know if you need anything."

Gabe drove away and Dave continued walking. When he reached the corner by the Seaside Café, he paused, worry pulling at him to turn and head back.

Why? He wasn't obligated to provide Nicole around-the-clock protective services. She wasn't going to stay past the time it took to decipher the data on the flash drive. Why the hell should he care?

She'd leave and he'd go on about his life as if she'd never slept in his bed, never showed such passion in his arms. Oh, who was he kidding? The woman had managed to slide under his skin in less than twenty-four hours. He spun on his heels. She'd just have to slide the hell out. His life didn't have room for a relationship. He was too messed up to be good for anyone.

Nicole woke to darkness, the only light coming to her through the open doorway to the living area. When she sat up, the sheet slipped down around her waist and cool night air brushed against her naked skin.

Had she really had sex with Dave? What had she been thinking?

That he was damned good in bed? That he'd been hard to resist, and that she'd gone long enough without some sort of physical release?

It wasn't as if he was going to steal secrets from her and sell them to the highest bidder. Hell, at this point she didn't have any secrets to sell. She pushed the sheets aside and scrambled off the bed.

Based on the silence, she assumed Dave had left. Standing naked in his bedroom should have made her shiver from the cold, but her body heated at the naughty feeling she had. She stepped into the living area, still naked.

What if Dave walked in right at that moment and saw her standing there? Would he insist they go back to bed and pick up where they'd left off? She pressed a hand to her breast, the skin there deliciously sensitive from beard-burn and being nibbled on. For a moment she hesitated, half hoping the cabin door would open to Dave and they'd continue with more of what they'd shared already.

When the door remained closed, she sighed, raided his T-shirt drawer for one of his older, worn T-shirts and pulled it over her head. It covered her body and halfway down her thighs and it smelled like Dave.

To take her mind off the man, she sat at the table and dragged her finger across the touchpad of Dave's laptop. The screen blinked to life, the decryption program still running with no data to show for it. The tracking bar indicated the code had passed through 22 percent of its processing. It would take time. Time she might not have. Worrying would do her no good.

Her stomach rumbled, the scent of tomato sauce reminding her of a dinner she hadn't gotten around to eating. Crossing to the pots on the stove, she touched her hand to one. It was still warm.

She pulled two plates down from the cabinet and scooped noodles onto one of them. Still no Dave.

Too hungry to worry about him, she dug her fork into the fragrant meal and was about to bite into it when footsteps sounded on the deck above.

Nicole laid down her fork on the plate and stood, grabbed a fillet knife from a knife-block on the counter then tiptoed to the cabin door where she waited for whoever was up there to come down.

The door opened above and jeans-clad legs descended.

Bracing herself, Nicole prepared to attack.

When Dave's dark, shaggy head appeared, she let go of the breath she'd been holding. "Thank goodness it's you."

Dave stared at the knife. "I'm glad you waited to verify before you filleted me."

"You could have let me know you were leaving," she countered.

"I didn't want to wake you." He glanced at the two plates on the table.

"Care to join me?" Nicole returned the knife to the counter.

He shrugged out of his jacket and hung it in a closet. "I'm not hungry. I have a charter in the morning."

"Suit yourself."

"Don't stay up too late," he said as he stepped through to the sleeping quarters. "You'll need to be up by five."

"Why?"

"You're coming with me."

"I can't go with you. You and I both know I can't leave this equipment and the decryption program running. What if whoever is looking for me finds it?"

"They won't."

"How do you know that?"

"Because you'll be on the *Reel Dive* with me all day. You can bring the computers with you."

"That's insane."

"It's not up for discussion. I'm not leaving you here.

You're not staying with one of your buddies who are already being watched. That leaves you with no other choice." He turned to face her. "Five o'clock comes early. When you're done eating, I suggest you get some rest." He stepped into the bathroom and closed the door behind him.

"I know when five o'clock comes. Sheesh," she muttered to the closed door. Then she sat at the table and forced herself to eat half the plate of spaghetti, no longer hungry but damned if she showed that man she was affected by his high-handedness. Who was he to order her around, anyway?

When he emerged, she'd scraped the rest of the spaghetti off her plate into the trash, combined the noodles with the sauce and stored it in the refrigerator. A regular freakin' domestic woman.

"One more thing…" Dave said.

Nicole held her breath, waiting for him to invite her to sleep with him so that she could tell him to go to hell. She raised her brows, daring him.

He grabbed a pillow from the bed and tossed it at her. "You might need this for the couch."

The pillow bounced off her face and she caught it on the way to the floor. A scathing comment rushed to her lips but she stopped herself from saying it.

Dave unbuttoned his jeans and shoved them down his legs.

Nicole forgot what she was going to say. Her mouth went dry and she swayed toward that gorgeous body.

With a slight curve to the corners of his lips, Dave climbed into his bed. Naked, he pulled the sheet up over his body and closed his eyes, ignoring her completely.

The bastard! How dare he walk in, give her orders,

then go to bed alone after they'd made love, not once, but twice?

Nicole's anger trumped her desire. Rather than let him know she was mad, she lifted her chin and turned her back on the man. She didn't need him, didn't want to share a bed with him.

It was *just sex*. Nothing more.

Apparently it was nothing more to him. She plumped the pillow and lay on the couch mad, twitchy and so hot her body might light the whole damned boat on fire.

For a long time she laid wide awake, her mind too active, her thoughts spinning around the operation, the men who'd followed Creed, and mostly around the naked man in the bed within throwing distance.

The whir of the fan motor on the laptop reassured her that sooner or later that damned program would finish its job and she'd be free to leave *Freedom's Price* and its owner. If she didn't need a place to stay out of the way and unnoticed, she would have left right then.

As her anger receded and her logic returned, she realized Dave had been right. And that made her mad all over again. Not at Dave, but, if she was honest, at herself for being disappointed that he hadn't wanted her to sleep with him. After what they'd shared, she thought it was a natural progression for her to share his bed. At least while they were in forced proximity.

Apparently he hadn't been as impressed with her as she had been with him. He'd set out to prove his point and, boy, had he!

The computer on the table beside her beeped.

Nicole sat up and turned the screen toward her. It hadn't done that before. Her pulse quickened. Had it decrypted the data already? If so, she'd be on her way before morning. Her hand hovered over the touchpad, her gaze shooting to the darkened doorway of the sleeping quarters. Would she miss him? Better question: Would he miss her? She brushed her finger across the touchpad. The screen lit up and she could read a message across the middle.

One quarter of the way through the process. Hang in there.

Cute, Zip. He'd programmed a note to reassure her the executable was doing its job.

But only one-quarter? Nicole groaned and lay back on the couch cushions. It would be a long night and possibly a longer day in the presence of Dave and his charter guests. What did she know about charter fishing? Not much. And she really didn't care to know.

She wondered what was happening in D.C. If Royce and Geek were being interrogated, would they be subject to torture? Would they point toward Cape Churn if given no other choice?

She needed the data on that flash drive as a bargaining chip to free her surrogate family. If going fishing with her host was the only way to stay safe until the data had been decrypted, she could suffer the ride. As long as her computers could keep running. At least she wouldn't have to worry about someone sneaking up on her outside the yacht. She'd be able to see someone coming from miles away on board the *Reel Dive*.

She finally closed her eyes and let go of the worry. The soft rocking motion of the boat relaxing her, the starlight shining through the slats in the blinds giving her just enough light to make out shapes in the darkness. For a moment the light flickered.

Had a cloud drifted over the moon? She listened for the sound of footsteps on the deck above or out on the dock beside the boat. When she heard none, she drifted into a troubled sleep where a dark figure followed her through the streets of Cape Churn.

Chapter 8

At the crack of dawn, before the sun had risen, Dave rose. He'd slept pretty well for someone who normally had nightmares about the streets of a certain Afghan village and woke in a sweat, kicking mad. He scooted out of bed, slipped into a pair of jeans and a T-shirt and padded barefoot out of the sleeping quarters into the living quarters of the yacht.

Nicole glanced up from the computer. "I'm ready when you are." And she was, dressed in the jeans and T-shirt he'd purchased for her the day before. He'd purposely selected a pink T-shirt, hoping to spark her ire.

To Dave, Nicole was a woman who brooked no arguments, took no prisoners and wasn't in the least a bit of fluff. Thus the pink T-shirt.

It didn't seem to faze her in the least, but it was doing funny things to him. And it didn't help that he'd woken thinking of her and all that they'd done in his bed the night before. His groin was tight and an erection strained against the fly of his jeans. If he didn't already have a group of Japanese golfers signed up to do a full day of deep-sea fishing, he'd have asked Nicole to join him for a pre-breakfast feast. If she'd have him after he'd gone to bed alone the night before.

Uncomfortable in his jeans and a whole day stretching in front of him in which he would have no chance of being alone with Nicole, his mood darkened.

"We'll leave in fifteen minutes," he said, his voice curt.

Nicole tsked her tongue. "Are you always this grumpy in the morning?"

"Only when I'm forced to share my living arrangements with an unwanted guest."

"You seemed to want that guest last night." She stood and stretched, her breasts pushing outward, the soft fabric of the T-shirt molding against her body.

Hell. She wasn't wearing a bra.

Dave could barely move, his jeans were so tight. So much for a relaxing day at sea. He spun toward the tiny kitchen, whipped out a skillet, cracked a couple eggs into it and beat them with a fork.

"I like mine over easy." Nicole stepped up behind him and peered over his shoulder, sniffing. "Smells good."

Dave groaned, wondering why he had thought going to bed the previous night without her had been a good idea. If he'd just had sex with her again, he might not be so hard and ready now.

"You're going to burn them." She reached around

him, her arm sliding against his waist, brushing his hip as she turned the burner down.

He twisted the control to the off position, abandoned the skillet and eggs and turned, all in a matter of seconds. Then he spun and gripped her arms. "You're making me crazy."

Her brows rose. "Me? I'm the unwanted guest, remember? The one you had sex with and then left to sleep on the couch."

"My mistake, obviously." His fingers tightened as he fought an internal war between pushing her away and kissing her until she was dizzy.

Finally he crushed her to his chest, his fingers twisting in her long hair, tipping her head back so that he could claim her mouth.

She met him, full-on, no hesitancy, no argument, her own hands wrapping around the back of his head, dragging him closer, her leg sliding up the back of his thigh.

His tongue pushed past her lips, sliding, tasting, caressing.

When he finally broke the surface for air, he pressed his cheek against hers, his hands sliding up her shirt, reveling in her smooth, soft skin. Cupping her naked breasts, he felt the weight of them in his palms.

She leaned away from him, yanked her pink T-shirt over her head and tossed it onto the back of the couch. Then she pushed his T-shirt up over his chest. "One thing you should know about me," Nicole whispered against his ear. "Though it's great…foreplay can be overrated."

"Good, because I might not make it past Go." Dave raised his arms and let her drag his shirt the rest of the way off. He yanked the button loose on her jeans and pushed them down over the swell of her hips.

She stepped out of them and kicked them to the side, then, backing away with her hands hooked in his waistband, she hiked her bottom up onto the table and parted her knees. "Let's do it."

Nicole flipped the button loose on his jeans and unzipped him.

His member sprang forward, hard, thick and ready. Dave thanked the heavens that she was willing to forgo foreplay as he stepped between her knees and nudged her entrance. Lost in the feel of her, he almost didn't hear her whisper.

"Protection?" She reached into his back pocket, removed his wallet and opened it. "Always prepared?" she asked, holding up the foil packet she found.

"Damn right." He grabbed for the packet, eager to get to his goal.

She held it out of his reach. "I've got this." After tearing open the package, she slid the condom down over him in one smooth glide, using both hands.

And none too soon. Once sheathed, he dove into her wet, slick channel. Holding her hips, he pounded into her, again and again.

Nicole leaned back on her hands, her head thrown back, her eyes squeezed shut. "Yes!"

Her passionate cry made him pump faster until his body tensed, teetered on the verge and then burst over the top. Thrusting hard into her one last time, he held her hips firmly in his hands, his member throbbing within her.

She fit him perfectly, her muscles contracting around him.

When he finally eased out, she sat up, closed her legs, hopped off the table and walked naked to the stove, a small, secretive smile curving her lips. "I'm hungry. How about you?" Nicole spooned the eggs out of the pan onto a plate. "Could you hand me my shirt?"

Dave pulled up his jeans, zipped, grabbed the pink T-shirt from the couch and stepped up behind her. "Are those for me?" he asked, reaching around her to cup her breasts.

She slapped his hands. "You have a charter to prepare for." Turning in his arms, she shoved the plate of cold scrambled eggs between them. "Sit and eat."

He took the plate from her and set it on the table behind him, then gathered her naked body against his. "That's the way to wake up in the morning. A man could get used to that."

Her quirky smile faded as she stepped out of his arms and pulled the pink shirt over her head, then jammed her legs into her jeans, sans panties. "It's just sex."

Dave felt as if she'd thrown ice water on the warm feelings he'd had a moment before. If that was the way she wanted to play it, so be it. "Right." He dressed in his shirt and shoes, and then sat at the table to eat his scrambled eggs that tasted like rubber. But he'd be damned if he'd let her see how her words had affected him.

Just sex.

Bull!

Nicole packed up the computer, the electrical cords, battery powered charger and the flash drive into a backpack Dave provided. Then she stripped, slipped into undergarments, jeans, T-shirt and the lined windbreaker he offered and stuffed her hair up into a baseball cap.

Dave left the boat first, claiming he wanted to check around before she came up on deck. Less than five minutes later he returned. "Coast is clear."

"I could have checked," she grumbled.

"I did it faster. I know all the nooks and crannies to search." He followed her up the steps onto the deck of *Freedom's Price*, admiring her derriere in the snug jeans. "Hurry up. I still have to load the bait before my clients come aboard the *Reel Dive*." Once they cleared the deck, he slapped her bottom.

Nicole covered her bottom. "Hey!"

"Just sex," he muttered, walking ahead of her, whistling.

He wouldn't let her go to the marina, allowing her to travel along the dock only as far as his fishing rig. "No use standing out in the open." He unlocked the cabin and held the door open. "Stay here while I go to the marina for my bait."

"Bossy much?"

He snorted. "Only when I'm looking out for the safety of my passengers…or babysitting snooty girls."

She swatted at him and he stole a kiss. "Just sex."

"What's wrong, Fish Boy? Does that bother you?"

He shook his head. "Not in the least. I just have to put up with you for a few more hours and I'm home free."

"And you can go back to your lonely, solitary life as Captain Ron. Going back to an empty, broken-down yacht and cooking your own eggs." She nodded, a smug smile on her just-been-thoroughly-kissed swollen lips. "Sounds pathetic, if you ask me."

"On the contrary. It sounds like heaven and, like you said…it was just sex." He grinned and slammed the door.

He let her chew on that.

Though he doubted she would. As tough and hard-core as Nicole "Tazer" Steele was, she wouldn't languish over a forgotten conquest. She'd move on to her next mission and wipe Dave Logsdon and Cape Churn out of her mind.

The thought pulled him down as he pushed through the front door of the marina.

"Morning, Dave," Sal called out from behind the counter.

"Running late?" Olie met him just inside the door with two five-gallon buckets of fresh bait. "Greenling and squid. Should be a good day for fishin'."

"Thanks. I'll get these." Dave relieved the older man of the heavy buckets.

Sal left her post at the cash register and walked toward Dave. "Had a couple gentlemen inquiring about you this morning."

Dave stiffened. "They say what they wanted?"

Sal shrugged. "At first, I thought they wanted to charter a fishing trip."

"At first?" Dave set the buckets down. "What do you mean?"

"I was giving them your contact information when they asked if you had a female assistant on your boat."

Alarm bells went off in Dave's head. "What did you tell them?"

Sal crossed her arms over her chest. "I told them no. It was none of their business if you have a female helper on your boat or not. Most times, you travel alone."

"Good." Dave lifted the handles of the buckets again and started for the door, stopping as he reached it. "If they come back, tell them I'm booked through the end of the week."

"What about the girl?"

He cast a direct glance at Sal and then shifted his gaze to Olie before replying, "What girl?"

"Okay." Sal smiled. "Got it."

Olie's brows knitted. "Got what?"

"Nothing." Sal hooked his arm. "Let the boy get ready for his customers. I'll fill you in later."

Dave exited and peered around the dock and the parking lot that had begun to fill. A dark van pulled to a stop and six Asian men stepped out.

His charter group. He'd better get a move on.

Dave carried the two big buckets to the boat, climbed aboard and dumped the contents into the bait tank. Once he finished, he strode into the cabin. Nicole wasn't there.

His heart beating hard against his ribs, he raced up the steps to the fully enclosed captain's helm. Nicole glanced up from the floor where she had the two laptops connected and the decryption software humming away. "I'll need to plug them in soon. With the CPUs running as fast as they can, they're chewing through the charge."

"Got it." He helped her set up and then glanced out the window. The six Japanese businessmen were headed down the boardwalk, smiling and talking, dressed in khaki slacks, matching windbreakers and deck shoes. All wore royal-blue baseball caps with Dodgers embroidered in bright white letters.

"Gotta go. Stay inside until we get well away from the dock."

Her eyes narrowed. "Something wrong?"

"Some men have been asking about you."

"At the marina?"

He nodded.

She sighed. "I'm glad we're getting away for the day. Hopefully the program will finish while we're out."

Dave dropped down from the helm onto the deck and greeted his customers on the dock, bowing and shaking hands. One of the men acted as the interpreter, translating Dave's safety briefing and instructions.

Once the gentlemen were all on board, Dave untied the ropes, started the engine and pulled away from the dock. Once he cleared the low wake area, he glanced back at the marina.

A dark SUV sat in the parking lot. Two men stood beside it, their hands raised to their eyes.

Dave lifted his binoculars and looked back.

The men were staring straight at them through their own sets of binoculars.

A trickle of apprehension slithered down the back of Dave's neck. If those men had narrowed their search for Nicole down to him and the *Reel Dive* it might not be safe to go back to the marina. Only he didn't have much of a choice. With six foreigners on board, he couldn't drop them off at the wrong marina.

That was if the men in the SUV had actually seen Nicole. In the meantime, they were safe enough out in the ocean. He had his pistol in a cubby in the helm and an ocean of space between him and the men onshore.

Dave headed out of Cape Churn into the open water and north, paralleling the coastline. His charter group wanted trophy lingcod and he aimed to show them where they were.

For the first twenty minutes Nicole sat in the seat

beside him, staring out at the water and the rocky shore to the east.

After a while, Dave broke the silence. "You can go out on deck if you'd like. It won't be easy to spot you from shore. You should be safe."

She rose from the chair and headed for the ladder leading down to the deck.

"If you see another boat approaching—"

"I know the drill. Get out of sight." She smiled. "I've been an agent for a while."

He nodded. "I know." Dave figured being an agent made her reluctant to put down any roots. Thus her insistence that what they'd shared was nothing to write home about. Purely physical gratification. She'd probably convinced herself of its truth.

Dave could relate. As a member of the Special Forces, he'd been just as hesitant to drag a woman into a relationship where she'd be alone for months, maybe even more than a year at a time. Special agents and Special Forces had that in common. Being foolish enough to have a family always meant heartbreak.

Most of the men he'd been deployed with were either divorced or on their second or third marriages. It wasn't a life conducive to long-term commitment.

While keeping his eye on the seascape, he couldn't help noticing Nicole as she moved around the deck, talking with the men. He expected her to find the interpreter, but she was speaking directly to them and they were laughing.

Not only was she beautiful and tough, she could speak Japanese. The woman never ceased to amaze Dave and he found himself wanting to get to know her even better—beyond *just sex*. What did he really know about her? Had she been hurt in the past? Was that why she was so adamant about no relationships? Or was it purely the job that made her keep her distance? Was she an only child? Did she like dogs or was she a cat person? Or no pets at all?

A million questions cluttered his mind as he watched his radar for any blobs indicating a school of fish. As he neared an area he'd successfully located lingcod in before, he slowed the boat. A large blob on the screen was just what he was looking for. He stopped the boat, turned off the engine and climbed down from the helm.

He'd prepared fishing poles with line and hooks; all he had to do was to bait them, show the men how to hold them and then help them reel in their catches. He went to work baiting hooks one pole at a time.

"How can I help?" Nicole asked.

"I've got this," he replied, handing off a pole to one of the men, showing him how to hold his thumb on the line before casting.

"Really, Fish Boy, I know how to bait and cast. Let me help."

"You do?" He looked at her again as if seeing her for the first time all over again.

"My father liked to fish. As an only child, and not the boy he'd dreamed of, I got to fish with him when I was really young." She lifted a pole out of the PVC holding stand, grabbed a squirmy greenling and ran the hook through it. "He left me and my mother when I was eight." Then speaking in Japanese, she showed one of Dave's customers how to cast.

He bowed, took the rod and cast the hook and bait into the ocean.

When they had all the men happily fishing, Dave asked, "Where did you learn to speak Japanese?"

"My stepfather was in the navy. I was a teenager when he was stationed in Japan. He insisted I learn Japanese by immersion. He put me in a Japanese-American school. We had immersion courses in speaking the language and many field trips to practice speaking."

"Did you get along with your stepfather?"

She shrugged. "At least he stuck around and we got to travel."

"A brat, huh?"

"Yes, a navy brat by marriage." She arched her beautiful brows. "And you?"

"Army brat. You could say I followed my father's footsteps." He nodded. "Hard to believe, right?"

"The haircut should have been a dead giveaway," she said, her voice laden with sarcasm. Then in a softer tone she asked, "I take it you didn't care for the army?"

Now that he'd started this conversation, he wasn't keen on finishing it. "What makes you think I didn't like the army?"

"You're not in it anymore."

He snapped back at her. "You liked traveling and sounds like the navy life suited you, so why didn't you join the navy or another branch of the service?"

She glanced out to the ocean, her face losing all emotion as if she'd drawn a curtain. "I did."

Just when he was about to dig deeper, she nodded toward one of the men. "He's got something big on his line."

Conversation on hold, Dave went to work helping his passengers reel in their catches. Between him and

Nicole, they were running between the men, scooping heavy fish out of the water with nets.

A quick picture of the fisherman with his catch and the fish was stowed in the holding tank. After a couple of hours they'd caught their limit and thrown the excess back in the ocean. Dave and Nicole collected the poles, cleaned the hooks and posted the poles in their stands.

The Japanese men downed bottles of water, smiling and talking rapidly about their conquests.

When he had all the equipment stored, Dave climbed up to the helm.

Nicole climbed up behind him and checked the computer. "I can't believe it's only halfway through the decryption."

Dave was strangely glad the program wasn't complete. It meant more time with her.

As he reached for the ignition, a rumbling sound caught his attention.

"Helicopter at six o'clock," Nicole said. She lifted the binoculars from the hook on the wall and pressed them against her eyes.

Dave hit the ignition. The boat engine roared to life and he set it in motion, making a wide turn to head back to Cape Churn. "Can you tell what kind of helicopter?"

"Looks like a Black Hawk." She studied it as it closed in on them. "Damn, the door is open and there's a gunner sitting inside."

"Surely they wouldn't—"

The gunner opened fire, the bullets hitting the water near the starboard, barely missing the boat.

"What the hell?" Dave spun the wheel, sending the boat west, and then turned it back to the east. He alternated, zigzagging east then west, all the while heading south as quickly as possible.

The businessmen were shouting inside the cabin.

"Go down and tell the group to stay inside and seated. If they don't have their life jackets on, have them put them on."

"Will do." She yanked the flash drive out of the computer and slid it into her bra. Then she loaded the laptops and the solar-powered battery charger into the backpack and slipped it over her shoulders.

"Nicole." Dave tore his gaze from the rough waters ahead long enough to stare into her eyes. "Stay down there with them. You're less likely to be hit by a stray bullet."

"What about you?" she demanded.

"I'll be fine. Besides, someone has to get this boat back to the dock."

"And if that SUV is still there?"

"We'll deal with it then."

More bullets cut through the water in a line headed straight for them.

"Get down there!" Dave yelled, jerking the wheel away from the bullets. Two hit the bow.

Dave pushed the throttle forward, skimming through the choppy water as fast as he could, knowing he couldn't outrun a helicopter. All he could hope to do was to get back to shore before those bullets poked enough holes in the hull to sink them.

"Before I go..." Nicole leaned against him.

He turned in time to capture her lips in a brief kiss, immediately returning his attention to the task of saving them all.

Behind him, Nicole hurried down the ladder and into the cabin below.

With several layers of fiberglass between the bullets and Nicole, Dave could better concentrate on escape and evasion tactics he'd never thought to employ on a charter fishing vessel.

One hand on the steering wheel, the other on his radio, Dave tuned the dial to the emergency channel and pushed the button to talk. "Mayday. Mayday. Mayday. This is Dave Logsdon aboard the *Reel Dive.* We are a charter fishing boat under attack and in need of assistance." He gave their coordinates, a description of the boat and their heading, then repeated the message.

The helicopter swooped lower and the gunner strafed the bow of the boat.

Dave whipped the wheel around, praying his passengers were holding on tight. He had to get them to safety soon.

"Reel Dive, this is the U.S. Coast Guard. Message received. A vessel is en route." The radio operator gave him an ETA and stayed on the radio while Dave navigated the shoreline, dodging the rocky outcroppings, while attempting to avoid being cut down by bullets.

On another pass from the helicopter above, a bullet slammed through the roof of the helm, scraping a line of skin off his arm. Another hit the radio.

Bleeding and cut off from the coast guard, Dave hunkered low, praying he'd get the *Reel Dive* to a safe harbor where the attack helicopter would be less likely to fire on him.

Chapter 9

Nicole stayed below in the cabin with the men, try-ing to calm them as the boat rocked wildly, speeding back to Cape Churn.

The men were surprisingly composed, smiling at her as they held on to whatever they could. Several times, someone would slip to the floor. The others would help him back to his seat and they'd stare out the windows at the helicopter swooping low again.

Wishing she could be at the helm with Dave, Ni-cole stayed put. He was better off without her up there. With her below, he wouldn't be as worried she'd get hurt and he'd be more able to concentrate on getting them to safety.

It didn't make her feel any better, though, not know-ing if he'd been hit or what was going on. Nicole wasn't good at sitting back and letting others take charge. In-activity left her with too much time to think.

Over the past day and a half, she'd been in Dave's company and her opinion of him and her feelings for him had evolved. He hadn't been too pleased at having her foisted upon him, but he'd kept her safe, bought her clothes and made love to her in a way she'd never expected from the scroungy boat captain.

Knowing that he had been in the army gave her a little more insight into his behavior that first night he'd tried to choke her. He most certainly had been traumatized by what had happened to his buddy. His reluctance to talk more about it only reinforced that belief.

Part of her wanted to soothe him, to let him know that he'd be all right. The other part of her shied away from lying to the man. She didn't know what he'd seen, where he'd been. Some men came back from war never able to cope with the transition back to the civilian world.

She'd be better off not letting herself be concerned about him, not getting involved. Still she was worried that he'd take a bullet. That he wouldn't make it back to shore before the gunner got the better of him.

Only able to see out the side portals, Nicole caught short glimpses of the sea ahead when Dave swerved to port or starboard.

In one of those swerves, she spotted an orange-and-white boat aimed directly for them at a swift clip. She wanted to cry with relief.

With the cavalry arriving, the helicopter swept away and disappeared.

The *Reel Dive* slowed to a halt as the twenty-five-foot coast guard boat approached, also slowing.

When the response boat got close enough, someone spoke over a loudspeaker. "*Reel Dive, Reel Dive,* turn off the engines and have all personnel step out on the deck with their hands in the air."

Huh?

Afraid she'd been caught and now would face the music of the felony she'd committed by stealing the data from Ryan Technologies, Nicole shoved the backpack under the bench seat and stood.

The interpreter had already translated the coast guard's instructions to the Japanese men and they all rose, their hands in the air.

Nicole pushed the door open and stepped out onto the deck, followed by the six men. Dave climbed down from the helm, blood streaking his arm.

Her heart dropping to the pit of her belly, Nicole rushed toward him. "Damn, you've been hit. How bad is it?" she asked.

"Woman on deck, hands in the air," the voice boomed through the loudspeaker.

She turned back to the other vessel, angry and not about to put up with any crap. "The man's bleeding!" she yelled and, ignoring the order, reached for the hem of her shirt.

Two coast guard personnel climbed aboard the *Reel Dive*, carrying rifles aimed at Nicole and Dave.

"Step aside, ma'am." A young guardsman waved his weapon at her.

Dave gripped her arms and set her away from him. "It's only a flesh wound. I'm okay."

"That's an awful lot of blood for a flesh wound." She let him push her to arm's length.

He let go and raised his hands, nodding at her to do the same.

Nicole did so, turning to face the sailors.

"Why are you taking *us* at gunpoint when *we* were the ones calling for assistance because we were under fire?" Dave demanded.

"You'll have to take it up with the coxswain," the guardsman on deck responded.

"Gladly."

In the meantime one of the guardsmen held them at gunpoint while the other patted them down.

Nicole bit down hard as the Petty Officer Third Class ran his hands up and down her legs, glad when he didn't pat down her breasts where the flash drive was wrapped in plastic and tucked into her bra.

By the time the PO3 completed his pat-down, another man in uniform climbed aboard.

"I'm Senior Chief Petty Officer Miller," he said to identify himself before nodding at the men with the weapons. "Did you check them for weapons?"

"Yes, sir," the PO3 responded.

"I take it you're the coxswain?" Nicole went on the offensive. If they were there to arrest her, so be it.

"Yes, ma'am."

"Do you mind telling us why we're being treated like criminals when a Black Hawk helicopter with a door gunner was shooting at us?"

"We received word that a boat meeting your description had known terrorists aboard with enough explosives to blow up a port the size of Los Angeles."

Nicole's chest tightened. If the U.S. Coast Guard and the U.S. Army thought they were terrorists, this scenario could have gone so much worse.

"Where did you get your information?" Dave asked.

"From the commandant of the coast guard," the coxswain replied.

"Intel from higher up justifies sending a Black Hawk helicopter to destroy a fishing boat?"

Nicole shook her head. Whoever had sent the message had power to contact a high-level commander as well as to approve use of deadly force.

"Go ahead." Dave waved toward the boat. "Search the vessel. Run bomb-sniffing dogs, the works. I promise we have no explosives aboard."

"We will." Miller nodded to another guardsman who stepped up onto the boat with a German shepherd on a lead.

The man and the dog moved throughout the boat, up to the helm and into the cabin. They also checked the engine compartment.

Nicole held her breath, concentrating on making her face appear calm. She glanced at Dave as if in passing and could see how tightly he'd clamped his jaw. Would they find the backpack under the bench? It looked like one of the bags the businessmen had brought on board. If they looked inside, they'd only find the computers and a solar-powered battery charger.

When the bomb-sniffing dog was done, the handler led him out on deck and told him, "Sit." The dog obeyed, glancing up at his handler for his next command.

"Nothing, sir," the handler reported.

"Looks like your intel was incorrect," Dave observed, his mouth tight around the words.

"Wait here while I report to my commander." The coxswain returned to his response boat and radioed to his commander.

Nicole could see the boat commander's lips moving,

but couldn't make out what he was saying. He stared at them the entire time, finally nodding.

When he returned to the *Reel Dive* Miller nodded to the men with the weapons. "Let them go. Apparently there was another boat meeting the same description. The police and a federal marshal will want to talk to you concerning the helicopter. We'll escort you to the marina at Cape Churn where they will be waiting."

"Are we in any way being detained?" Nicole asked.

"That's up to the police and the federal marshal. My orders are to escort you to them," the senior chief said. "Two of my men will ride with you."

Dave nodded. "Then let's go. I need to get these gentlemen back to Cape Churn. I'm sure they're not happy about being stopped in a foreign country by armed men."

Nicole almost laughed. When the weapons were lowered, the Japanese businessmen relaxed and talked among themselves.

By the time they made it back to Cape Churn, the sun was setting on the ocean, as if it was melting into the water.

As promised, a federal marshal, Cape Churn's chief of police and Officer Gabe McGregor were there to question them. An ambulance was there, too. Nicole was thankful the medic treated Dave's wound. As he'd indicated, it was only a flesh wound.

She shivered. If that bullet had been fired a second sooner, it could have hit his chest or gone into his skull. He was lucky to be alive.

And the relief she felt was far greater than she'd expected for someone she'd only known for barely two days.

The parking lot at the marina was full of vehicles with too many headlights shining for Nicole to make out if one of them was the black SUV that had been following Creed and Emma the night before.

Staying in the background, sure to keep moving, even if only a little, Nicole shouldered her backpack and held on to it while staying out of what she considered the range of a sharpshooter. With as many lights shining as there were, she couldn't stay hidden.

Now that the police had her name and Dave's, her cover would be compromised. The decryption program had not completed and she was at risk of losing the data if she was arrested or killed. One thing was certain: as soon as the cops and the marshal had her statement, she'd have to get lost. It was time to move on.

Dave watched the expressions on Nicole's face go from wary to resolute. He wished he could have spared her the crowd of people and the exposure. But he hadn't known any other way to get the helicopter off his back but to call for help.

The U.S. Coast Guard cleared the area first, reporting back to their base of operations. The ambulance left next.

Much to Dave's surprise, the businessmen thanked him profusely, commending him for delivering them safely back to Cape Churn and for the most eventful fishing trip of their lives. Their translator told Dave they'd considered they'd gotten a little of the Wild West out at sea. Given that they were uninjured, they appreciated the opportunity to share a great story when they returned to Japan.

They tipped Dave well and left in their black van, laughing and smiling.

"Seriously? They thought it was all part of the package." Nicole shook her head. "Can we go now?" she whispered to Dave.

The federal marshal shook Dave's hand. "I have a call out to the local military bases to find out who authorized that helicopter. In the meantime, I'd like you two to stick around in case we have more questions."

Dave nodded, without promising to stick around.

The marshal left, leaving Chief of Police Taggert and Officer Gabe McGregor. "If you don't mind, we'd like to take this indoors." Dave pulled Nicole into the protection of his arm and ushered her toward *Freedom's Price*.

"Let me go first," Gabe insisted as he stepped aboard.

Dave handed him the key and waited.

Gabe descended into the yacht and started to put the key in the lock. "Uh, the lock's been broken."

A spike of adrenaline sent Dave hurrying forward.

Gabe raised a hand. "Let me check it out." A few minutes later he emerged, shaking his head. "It's not pretty. Someone's been inside and trashed the place."

"Damn." Dave stepped around Gabe and dropped down the steps into what could only be classified as a complete disaster.

Everything in the yacht had been moved, flung, thrown, bashed or slashed. Nothing had been left untouched. It looked as though someone had exploded a grenade in the middle of the only place he'd called home in the past two years since he'd left the Special Forces.

Nicole laid a hand on his arm. "Dave, this is my fault. I'll make this right."

He jerked his arm away and closed his eyes. Anger

made his heart race and his fists clench as he blasted into a full-fledged panic attack made worse by the fact that he couldn't control it.

Chief Taggert entered the cabin and whistled. "Don't touch anything. If we can lift prints, we might be able to find out who did this."

"No." Dave raised his hand. "I'd rather not make this part of public record."

"Why not?" the chief asked.

"It's not worth it," Dave responded.

"You were shot at and your home has been vandalized," the chief pointed out. "Whoever is responsible needs to be stopped before someone is hurt."

"I don't want it made public," Dave insisted. While he stood, rooted to the spot, unable to stop the feeling that his heart would explode in his chest, Nicole stepped around him.

She lifted a cushion and placed it back on the couch, ripped side down. The next cushion, she placed beside the first. One by one, she righted the wronged items, slowly setting the cabin back in order.

Gabe and Chief Taggert joined Nicole, and the room began to take on a feel of normalcy.

As Dave watched Nicole move methodically around the cabin, his racing heart slowed. A minute passed, then two, and he was back in control. With a deep breath, he dove in, placing canned goods on the shelves, setting the unbroken dishes in the sink and cleaning up spilled boxes of cereal.

Soon, only the sleeping quarters needed straightening.

"We can handle it from here," Dave said.

"Are you sure you don't want me to file a report?" Chief Taggert asked.

Dave shook his head. "Please don't. It's nothing that can't be fixed."

"Then I'm headed to the Café. Nora will have my dinner ready. Anyone care to join me?"

"Thanks, but I think we'll stay around here and finish cleaning," Dave said.

The chief nodded and left.

Gabe said. "I need to get home. My shift ended an hour ago."

"Go. Kayla will need you to help with the baby."

"Thanks. Call if you need me. And be careful." Gabe nodded toward Nicole. "There are enough people who now know where Tazer is. It won't be long before someone comes after her."

"I know. I plan on doing something about that."

Gabe nodded. "Again, let me know if I can help."

Dave shook hands with the officer. "Hopefully, this will all be over soon."

When Gabe left them alone at last, Dave faced Nicole, his expression solemn.

Before he could speak, she said, "I need to leave."

His heart squeezing, he nodded. "I know."

She swallowed hard. "Is my motorcycle working?"

He shook his head. "I doubt Olie had time to tinker with it."

"Then I'll find another way. I've caused you enough grief you didn't deserve." She slipped the backpack straps over her shoulder. "I'll get your laptop back to you as soon as this mess is cleared up."

Dave cupped her face, brushing his thumb over her cheek. "I'm not worried about the laptop."

She stared at him, biting her bottom lip. "No?"

"No." He pulled her into his arms, wrapping his hand around her waist. "You're not leaving."

She tried to push away. "I have to."

He held tight, stroking her long blond hair that had fallen out of the baseball cap. "*You're* not leaving. *We're* leaving."

She shook her head. "I've put you in enough danger. I need to get out of your life and go someplace no one will find me."

"I know just the place. As soon as I can gas the tanks, we'll be on our way."

"What tanks?" She looked up into his eyes. "Not that I'm agreeing that you're going with me."

"You have to take me if you want to go in the *Freedom's Price*."

Her eyes widened. "In this?" She glanced around at the dilapidated furnishings made even less habitable than before by the damage. "Is it seaworthy?"

Dave laughed. "I told you. I refurbished the hull and engines first. Not only is it seaworthy, it's fast."

"You've done enough. I can't ask you to do this."

"You don't have to ask me. I'm volunteering." His lips twitched. "Something I swore I'd never do again."

"It's too dangerous. Look what happened today. Someone has power. The kind that can call in the military to do his bidding."

"Even if I wasn't worried about you, I'd want to see this operation through. If someone in the government is corrupt enough to want to keep information about arms sales from getting out, that person needs to be exposed for the traitor he is. Our soldiers, our brothers in arms, are dying because of him. I won't stand by and let it continue."

Nicole slipped her arms around his middle and pressed against him in a tight hug. Then she stepped back. "Okay then, how do we get this thing moving?"

Chapter 10

It was still early in the evening, but they had a lot to do before they could set sail in the middle of the night. He had to stock up the yacht with fresh supplies. Cape Churn's stores had long since closed. The only way he could stock up was to call his friends for help.

Dave left Nicole straightening the sleeping quarters while he hurried to the marina and climbed the back steps to Sal and Olie's door.

After only a brief knock, Olie arrived at the door, carrying a loaded shotgun.

"Going hunting?" Dave asked.

"No, but I heard your charter boat was attacked. Got me worried."

"Keep that gun handy." Dave tipped the nose of the weapon to the side. "I need to borrow your cell phone."

"Something wrong with yours?"

"No. I just don't want anyone to trace back to me."

"Come in." Olie moved back.

"If it's all the same to you, I'll stay here. I want to keep an eye on my boat. Someone ransacked it today."

"Well, dadgum it. I told Sal we needed to install a security system." He turned to yell at Sal, "Did you hear that?"

"Yes, you don't have to yell." Sal stepped up behind him. "I'm not hard of hearing." She handed Dave her cell phone. "I have unlimited minutes. Use what you need."

Dave placed a call to Emma.

She answered on the first ring. "Sal, Olie? You two okay?"

"It's me, Dave."

"What are you doing on Sal and Olie's phone?"

"We need to meet and I'll need you to bring some stuff."

"Name it, I'm there."

He told her what he needed and to meet him in two hours in front of the police station, the only place they might not be shot at. "Spread the word to Valdez and Molly."

"What about Gabe and Kayla?"

"Leave them out of it. I don't want to draw them away from their children. Gabe's done enough today, and the less he knows of what's happening, the better."

"Got it."

When Dave hung up, he turned to Olie and Sal. "I need to gas up my yacht."

"I'll get the keys. It'll only take a moment to unlock and get the pumps started."

"Not now. At midnight."

"Why so late?"

"I have to leave and I can't let anyone know I'm going."

"You in trouble with the law, Dave?" Sal asked.

"No. I just need to get away without anyone following me. I'll need you to move the yacht around to the pumps and fill the tanks. I'll be back by midnight."

He handed Olie the key to the ignition. "Be sure to wait until after I leave this evening. I'll honk my horn as I head out."

"You taking your girl with you?"

He didn't have time to explain to these older people that Nicole wasn't his girl. Besides, he kind of liked the sound of it. Maybe too much, considering she'd always been level with him. Once the decryption was complete, she'd be gone.

"What about the motorcycle in the storage shed?" Olie asked.

"Any chance of getting it running?"

"I'll look at it first thing tomorrow."

"Thanks." It didn't hurt to have a backup plan.

Having given Olie his marching orders, Dave returned to the yacht and went over the engine and the radio equipment, testing to make sure they hadn't been tampered with. He topped off the water-holding tanks with the hose outside. Working in the dark made it more difficult, but the sky remained clear and the moonlight helped.

Nicole had the decryption software humming and had gotten the sleeping quarters squared away. Other than a few torn cushions that needed replacing anyway, the old yacht didn't look too much worse considering the tossing it had taken.

An hour and a half passed quickly and Dave finally had everything but the gas taken care of. He descended into the cabin one last time.

Nicole had the inside straightened and had turned off all the interior lights, including the laptop's screen. She peered through the tattered blinds, keeping a watch out for movement on the dock.

Dave glanced around at how well she'd cleaned up, his gaze zeroing in on the 9 mm pistol he'd salvaged from its hiding place on the *Reel Dive*. "I want you to keep the gun."

She didn't look at him, her attention on the world outside the yacht. "Do you think they're out there?"

He closed the distance to her and glanced out the window. "I'd bet money they are."

"Why haven't they come after me like they did Royce and Geek?"

"Maybe they're afraid you've stashed the data somewhere." He glanced down at her. "They might be waiting for a time they can capture you while no one is around so that they can get it out of you."

"It's just been you and me for the past hour." Her gaze locked with his, the starlight shining through the window glimmering in her eyes. "The status bar indicates only 50 percent complete. I can't stand the waiting."

"We have another thirty minutes before we're due to be there."

"I don't understand what you have in mind."

"And I don't want to tell you if we missed a listening device." He pulled her to her feet and into his arms. "I know how we can get through the next twenty minutes."

"Oh, yeah," she snorted. "I can guess what you have

in mind." She reached for the hem of his T-shirt and lifted it over his head. "It would definitely take my mind off what might happen next."

He let her pull his shirt off and toss it to the couch. "We don't have to do this."

"Yes. We do." She pulled her shirt over her head, sending the decision out of his head and farther south in his body.

When she unclipped her bra, his breath left his lungs. The tension in the air added to the tension in his body and groin. "We need to hurry."

"I'm so hot, it won't take me long to get there," she assured him. She flicked the buttons loose on his jeans and he sprang free into her palm. "And based on this, you won't take long, either."

She reached for the button on her jeans, but Dave brushed her hands away.

"I've got this." He pushed the rivet free and slid the zipper down. Instead of stripping the jeans off her, he slipped his hand into her panties and cupped her sex. "You're hot and wet."

"Something about you does that to me."

"Can't let it go to waste." Dave pushed a finger into her, sliding deep into her slick channel.

Nicole rocked her hips toward him, moaning softly.

He slid a second and third finger in with the first and swirled around her juices, pumping in and out. She was ready and that was something he loved about her. The urgency of the situation and of the heat raging through his body pushed him past playing. Dave shoved the jeans and panties down over her hips and off her legs.

She kicked them aside.

He pulled her into his arms, his hand sliding over

her naked buttocks. Driven past coherent thought, he cupped the back of her thighs, hiked her up his body and wrapped her legs around his waist.

She sighed. "That's better." Then she lowered herself down over him, taking him into her until he was fully sheathed by her warmth.

Nicole threaded her fingers through his hair and bent to kiss him. "I'm beginning to like your long hair." She tugged on it. "The better to pull."

"Ow. Remind me to cut it." He smacked her naked bottom, the sound reverberating against the walls.

"Mmm. I kind of liked that. Are you going to do it again?"

"I'll do better than that." He backed her against the wall and drove into her again and again until he peaked and she cried out.

At the last minute he withdrew, sliding her down to her feet and angling her toward the table.

"Is it time?"

"To get you there?" He laid her on the table, caressing her thighs, his hands trailing over her body to tweak the hardened peaks of her nipples. After a quick glance out the window to the dock outside, he parted her knees and knelt between them.

"Shouldn't we be going?" she asked, her breath catching on a gasp as he parted her folds and stroked her swollen bundle of nerves.

"Soon," he said. Then he leaned in and flicked his tongue across her, licking from her center to that nubbin of tightly packed bundle of nerves.

"Oh, baby, don't," she cried, her fingers threading through his hair, urging him to continue.

He paused. "Don't what?"

"Don't stop!" She pressed the back of his head, dragging him close to continue what he'd been doing.

He laughed and blew a warm stream of air over her wet parts and resumed the task of launching her into to the stratosphere.

Once, twice, he licked her, tongued her and nibbled at that small strip of flesh.

She progressed from pulling his hair to digging her fingernails into his scalp to arching her back off the table, stiffening as she called out, "Dave!"

He didn't let up until she lay back against the table and let out the breath she'd been holding. "That was too…too…"

He rose to his feet and bent over her, pressing a kiss to the wildly beating pulse in her neck. "Too much?"

"Too intense," she said in a rush. "I've never been that…"

"Turned on?"

"Yes."

A shadow moved past the window and Dave froze.

"What?" Nicole tried to look behind her, twisting beneath him to see out the window. "Did you see something?"

"I think so." He eased off her and pulled her down behind the table. "Though I love feeling you naked beside me, it's time to get your clothes on. We need to get out of here."

She grabbed her T-shirt and slipped it over her head.

Dave caught it before it covered her breasts and sucked one nipple into his mouth for one last taste. "Sorry. I couldn't resist."

She laughed. "Animal."

"That's me." He patted her bare bottom and returned

his attention to the window, dragging his own T-shirt over his head and shoulders. Then he buttoned his jeans and reached for the gun on the table.

Nicole knelt beside him on the floor, fully clothed, wrapped the flash drive in a plastic bag and tucked it into her bra. "Ready?"

"With you? Always." He nodded toward the door. "I'll go first. Follow close behind and make a run for the car."

"And if someone gets in the way?"

"We'll shoot our way through. You in?"

"I'm in."

Dave climbed the stairs up onto the deck and squatted low, his pistol aiming toward the dock. Other boats rocked in the slips next to his, but he didn't see any shadows moving. After a moment he clicked his tongue. "Come."

"I'm not a dog," she muttered as she emerged onto the deck, bent low to keep from being a target. "Now what?"

"We run." He grabbed her hand and leaped onto the dock.

Just as nimble, Nicole landed beside him and ran for the parking lot.

Shots rang out from the deck of one of the boats. "Gotta bail."

"What?" Nicole asked.

Another shot popped off nearby, hitting the wooden dock at their heels.

They'd never make the parking lot without being hit.

Dave's grip tightened on Nicole's hand. "Jump!"

He took a flying leap, Nicole beside him, into water deep enough for deep-hulled sailboats. As he hit, the cold Pacific water took his breath away and he sank toward the bottom, keeping a firm grasp on Nicole's hand. Then he kicked hard, headed up, the lights from the dock above guiding him to the surface. Only he didn't want to come up right where he'd gone down. They needed to come up beneath the dock to avoid the shooter's bullets.

Apparently, Nicole had the same idea and swam toward the darkness beneath the pier.

They came up beneath the boards.

Dave snatched a breath of air and listened, the cold seeping through his clothes and into his bones. They wouldn't last long without wet suits.

"Do you see them?" a raspy male voice whispered.

"No, do you?" another responded.

"No. I think they went under the dock."

Dave tugged at Nicole's hand, indicating they should move toward the marina store.

A light blinked on, shining from the direction of the store. "What's goin' on out there?" Olie's gruff voice called out.

The figures on the dock froze. "Want me to shoot 'im?" the raspy voice whispered.

"No. We don't need any more questions asked than necessary."

"I'm callin' the police," Olie yelled, then slammed the door.

Footsteps pounded on the deck above as the two men hurried to get off the marina grounds before the Cape Churn police showed up asking questions.

Dave let out the breath he'd been holding when he heard the sound of an engine and the crunch of gravel as the vehicle sped out of the parking area.

"Come on," Dave said. "We need to leave before the police arrive."

He and Nicole climbed a ladder up the side of one of the piers and slogged across the dock to the parking lot.

They scooted into Dave's old truck and drove south as a siren wailed toward the marina.

Dripping wet and cold, Dave cranked up the heater.

"You gonna tell me your plan now?" Nicole asked.

"Not yet. When we get where we're going, I will."

Nicole sat back, twisting the hem of her shirt over the floorboard, trying to get as much of the saltwater out of it. It lay cold against her skin. If not for the heater blasting out warm air, she'd have been shivering.

She recognized the direction they were headed. "The McGregor B and B?"

He nodded. "Call Valdez and tell him we're on our way." Dave handed her the cell phone he'd left in his truck since he'd gone silent.

"Are you crazy? If someone's monitoring his phone, it will alert them that we're coming."

"Yup." Dave drove, without glancing her way. "We want them to find us."

"We do?" She shook her head. "I must have water in my ears. I thought you said you wanted them to find us."

"I do." He grinned.

"I don't understand. I need time to finish the decryption. How will I be able to do that if I'm in jail or dead? What happened to the idea of going in the yacht?"

"Change of plans."

"I'm not sure I like this idea."

"I'm sure you won't like the idea." His grinned broadened.

"I take it you're not telling me anything else, am I right?"

"Bingo."

Nicole crossed her arms over her chest and stared ahead as the road curved along the coast headed toward the B and B.

When they pulled up in front of the B and B, lights shone from every window and music blared.

Molly and Valdez emerged, carrying boxes that they stashed in the backseat of Dave's truck. "I stripped my pantry of everything nonperishable."

"Hopefully, we won't be gone that long, but thanks." Dave kissed Molly's cheek and shook hands with Valdez. "Thanks for agreeing to do this."

"Hopefully it'll work." Molly stared at them, her eyes widening. "You two are soaked."

"We had a run-in at the dock. All the more reason for this to go off the way we planned."

Valdez nodded, his gaze shifting to the headlights turning off the highway and shining on the drive into the B and B. "You two might want to go inside and change in case this isn't Creed and Emma. I might have something to fit you."

Molly hooked Nicole's arm. "I'm not as tall as you, but I have some slacks that are too long for me."

"Thanks." Nicole allowed Molly to lead her into the house and up the stairs to the master bedroom she and Valdez shared.

Dave followed.

A party was in full swing in the main living area, with laughter and dancing, the music loud, the guests focused on a couple at the center of the crowd.

When she saw the happiness in the young couple's

eyes, something tugged at Nicole's heart. Why couldn't she be that happy?

Because she was a special agent, prone to assignments that led her into danger and away from home more days than not. A life unsuitable for owning pets or being in a relationship.

Molly opened the door to the master bedroom and stood back as Nicole and Dave entered. "Get in the shower and rinse the saltwater off while I get you some clothes."

"You go first."

Molly laughed. "You can both go. The shower is big enough for two."

Nicole's face heated. "Oh, no. We're not…" She swallowed hard on the lie.

Molly clucked her tongue. "Yeah, right. I'm sure you two haven't been all over each other. I mean, look at you. Both good-looking, both single. What's to keep you from jumping each other's bones?" She smiled slyly. "And your reaction gave you away." She turned Nicole around and gave her a shove. "Go on. It'll save time." Her hand on Dave's shoulder, she aimed him for the bathroom and gave him a push. "Sheesh, you'd think you were pretending to be virgins. But wait."

Molly ducked out of the room and was back in less than a minute. She slapped a condom into Nicole's hand. "Better safe than sorry."

Nicole's cheeks burned as her fingers closed around the packet.

Dave chuckled. "Molly thinks of everything. Doesn't she?"

Nicole stepped into the spacious bathroom and waited for Dave to close the door behind him.

"You heard the woman. It'll take less time if we take one together. Here, let me." He gripped the hem of her shirt and dragged it over her head. "Better?"

The warm air of the bathroom helped to dispel the chill of having wet fabric against her skin. While Dave shucked his shirt and jeans, she struggled out of her wet ones and turned the knob on the faucet.

Hot water steamed the air. Then she finally faced Dave.

Cold water and damp clothes hadn't had much affect on his lower extremities. His member jutted out, straight and proud.

He shrugged. "I can't help it. You turn me on."

Her body instantly warming, she stepped into the shower and reached out to pull him in beside her. She set the foil packet on the soap dish, then grabbing a bar of soap, she lathered her hands and handed the bar to Dave. Starting at his neck, she worked the lather down the hard contours of his chest and across his taut abs. As she angled lower, he started his magic on her shoulders, moving slowly downward to the rounded swells of her breasts.

She circled his member as Dave tweaked her nipples.

"Molly will be waiting," she said.

"I doubt it." Dave took the condom from the soap dish, tore it open and rolled it down over his erection. Then he lifted Nicole.

She wrapped her legs around his waist, sinking down over him.

He backed her into the cool tiles of the shower and thrust into her slowly, once, twice, then faster and faster.

Nicole braced her hands on his shoulders and rode him, her slippery body sliding against his, bubbles slid-

ing down the drain. She loved how wild and spontane-
ous it was to make love to Dave and she never seemed
to get enough.

As he thrust one last time, she tightened her channel
around him and held him there, relishing the feel of his
muscular chest against her softer one. He was all cave-
man and she liked it.

Almost too much.

When they finally returned to earth, Nicole helped
him rinse the soap off his body and out of his hair, and
he returned the favor.

What felt to be a long time had only amounted to
a few minutes and they were out of the shower drying
each other off.

"I have clothes on the bed when you're done in
there," Molly said through the door. "Everyone is here,
waiting downstairs."

Nicole ran a brush through her wet hair, twisted it
into a braid and left it hanging down her back. Then
she opened the door and stepped out of the bathroom
into the empty master bedroom.

Dave's arms wrapped around her middle and he
hauled her back against him. "Whatever happens, this
doesn't end here."

"Doesn't it?" she whispered, tilting her head to the
side to give his lips access to her throat.

"Not if I can help it. But for now, we're going to do
a little diversionary tactic."

"I'm listening."

"I'll let you in on the plan when I brief it to the others."

Nicole had to be satisfied with his promise. She
stepped into the jeans Molly had provided. They were

a little short and loose on her hips, but they would do. She'd also provided a bra and shirt. The bra was also big, but the shirt would hide that. Thankfully, she and Molly wore the same shoe size and she slipped her feet into socks and a pair of sneakers.

Once complete, she faced Dave, dressed in Casanova Valdez's clothes.

"Didn't realize we were the same size." Dave glanced at the black T-shirt, black jeans and the lightweight jacket Valdez had provided. "The boots are tight, but not too bad."

"At least they're warm and dry."

"Right." He pulled her into his arms and kissed her soundly. "Let's go." He headed for the bedroom door. "The sooner we get out of Cape Churn, the better."

Nicole muttered behind him, "Alive would be preferable."

Chapter 11

Dave and Creed had left enough of a gap between their vehicles to provide a protected meeting place. The group gathered in the middle and ducked low to the ground, hopefully out of range of sniper fire.

With a long stick, Dave drew in the dirt and gravel, laying out his plan. "It's simple, really. We split up and hopefully whoever is following us will chase after the car they think is carrying Nicole."

"And how are we going to get them to do that?"

Molly held up a bag. "With these." She pulled out baseball caps with McGregor B and B embroidered across the front. "I've got tons of them and no one ever buys them." She handed one to each of them. Then she dug into her bag again and brought out three matching jackets, all with McGregor B and B written in silk print across the back. Her lips twisted. "What can I say? It was an effort at marketing. I can't think of anything better to use in this case." She handed one to Emma and Nicole, keeping one for herself.

Nicole shook her head. "I can't let you do this. What if they shoot at one of you?"

"We have to stay a step ahead," Creed said. "When we leave here, we head toward Cape Churn. Once in the city limits, Dave and Nicole will head toward the destination while the rest of us take different routes, all leading toward the police station."

"Nicole and I will go lights out, ditch the vehicle we're in and head for *Freedom's Price*."

"What if they're watching it?"

"That's where we come in." Valdez grinned. "We're going to set off an explosion."

Nicole sat back on her heels. "You can't do that in Cape Churn."

"We can and we will. It'll be contained in a trash can and will make more noise than anything." Valdez raised his hands. "No humans or animals will be harmed in this pyrotechnical display."

Molly nodded toward Dave. "I know you didn't want Gabe involved, but he's primed the police chief. They're working together on this to give you both a safe send-off. They will be the ones to set off the explosion as an unscheduled, surprise part of a local disaster preparedness exercise. He'll recall all of the fire and emergency staff. That ought to lead to a lot of confusion and vehicles on the road."

"Perfect." Dave knew Chief Taggert and Gabe well. They could be trusted. "Then let's get this ball rolling."

The ladies all slipped into the jackets and every one

pulled a cap over their heads, the women tucking their hair inside it.

"Ready?" Dave asked.

Each person of the diversion team nodded.

"Is this what it feels like to go on a mission?" Molly asked, a smile spreading across her face.

Valdez frowned. "We've had training in escape and evasion. If anyone comes after us, you're to get down in the seat and stay down."

"Yes, sir." Molly saluted Valdez.

Dave was second-guessing his use of Molly and Emma. They'd never been trained in tactics or warfare. Was he putting them into unnecessary danger? "You know, Nicole, Valdez is right. We shouldn't put the women in danger."

"The hell you won't." Emma slapped his arm. "Let us decide." She nodded at Molly. "You and I have been the targets of crazies lately. I think we've earned our wings."

Molly wiped the smile off her face and straightened. "Damn right."

"Are you in?" Emma asked.

Molly gave Emma a serious look. "I'm in." She ruined it when her face cracked into another smile. "I'll be careful, Dave. Nova won't let anything bad happen to me, will ya, sweetie?" She leaned into him.

"No way."

"Well, then, *sweetie*," Dave said, "let's go. I have a boat being gassed up as we speak."

Creed handed him the keys to his SUV. "I'll take your truck."

"I can't guarantee where I'll leave yours."

"Don't worry." Creed clapped Dave on the back. "Cape Churn is not so big I won't find it."

"You sure you don't want me to get Tazer out?" Valdez asked. "This is SOS business. We should never have involved civilians. Even more so now that we know someone is willing to play dirty to get to that data."

"You don't know the islands like I do and you've never navigated in a yacht. Unless you're holding out on us."

"No, but I could try to get her out on land."

"Stick with the plan. We only need another day or two without interruptions and the decryption will be complete." Dave pulled his cap down low and clapped his hands once. "Let's load up and head to town."

He slipped into Creed's SUV and waited while Nicole climbed in beside him. The three vehicles headed north toward Cape Churn, spilling out on the highway like a convoy of military vehicles headed into battle.

Nicole kept watch through the front windshield and also twisting in her seat to get a look at the road behind them. They were the last vehicle in the convoy with Dave's beat-up truck in front of them, sandwiched between the two SUVs.

Adrenaline had her sitting forward, ready for anything. She would have preferred to do the driving. Anything to be an active participant in this part of the operation.

Halfway to town, she glanced back.

"We have a tail," she said, her voice flat.

"I know." He'd noticed when the starlight glinted off the shiny surface almost as soon as they'd left the B and B. "They've been following since we left."

"Why didn't you tell me?"

"They were keeping a safe distance from us." He shrugged. "If they'd tried to catch up to us, I would have told you."

"I really think I should have appropriated a motorcycle and left by road."

"No one will be able to find you on the island I'm taking you to. It has no electricity, no other buildings but the small hunting and fishing cabin I built there. You'll have time for the software to complete."

"And then?"

"And then we nail the bastard."

"Uh, one thing."

"What's that?"

"We have to get that information to someone who cares."

"Let's cross that bridge when we come to it. First thing we need to do is to get you and that flash drive out of Cape Churn."

"Uh, Dave?"

Something in her voice made him glance in the rearview mirror. "Hold on."

"I'm holding." She held on to the handle over the door and braced herself.

Dave held the steering wheel so tightly his knuckles turned white.

The vehicle behind them sped up as they neared a particularly treacherous curve in the highway, the east side a towering wall of solid rock, the west a sheer dropoff into the rocky coastline.

The vehicle behind them slammed into their left rear bumper, sending them careening toward the edge.

Dave held steady, easing the SUV back toward the right side of the road. The vehicles ahead of him picked up speed, barreling down the highway, taking the curves faster than was safe.

Again, the vehicle rammed into them. This time Dave swerved toward the cliff face, skimming the passenger side of the SUV against the rock, metal on rock screeching and sending up sparks.

Nicole leaned toward Dave, her face tense.

While Dave struggled to keep the vehicle on the road, the SUV behind them pulled around and slammed into the driver's side. It was all Dave could do to keep from wiping out on the rock wall.

"That's it." As soon as the SUV let up, Dave jerked his wheel to the left, hitting it hard in the side.

The driver hit the accelerator and sped ahead of Dave as they cleared the cliffs and drop-offs and headed into town.

Valdez, who was in the lead, broke off to the east, taking a corner fast onto a residential street.

The vehicle in front of Dave rear-ended Dave's old truck, sending it up over a curb and onto the sidewalk.

Creed jerked it back onto the road seconds before they would have hit a tree.

The SUV slammed into them again.

Dave turned west, away from the fight in front of them, praying they reached safety before anything really bad happened to them.

"We can't leave them to fend for themselves." Nicole twisted in her seat, her gaze following the drama of the SUV hitting the back of Dave's truck. "What if they're hurt?"

"They're headed for the police station. It's only two more blocks. They'll be okay. We only have a few minutes to get to the marina before the diversionary bomb goes off."

Dave zigzagged through the streets until he found an empty carport and pulled in, shutting off the engine and killing all the lights. "Out!" He shoved the door open and dove out.

Nicole did the same, tripping over her own feet and falling onto the ground. She was up and running before Dave rounded the outside of Creed's SUV to her side.

Dave led the way, more familiar with the layout of Cape Churn than Nicole. She was content to follow, unless more of the men showed up. Then she wanted to be in front, kicking ass. Dave hadn't signed up to take a bullet for her. He shouldn't even be in this mess.

If something happened to him, Nicole would never forgive herself.

As they neared the marina, Dave slowed and ducked behind buildings and bushes, checking the road ahead for signs of vehicles or movement.

They were able to get within sight of the marina before they noticed the dark sedan parked on the side of the road. A red glow briefly lit the interior as someone inside lit a cigarette.

Dave ducked behind a thick bush, pulling Nicole in behind him. He glanced down at his watch and pressed a button that illuminated the face. "One minute."

Thirty seconds later an explosion ripped through the quiet coastal town.

Lights blinked on in the houses and doors opened. The brake lights on the sedan parked on the side of the road blinked and the vehicle rolled forward, headed back toward the center of town.

As soon as it was out of sight, Dave motioned for Nicole. "Let's go."

They ran down the hill toward the marina, keeping to the side of the road and the shadows.

When they reached the marina, they had to leave the concealment of the shadows and break out into the open.

In top condition, Nicole wasn't concerned about being fast enough. Dave kept up with her, bringing up the rear.

"Hustle, woman," he said.

When they hit the dock, they ran across the board-walk to the end and leaped aboard the yacht. While Nicole untied the yacht from its mooring, Dave climbed up to the pilothouse to start the engines.

Nicole held her breath and let it out as the engines engaged on the first try.

The yacht pulled away from the pier as a vehicle skidded sideways into the parking lot and raced up to the marina.

Three men exited the vehicle and ran toward *Freedom's Price,* firing handguns. A fourth man got out of the car carrying what appeared to be a military-style rifle. With slow deliberation, he took a knee on the dock and aimed.

Her heart pounding, Nicole threw herself to the deck as wood splintered from the walls behind her. If she'd been standing, she'd have been hit.

The yacht picked up speed and soon was out of range of the shooters.

Nicole dared to look up over the side of the rail. In the light from the marina, she could see the men clambering in and out of boats.

Finally one of them pulled away from the marina and came after them.

Her pulse racing, Nicole hurried up to the pilothouse. "We have a tail."

"Thought we might. How big a boat?"

"Looks like it can't be more than twenty feet. Like a small fishing boat."

"If we can make it out to the open sea before they catch up, they'll have a tough time keeping up with us. The sea is supposed to be heavy. A storm was predicted for later this evening."

"Is that going to be a problem for us?"

"No. I'm headed north. The course of the storm is due east. It'll barely make it far enough north to hit Cape Churn, but it'll make for rough seas. How's your stomach?"

"Never had motion sickness a day in my life."

"Ever been out on eight-foot seas?" Dave asked.

Nicole shrugged. "Guess I'll find out how seaworthy I am."

He handed her a set of binoculars and she pressed them to her eyes, scanning the cape behind them for the boat in pursuit. "Damn. They're getting closer."

"Just a little farther and we'll clear the cape and be out in the open sea."

"That doesn't mean they will quit following us."

"No, but they'll have a harder time of it in that little boat. It will slow them down. And if they're not used to being out at sea, they won't last long."

"That's a lot of ifs."

Dave maneuvered the yacht past the rocky point and out into the open sea as the small boat came within shooting range.

One man drove while the others fired at them.

The waves were heavy, as Dave had predicted, and the yacht rose and fell with them, powering through the water like a newer vessel.

The little fishing boat fell behind and finally turned away.

Nicole set the binoculars down on the console and took a seat beside Dave. She rolled her neck, releasing the tension. "That was close."

"Too close."

"I hope the others are okay."

"To keep ourselves safe, we won't know how they are until we return to Cape Churn."

"Where exactly is your cabin?"

He smiled down at her. "Up off the coast of Washington."

"It's a cabin?"

"Yes."

"Let me guess…no latrine and no running water, right?"

"We'll have the yacht for backup, but the cabin is comfortable with a bed, candles and a fireplace."

"You go there often?"

"After the summer season ends, I spend a couple weeks out there."

"By yourself?"

"I like the peace and quiet."

She sighed and leaned back. "I could do with a little peace and quiet after today. At least until I get that data decoded. Hopefully, it won't take too long. Speaking of which…" Nicole descended to the cabin below and unpacked the backpack, setting up the computers and plugging the flash drive in, then clicking the control to continue the decoding process. The program could run all night as long as they weren't attacked.

With a blanket in hand, she climbed back up into the pilothouse and settled into the seat beside Dave.

"You should sleep in the bed."

"I like it up here. I feel like I'm closer to the stars." *And to you.* She'd gotten used to having him near and didn't feel like changing it now.

She enjoyed being alone with him without the stress of being followed or thinking about what could happen next.

In the boat on the open sea, they might as well be on another planet.

Nicole yawned and curled up in the blanket. "What happened when you were deployed that makes you have nightmares?" she asked. For a moment she thought he'd ignore her question, preferring to maintain the silence.

His gaze remained on the ocean ahead. "We were sent out on a mission to take out a Taliban stronghold in an Afghani village in the mountains." He paused for a long time, as if he was back in the action, reliving the event.

Nicole waited. If he wanted to finish the story, he would. If not, he wasn't ready.

"Our intel gave us specific homes to target. We were to go in, hit hard and take no prisoners."

His fingers tightened on the steering wheel of the big yacht as the rough seas tossed them from one wave to the next.

"One of our target houses was supposed to be filled with Taliban, not civilians. I kicked in the door and pulled the pin out of a grenade. Just as I tossed the grenade into the open doorway, a small child appeared in the door frame."

Nicole's heart fluttered and her gut knotted, knowing what came next was going to be bad.

"We should have ducked behind the building, but I couldn't. I stood there, staring at that kid, knowing it was too late to save him. Michael Steadham, my best friend since Ranger and Special Forces training threw himself on the grenade to save the kid and me." Dave's words left his lips as if they weren't coming from him at all. They were cold, empty and hopeless.

A tear slipped from the corner of Nicole's eye, followed by another and another. She wiped the moisture from her cheeks. It hadn't been her buddy who'd died. It had been Dave's. And yet she felt his pain, the agony of losing someone close to him.

"What got me almost as much as losing Mike was that the intel was wrong and no one took responsibility for it. Someone up the chain wanted that village wiped off the map just to keep the Taliban from taking it and using it as a stronghold. It didn't matter to them that there were defenseless women and children in those homes. It mattered to me and Mike."

Nicole got up from her chair and laid a hand on Dave's shoulder as he maneuvered the yacht through the rough seas, heading north. She balanced on the balls of her feet, but she didn't sit again until he finally said, "I'm okay. You can go to sleep."

She knew better. The man was still grieving for his friend and angry at the senselessness of killing. "I'm staying up here with you."

"Suit yourself."

Her heart aching for Dave, Nicole curled up again in

the chair beside him and stared out at the ocean. Soon the rocking motion of the boat lulled her to sleep.

In her dream, children cried and mothers wailed around a dead soldier who'd taken a grenade to protect them.

Nicole cried, along with the other women, at a world where children died for what? A cause that made no sense? Where friends were blown away in front of you and where the nightmares never ended?

Dave stood in his combat uniform, covered in his friend's blood, his eyes open, but blank.

She reached out to him, yelling for him to look at her, to take her hand.

He raised his arm, but before their fingers could touch, she was knocked out of the dream when the world erupted around her and she fell out of her seat.

Chapter 12

"Hey," Dave's warm, deep voice sounded above the rumble of the yacht's engine. "Are you okay?" His hand gripped her arm and helped her to her feet.

Nicole leaned into him, pressing her face into his chest, afraid to open her eyes, her throat locked around a lump the size of her fist.

"You were having a bad dream," He smoothed the hair out of her face with one hand. "And I thought I was the only one who had those."

She swallowed hard and dared to open her eyes. The gray light of dawn filled the sky and they were headed east toward the lightening horizon.

"Where are we? How can we be going east?" Then she glanced to the left and right and could see the dark silhouettes of land on either side.

"We're in the Strait of San Juan de Fuca."

"What?" She rubbed her eyes and glanced out the window again. "Between Washington State and Canada?"

He nodded, his eyes red, his face appearing tired. "I'm headed to an island in the strait."

"Won't there be too many people around?"

He snorted. "It's a very small island and there aren't many people on it."

"What about the aerial view? Won't we be easily detectable from above?"

"There are a lot of islands and a lot of yachts in this area. It'll be hard to pinpoint us."

She let go of the tension of the dream and waking in a strange place and glanced up at him. "You stayed awake all night?"

"Someone had to navigate."

"You sleep as soon as we park this boat."

"Yes, ma'am." He saluted her, his hand still resting on the steering wheel. "I could use some coffee."

"On it." She stretched and pushed her hair behind her ears, then descended into the cabin below.

First thing she checked was the decryption program. The status bar indicated seventy-five percent complete. "Really? After running all night?" She turned to the task of making coffee, the aroma of fresh brew stimulating by itself. While she waited for the coffee, she searched the cabinets for the pots and pans, found a skillet and whipped up a couple of omelets.

By the time she returned to the pilothouse with a steaming cup of coffee, Dave was maneuvering around a small island covered in a thick forest of trees. On the eastern side, the curve of the land created a cove. The water there was still, free of the heavier swells out in the open.

"I cooked eggs and toast."

"Sounds like heaven.

Dave slowed the yacht, bringing it to a standstill in the middle of the cove.

"We take the dingy from here."

"You sure it'll be safe?" The cove seemed deserted, but small enough to hem them in.

"The cabin is tucked beneath a stand of trees on a ridge. We'll have a three-hundred-and-sixty-degree view of everything around us and it's hard to see from the sea and above."

"Sounds like a great place for a stronghold."

"It is. And I'll set up some early warning devices if we miss anything."

"Okay. Let's eat breakfast, I'll pack a lunch and jam a few things into my backpack."

"I need to lock things down here and lower the anchors before I eat."

They went about their planned activities, meeting again over omelets Nicole reheated in the microwave.

Thirty minutes later they climbed down the ladder into the white inflatable dingy with the 3.5 horsepower motor attached.

As Dave set a course for the rocky beach, Nicole hugged the backpack to her chest, wondering if the data on the flash drive was worth all the trouble she'd caused Dave.

"Will your business suffer while you're away?"

"I didn't have any charters on my schedule for today. Kids are back in school, so things in Cape Churn will be shutting down."

"Yeah, but this is above and beyond putting me up for a night or two."

"If I hadn't come to my fish camp now, it would have only been a matter of days before I did."

Nicole sat for a moment in silence, the shore getting closer. "I'm sorry I've disrupted your life." She paused a second, then added, "But I'm not sorry I met you."

His hand tightened on the steering handle. "I think I needed to be disrupted."

Nicole snorted. "No one needs the kind of disruption I've brought."

"Anything less wouldn't have gotten me out of my rut." He stared at the shoreline.

"Look," she went on, "I'm not good with people. I usually push them away before they have a chance to get to know me. I just wanted you to know that I appreciate all you've done."

"It ain't over yet."

"I know. But you could walk away now and I'd understand."

"And leave you stranded on an island?"

Her lips twitched on the corners. "Well, maybe on the mainland."

"Let's get through that decryption and go from there."

"Agreed."

He drove the front of the dingy up on shore and jumped out, pulling it the rest of the way up before extending a hand to Nicole.

She slipped the backpack straps over her shoulders before standing and taking Dave's hand.

When their fingers touched, the electricity of the connection was not lost on her. What was it about the man that made her crave contact with him? From holding hands to pressing her naked body against his, she couldn't seem to get enough.

Dave didn't let go of her hand; he dragged her closer until they stood chest to chest. "I'm not good with people, either." He kissed her, his hand rising to cup the back of her head. His tongue skimmed the line of her lips until she parted them, letting him in. Then all thought escaped her, flying from her mind.

In his arms was where she wanted to be. It didn't matter if it was on the *Freedom's Price* or in a primitive cabin on a small, tree-covered island. She wanted to feel his arms around her, his mouth crushing hers in a ravenous, sensuous kiss.

When he stepped away, she swayed toward him as if her body were following his.

"We need to get that program running." His urgent words acted as a splash of cold water in the face of her lust. When the decryption was complete, he had no responsibility toward her. She'd go back to being an SOS agent. When she wasn't working an operation, she'd return to a cold, lonely apartment where she'd eat alone, sleep alone and have no one with which to share a glorious sunrise.

She glanced back at the east. The purples and mauves had graduated into a brilliant orange as the sun made its appearance.

"Beautiful," Nicole whispered.

"Beautiful," Dave confirmed.

When Nicole turned toward him, his gaze was not on the sunrise, but on her.

A rush of something that felt like happiness zipped through her veins.

Dave looked down at the rubber dingy. "We need to stash this in the woods. If we're found on this island, it would be good if we have a way to get off."

"You think someone will find us?"

"They found the *Reel Dive.* I hope we got far enough away we won't have to worry. But I'd rather be on the safe side. I don't particularly like being shot."

A cold shiver trickled up Nicole's back. She sure as hell hoped no one found them on the island. If they did, she hoped like hell they'd have a chance of getting off it in time.

They dragged the inflatable raft behind trees and piled branches over it, camouflaging it from casual observers.

Then they climbed to the top of the hill where a log cabin nestled beneath the trees, the canopy of leaves completely shading it, provided concealment from any aircraft flying overhead. Rustic, plain and small, the cabin had the most incredible view all around, just as Dave had described.

Nicole turned, examining all possible trails leading up to their perch on the hill. "I'll have to set up the solar battery charger someplace sunny."

"Over here." He led the way to the edge of a rocky escarpment, falling away toward the west side of the island. Because of the large boulders, there were no trees on this side, just a few scraggly bushes clinging between the rocky crevices.

"For now, I can run the laptop on the battery charger. If the program continues to run into the night, I'll have to rely on the laptop's batteries."

"If you want to conserve battery life at night, you can run one computer at a time."

She nodded. "It'll slow the processor, but slow is better than no progress. Hopefully we won't have to go past dark."

Dave removed the solar charger from the backpack, set it out in the sun and then ran the cord to the laptop.

Nicole opened the laptop and resumed the decryption execution module.

"Eighty percent," she said.

"Hopefully by the end of the day, you'll know something."

"If it actually decodes the file. At 80 percent complete without a hit on the decryption, it could end up without a hit."

Dave patted her hand. "Think positive."

"Hard to when you have no idea if this thing is going to work." She stood and walked to the edge of the cliff, staring out at the other islands in the distance. "What if it doesn't? What will happen to Royce and Geek?"

"You can't worry about them. You should only focus on what you *can* control."

"Which amounts to what? Keeping a computer running?" Nicole faced him and shook her head. "I've always prided myself on the ability to take charge of a situation. I find myself relying on you for just about everything."

"Is that such a bad thing?"

"Yes." She cupped his cheek. "I might get too used to having you around."

"You have a point." He caught her hand, pressed a kiss into her palm and stepped away from her.

"I do?" The disappointment was palpable. What did she expect? They weren't going to be together forever. He hadn't wanted her in his life to begin with. And three days together wasn't going to change that. "Yeah. I have my life. You have yours. I live in D.C. and you live in Cape Churn."

He nodded. "Opposite ends of the world for all intents and purposes."

She studied his face, wondering what was going on behind those dark eyes. Was he sad she wouldn't be around? Or was he counting the minutes until the program completed and the data was revealed?

The man was hard to read. Bloodshot eyes and dark circles beneath his eyes reminded Nicole that Dave had not slept at all.

"If you want to sleep, I'll stay out here and keep watch."

"I think I will." Dave disappeared into the cabin. A moment later he emerged carrying a rubber mat and a wool army blanket. "I used to sleep on this before I built a bed frame in the cabin. It's actually big enough for two. And the blanket's a little itchy, but it's warm." He rolled it out on the ground and lay down, patting the space beside him.

"Maybe after a while." She tipped her head to the right, then the left. "I want to work out the kinks of sleeping sitting up in a chair all night."

Dave crossed his arms behind his head and laid back, closing his eyes. "I'll save you a spot." Within minutes his breathing grew deep and steady.

Nicole resisted joining him, knowing that if she did, she'd keep him awake when he needed to sleep. If something happened, he would need to be fully alert and ready to go.

She checked the computer, satisfied that the batteries

remained at 100 percent and the decryption program seemed to be running fine.

With an entire day in front of her and most likely a night spent on the island, she couldn't imagine sitting around doing nothing. She set out to explore the hillside, looking for all avenues of escape should they need to make a run for it.

The path up from the cove was the easiest, a long, gentle descent. The rocky cliff to the north where they'd set up the solar charger would be treacherous and leave them exposed as they picked their way down the side of a steep hill with no cover or concealment from the trees. The last twenty feet would be a sheer drop into a rocky shore. The west was just as dangerous.

On the south side of the little island, they'd have to travel along the ridge for several hundred yards, then they could descend into the trees and out to the water. If they had to, they could circle around to the cove, the safest place to bring a boat in.

Her thorough exploration of the little strip of land and trees had taken less than two hours, moving slowly and methodically. If they had to leave at night, she'd need to be sure of her footing. Running in the dark, she wouldn't want to run right off the edge of a cliff.

As she studied the terrain, she could understand why Dave loved to come here. Nothing stirred but the birds roosting in the trees. Every once in a while she spotted a boat in the strait and ships moving along the channel. The silence was exceptional and the view of the other islands breathtaking. After a summer of charter fishing, this would be a haven of quiet where Dave could relax and recharge.

Nicole could almost imagine what it would be like

to stay on the island with Dave, soaking up sunshine, dropping a line in the water, taking the dingy out on the cove. Even though her father had left her and her mother, he'd given her a taste of the outdoors, instilling in her a love of nature, sports and fishing. Her stepfather had also loved being outside and insisted she and her mother run, walk, ride bikes and otherwise spend time with him in the sunshine. She could be content spending time here. With Dave. They wouldn't even have to talk.

Her body flushed with heat. There were a lot better things to do than talk. And the moon and starlight overhead would be uninterrupted by streetlights and the noise of the city.

They could make love under the stars. Nicole picked up the pace in an attempt to work the lust out of her system. As idyllic as the island was, fooling around would only make them lose focus. Still, the image of lying naked in the sunshine with Dave had her steamy all over.

After walking all over the island, Nicole returned to the hilltop, feeling a combination of refreshed from the exercise and frustrated with her naughty thoughts.

Dave stirred long enough to acknowledge her presence and went right back to sleep. Damn the man. If he'd woken and patted the mat beside him again, she'd have been helpless to resist.

To be fair, two hours was not enough sleep. Nicole strode past him to explore the cabin. The log structure consisted of one room with a stone fireplace at one end and a rough-hewed bed on the other. A lightweight metal folding table took up one wall. An old footlocker worked as a bench on one side of the table.

A single plank shelf on the wall next to the fireplace

had a row of canned goods, most of them beans. It was a good thing she'd brought enough food for lunch and dinner.

Along with the cans were two worn paperback novels. Nicole lifted them, read the titles and smiled. Action adventures. She supposed Dave might still have the longing for the adrenaline rush he'd get from battle. He probably got some of it from deep-sea fishing. The rough seas were a challenge to anyone, including an experienced boater.

Several cans were stacked in one corner of the floor, stripped of their labels, clean and empty. A couple of old fishing poles hung on hooks over the door. If they were going to be there overnight, they might not have the three-hundred-sixty-degree view. Clouds were building in the west, moving closer to the island. If it didn't rain before nightfall, there wouldn't be any light from the stars. If a boat just happened to find its way to the island, and someone decided to climb the hill to the top, they wouldn't know it until it was too late.

Maybe she was being too paranoid, but she needed something to occupy her hands and mind or she'd go stir-crazy.

Nicole found a knife in the footlocker and went to work on the cans, poking holes in the sides. She appropriated fishing line from the fishing poles and ran the string through the cans at intervals. Armed with her cans and lines, she tiptoed around Dave's sleeping form and headed back along the worn path toward the cove. Halfway down the hill, she stretched fishing line across the path and placed the cans along the line but out of sight of the path. She then put a handful of pebbles in each can.

Satisfied with the effort, she walked back up the hill and pulled two sandwiches out of the backpack.

Dave's eyes blinked open. "Do I smell food?" He stretched and sat up.

Nicole dropped down beside him and handed him one of the sandwiches and a bottle of water.

He glanced down at his watch. "Three hours. Did I snore?"

"I wouldn't know. I went for a walk." She bit into the sandwich and chewed, staring out at the clouds building to the west. "We might get rain tonight."

"Hopefully the sun will stay out long enough for the battery to stay charged."

"So far it's still running at 100 percent."

"Where is it now?"

"Creeping up on 90 percent complete." She sighed. "What worries me is that it hasn't broken the code and there is only 10 percent more of the program to run. I'm beginning to think it won't decode the data. Zip gave me his best, but he made no guarantees."

"You have to believe." Dave polished off the last bite of his sandwich and wrapped his arm around her shoulders, urging her to lean against him.

She liked the solidness of his body next to hers. Before Dave it had been a long time since she'd leaned on anyone. "Royce and Geek are depending on me. Whoever wants to keep me from deciphering it must be in a pretty high position to have pulled as many strings as he has."

Dave's arm tightened around her. "All the more reason to expose him. That much power corrupts a person."

Nicole nibbled on the last half of her sandwich, no longer hungry. While she'd been trudging across the island, she'd pushed aside the ramifications of revealing a traitor in the U.S. government. "What if we decipher the data, but can't get it into the right hands?"

"What is it your teammates call you?"

"Tazer."

"I take it you earned that moniker because you kick ass and take no prisoners."

"Damn right."

"Then why question yourself now? You're tough."

"Tough enough to go up against the U.S. government?"

"Just another walk in the park." He squeezed her shoulder. "Besides, you have me."

Her body warmed. "Are you signing on to help me see this through?"

"I told you. Once I commit to something, I don't back down. Plus, they shot up my fishing boat."

"You'd go all the way to D.C. if that's where it takes us?"

"All the way."

She slipped an arm around his waist. "Good. Because this is one time I don't think I could do it on my own."

"You don't have to."

"What happened to being your own island?"

"I saw power abused once and I didn't like it then. I still don't like it."

"Did you find out who gave the faulty intel?"

"Yes." His jaw tightened. "The theater commander. And that after he told a bald-faced lie to the local authorities that he would do his best to ensure his men didn't kill innocent women and children."

"Did you confront him?"

"Damn right I did."

"And?" Nicole asked.

"He denied it. I threw a punch and I was out of the military."

Nicole's arm tightened around Dave's waist. "I probably would have done the same."

"Now that you know my story, what happened with you and the FBI that made you part ways?"

"Is this time for confessions?"

"Might as well, we don't have much else to do."

"We could go fishing."

"You're stalling."

Nicole removed her arm from around Dave's waist, stood, rewrapped her sandwich and set it aside. She stared out at the trees, the sky and the water surrounding the island. As it always did when she thought back to how she'd left the FBI, her chest tightened so much that she could barely breathe. "I loved being a part of the FBI. Since I was a small girl, I'd dreamed of serving my country as an agent. My mother and stepfather were so proud when I was accepted and went to Quantico for my training."

"If you loved it so much, why did you quit?"

This was the part where he'd look at her with disappointment in his eyes and she'd relive the pain of having failed her country, the other agents and herself. "I didn't quit. I was fired."

Chapter 13

Dave remained seated, his chest tightening at the sight of the pain in her face. He wanted to reach out to her, take her into his arms and hold her through her confession, but he didn't dare. This was something that she had to do on her own. Sympathy, or even empathy, would only make her angry. Possibly at herself more than anyone else.

So he gave her the chance to explain or not. Her choice. He promised himself he wouldn't judge.

After a long two minutes she said, "I met this guy. He was smart, sexy and gorgeous. He liked to hike, bike, fish, ski and read thriller novels. All things I loved doing." She pushed her hand through her long hair. "He told me he loved me and wanted to be with me always. I'd never felt so…cherished. I was so in love with him, I didn't realize he was only playing me."

Her jaw stiffened and her lips pressed into a straight line as she paused. "One night, after…after we'd made love, I fell asleep. He must have stolen my card and made a print of my thumb. Days later, at night, he entered FBI headquarters disguised as me, logged into my computer and downloaded data on a case I'd been working with one of our undercover agents. This guy I thought I was in love with worked for the man we had been investigating.

"The data he stole compromised our undercover agent's position. The agent was beaten to within an inch of his life and left for dead. A year of undercover ops and data collection was wiped out. The criminal walked free. All because I was stupid, gullible and supposedly in love."

"What happened to your partner?"

"He lived." She glanced down at her fingers twisting the hem of her shirt. "He lost a lung, but he lived."

She inhaled and let the breath out in a long, shaky stream. "Even after the attack on my partner, I didn't want to believe my boyfriend could have been so deceitful. But all the evidence pointed back to me, my ID and my computer. If my mother hadn't been sick the night he broke into FBI headquarters, I wouldn't have had an alibi, I'd have taken the fall completely and no one would have looked into my boyfriend." Nicole shook her head. "It didn't matter. I was as guilty as if I'd done it myself."

"You didn't betray your partner."

"I did by not following protocol. I shouldn't have trusted him. I was put on suspension, but I left the FBI. I couldn't face them. I'd betrayed them and my partner nearly paid the price for my stupidity."

"So you weren't fired, you quit." As he'd quit the army. "And now you push people away, rather than trust them." The similarities of their situations made him even more attracted to her, rather than less. She knew loss and disappointment in people she trusted.

Nicole pushed her hair back and faced him. "I refuse to make the same mistake twice."

"How do you know I'm not sticking around for the data?"

"I don't."

His lips twisted. "Fair enough."

"If you'd wanted to take it from me, you would have done it already. You've had plenty of opportunities." She turned toward the west as the sun began its descent.

"Does that mean you trust me?"

Dave stilled, waiting for her answer, not sure why it meant so much to him.

"No," Nicole said. "Not really."

He'd expected that answer, but it hurt nonetheless. "Understandable." Too restless to sleep anymore, he rose and stretched. "You must trust me enough to go with you to D.C."

"You've proved yourself resourceful."

"Oh, so now I'm resourceful." He chuckled. "I'll settle for that. One step at a time. That's what it'll be." He started for the trail leading down to the cove.

"Where are you going?"

"To check on things and set some booby traps."

"Watch out for my early warning system on the trail."

"I heard you setting it up." His brows rose. "Rocks and cans?"

Her brows furrowed. "Don't you laugh at me."

"I'm not laughing. It's…what was it you called me?" He tapped his chin. "Ah, yes, resourceful."

"What did you have in mind?"

"Just a few pyrotechnics."

"You have explosives?"

"Maybe. But not what you think."

"You're going to leave me guessing?"

"Yup." He sauntered away. Let her wonder.

So, she didn't trust him. He couldn't really blame her. Who could she trust after the man she'd thought she loved betrayed her so badly?

It would take a lot for any man to breach the barriers she'd erected since that incident. Not that Dave was thinking along those lines. Hell, he wasn't anything to write home about. Having quit the Special Forces, he was still mired in dreams that left him angry and lashing out. How could he expect her to trust him when he didn't trust himself?

A fine pair they'd make; a couple of emotionally deficient individuals who had been muddling through life.

"Hey, what if I don't want to stay up here alone?" she called after him.

He turned. "Someone has to watch out for the computer."

"Humph. Like you were watching it while you slept?"

He laughed. "Jealous?"

"Of you? Hardly."

When he looked back, she was checking the computer, her long hair falling over the side of her face.

He had the urge to charge back up the hill like a hero, storm her defenses and show her that not all men were dumb asses. Trouble was, *he* could be classified as one.

Dumb ass, not hero. He baited hooks for a living. He wasn't hero material. If he were, his best friend wouldn't have died while he'd stood there gaping at a child.

He kept walking down the trail toward the cove, his mind on a lot of things but not on what he should have been doing.

Halfway down the path he tripped over something and a loud rattling sound shook the silence of the island.

"Damn."

"Ha!" Nicole shouted from atop the hill.

He glanced up to see her standing with her arms crossed over her chest, a smug smile on her face.

"Yeah, yeah, so it was loud and it worked," he muttered as he checked the line, tightening it after he'd fallen over it.

He hated to admit it, but the alarm system she'd built was crude but clever. If someone came up the path, he and Nicole would definitely know they were coming once they hit the trap.

He had some other surprises in store for them if he could get out to the yacht and back for his supplies.

Hopefully, none of their efforts would be needed, but just in case, he'd like to be prepared. The things they did wouldn't stop anyone, but might confuse them long enough for Nicole and him to make it to safety.

In a few short hours the sky would be completely dark, the rain might come and drench the island. He hoped the decryption would be complete by then. He wasn't sure the computer batteries would last very long into the night. The clouds were cloaking the sunshine as he pushed the dingy out into the water and the wind had died down to nothing…like the calm before the storm.

* * *

Nicole was glad Dave had tripped over the early warning system. It proved that not only could she hear the cans rattling but that it was loud and effective at warning her of someone climbing up the trail.

Fortunately, or maybe unfortunately, because the island was small, there really was only one way on and off. The trees covered the island. A helicopter would not find a clear spot to land. A gunner could shoot from the chopper, but would find it difficult to locate them beneath the cover of the trees. Although, if they strafed randomly, they stood a good chance of hitting something.

The status bar indicated the decryption code was at 94 percent. Her hopes dimming, Nicole checked the battery charger. Also 94 percent. She lifted her face and felt for the wind. A light breeze had sprung up, a little cooler and smelling of rain. The clouds were closing in on the sun. The solar charger would be defunct once the sun was cloaked.

The rain came before the clouds completely covered the sun. Nicole hurriedly gathered the equipment as the first drops fell and moved it to the cabin. Ninety-six percent complete and still the encryption hadn't been decoded.

Her heart heavy, Nicole wondered who she could go to next. The FBI had resources for breaking encrypted data. She could tap on some of the people she'd worked with in the past, if they'd even talk to her.

Hell, she hadn't spoken to them since her exit from the Bureau. She hadn't even spoken to her mother and stepfather about the whole fiasco. Any phone calls she'd made to them had been short and excluded anything to do with work.

They had been so proud of her, she hated to disappoint them, so she hadn't been to visit in two years. Phone calls had become fewer and farther in between.

And she missed the only family she had left. Her stepfather had filled the shoes her father had left empty.

If she dug her way out of this mess, she should visit. It would mean letting them know what a failure she'd been in the FBI. But she could sure use a hug from her mother right about now.

More than an hour went by before Dave returned, raindrops dripping off his hair and face, a large black trash bag slung over his shoulder. "The yacht is still there."

"I should hope so."

He dropped the trash bag on the floor of the cabin, shed his dripping jacket and hung it on a hook on the wall. Then he untied the bag. The first thing he pulled out was a sleeping bag. "Thought it might get cold tonight and that wool blanket might irritate your tender skin."

Before she could open her mouth to tell him she wasn't a delicate female and that the wool blanket wouldn't touch her skin since she was fully clothed, Dave winked at her. "Okay, so my skin is sensitive to itchy wool. Don't get your panties in a twist."

A smile tugged at her lips at the thought of Dave being sensitive to wool. The blanket was all he'd left in the cabin. She was sure he'd used it when he came to rough it.

Dave continued to remove items from the bag. One of them was a plastic container. "I brought dinner."

He opened the top and the rich aroma of spaghetti filled the air. "Hope you don't mind leftovers. I nuked it in the microwave before I left the boat. It should still be warm."

Paper plates, plastic forks, a bottle of wine and two plastic cups were the remaining contents of the plastic bag.

"A regular feast," Nicole declared, her stomach rumbling. She took over, serving the spaghetti on the paper plates while Dave poured the wine.

Darkness had settled in around them. Dave unearthed candles and matches, setting them up in cans on the table. The soft glow of candlelight made the atmosphere even more intimate. They sat beside each other on the footlocker and touched plastic cups.

"To success," Nicole said, feeling less confident of Zip's code now that they neared the end of its capabilities.

"To us," Dave said. "Two messed-up individuals, tied together by the need for truth."

She nodded. "To us."

Dave lifted his cup and drank the wine, then nodded toward the computer. "Anything?"

Nicole swallowed the sip she'd taken and shook her head. "Not yet. We're at 97 percent complete. It's probably time to consider my next alternative. You don't happen to know anyone who can hack into data, do you?"

"No," Dave responded. "Fresh out of hackers. I didn't meet any in the army and I might have met some on the *Reel Dive,* but they weren't advertising." He tipped his glass toward her. "What about you? And buddies from your FBI days?"

"I'm afraid to take it back there. Whoever sent the coast guard and the Apache helicopter after us has some big pull in the government. If I try to tap some of my old FBI contacts it could lead them straight to us."

"Then we have to hope the last 3 percent of the decryption software reveals the data." He held up his wine cup. "To the last 3 percent."

She touched his glass and drank the wine, warmed by the alcohol and Dave's smile and his optimism in the face of their potential defeat.

The spaghetti was still warm and welcome, given the cool, damp night air seeping through the gap she'd left in the window to better hear the rattle of cans.

After consuming all of her portion, Nicole sat back with her glass of wine, a chill rippling down her spine.

Dave wrapped his arm around her, pulling her close. "Why don't you climb into the sleeping bag and take the first shift sleeping?"

"You're the one who had less than three hours of sleep," she said. "You should go first."

He didn't move and Nicole was glad. His arm around her waist felt good and she knew as soon as he removed it, she'd be fighting the cold.

For now, she was content to be close to him. Though content might not be the right word to describe what she was feeling. More disturbed by the rising heat generated by his body and her body's reaction to him sitting so close.

She stared around the one-room structure, trying to think of something to say to keep her from diving right into those lusty thoughts of making love to Dave. "What do you do at night in the cabin when you're all alone?"

"Sleep." His arm tightened around her waist. "But I'm not alone now."

The low, sexy tone he delivered those words with set off a spark, igniting her desire.

Alone with Dave, with nothing but candlelight, a sleeping bag and wine stirring her blood, had an immediate and sensuous effect on her. Add the real danger of guys with guns trying to find them and sleep was the furthest thing from her mind.

She slipped her arm around Dave and leaned into him. "So, you're not alone. What do you do when there's nothing else to do?"

"This." He turned toward her, tipped her chin up and claimed her lips in a long, deep kiss that left her breathless and wanting more.

"If we do what I think we're about to do, aren't you worried about someone finding us? Possibly naked?" she whispered, a shiver of desire spreading through her body.

"Your early warning device will give us plenty of time to dress and get out."

She laughed. "You think so?"

"I know so." He leaned back, staring into her eyes. "What do you say? I'm willing to risk it if you are."

"At this point, what do we have to lose?"

"A few clothes." He trailed a line of kisses along her jaw and dropped down to press his lips to the pulse beating in the vein at the base of her throat.

"Expendable." Nicole moved her hands to the jacket she wore and unzipped it.

Dave pushed it over her shoulders and let it fall to the floor. "I don't know about expendable, but they're definitely in the way." He removed her shirt and tossed it over the back of the footlocker. With a quick flick, he unhooked her bra and then tossed it aside, as well.

She stood, feeling amazingly free, half naked in a strange place with a man she'd only known a few short days. Nicole extended a hand. "Your turn."

"Mmm. Not so fast. I'm still hungry." He parted his knees and pulled her between them, placing her breasts within range of his mouth. He tongued the tip of one.

The cool night air and the touch of his warm, wet tongue made her nipple harden into a tight little bead as her lower regions flamed with need.

Nicole threaded her hands through his shaggy hair and pulled him closer, urging him to take more.

With one hand on her hip, holding her in the V of his legs, the other traveled up her side and cupped the other breast. While he sucked on one nipple, he fondled the other, tweaking and pinching until her breath caught and held.

Finally he stood and ripped his shirt off. Then he tugged the zipper on her jeans and pushed them and her panties over the swell of her hips.

Nicole toed off her shoes and socks, and stepped free of the jeans. Naked and not the least bit self-conscious, she dodged his reach, grabbed the sleeping bag and untied the strings holding it in a roll.

"Seems to me you're overdressed, soldier." She pressed the bag to her body and unzipped the long zipper with deliberate slowness, letting the bag drop down in front of her, revealing her naked body.

Mimicking the slow descent of her hand, Dave unzipped his fly and pushed his jeans down his body, kicking them off along with his shoes. For a long moment he stared at her in the candlelight.

The smoldering look in his eyes made her body heat in the cool confines of the cabin. His body was bathed in a soft glow but there was nothing soft about him. He was all hard muscles, tight abs and solid, broad chest, even down to his rigid staff, jutting forward.

Eager to feel him inside her, she bent to spread the bag over the mattress.

Before she could straighten, he was behind her, smoothing a big, coarse hand over her bottom and around her to slide between her legs and cup her sex.

When she started to straighten, he held a hand in the middle of her back. "Not yet."

The hand cupping her sex slid up between her folds, stroking the sensitive strip of skin until Nicole arched her back, her body tensing.

Dave pressed his member to the slick opening of her channel, nudging her with the velvety-smooth tip.

She leaned back, wanting him to take her, to ride her hard and fast, to master her in a way only he could do.

He slid in, his fingers stroking her at the same time, the combined intensity spiking her senses, strumming her body to life.

"Please," she begged.

He leaned over her and pressed a kiss between her shoulder blades. "Please what?"

"Faster," she said on a gasp. "Harder. Just do it!" Holding the edge of the bed, she rocked back, forcing him deeper, her channel clenching around him.

In a dark cabin, in the middle of nowhere, with a man who made her come alive, she couldn't stop herself, couldn't let the moment end.

* * *

With his hands on her hips, Dave slammed into her again and again. The feel of her encasing him like a warm, wet sheath made him drive harder and faster. Before long, Nicole's cries of ecstasy sent him shooting over the edge. He pulled free at the last moment, aware even through the fog of passion that they hadn't taken any precautions.

Nicole collapsed onto the bed and rolled onto her back, laying her arm over her eyes. "Wow. I could get used to that."

For a moment he said nothing, still too tense from the force of his own release. When he regained his control and could move again, he laid beside her on the bed, resting on his side, propped up by his elbow. "I've only just begun to rock your world."

Then with slow deliberation, he mounted an assault on her body that would leave her memories forever marked.

He trailed his fingers over her breasts, stopping to tweak first one then the other. His lips followed suit where he rolled the tip of one nipple between his lips, flicking his tongue over the hardened bud.

"I see what you mean," Nicole said, her voice hitching as he applied the same technique to her other nipple, sucking it into his mouth and pulling hard.

She arched off the bed, his suction eliciting an answering call to her lower regions, making her squirm against the soft fabric of the sleeping bag.

"Is that all you have to show me, Fish Boy?" she asked, daring him to take it farther, to lay her open and exposed to his machinations.

"Don't you worry. I have a few more tricks up my

sleeve, sweetheart." As if to prove it, he eased down her body, nipping her skin, tonguing and kissing as he traversed her torso, belly button and finally the mound of curly hair over her sex.

Pushing her thighs wide, he lay down between her legs and dragged the tips of his fingers from the back of her knee up to her center.

"Okay, you've made your point," she said, barely able to breathe past the tension stretching her body as taut as a bowstring.

"No, now I will." He parted her folds and flicked her with his tongue.

Nicole dug her heels into the mattress and rose off the bed.

The second time he touched her there, she gripped the headboard and held on.

Having primed her, he revved her engine with a succession of nibbles, licks and taps that rocketed her to the heavens. "Oh, Dave!"

He didn't let up until she fell back to earth, her heart hammering and bells pinging in her ears.

"What's that?" Dave lifted his head, tipping it to the side.

When the fog of passion cleared, Nicole heard it, too. A bell pinging on the other side of the little room. She jerked to a sitting position. "The decryption."

Dave shot to his feet, Nicole right behind him as they ran for the computer and leaned over the screen.

DECRYPTION COMPLETE. HIT ENTER TO VIEW DATA.

Nicole glanced up at Dave. "This is it."

She pressed Enter and waited as the screen filled

with file folders, each labeled presumably by customer. Some of them were names Nicole recognized as members of al Qaeda. Others were names of corporations known for dealing with al Qaeda. Another folder was labeled Contacts.

Nicole opened it and clicked on a spreadsheet of names. As she skimmed down the list, one stood out among the rest and her heart sank to her knees. "Are you kidding me? How do we go up against the President's chief of staff?"

Chapter 14

Dave's chest felt hollow, his faith in the U.S. government taking yet another huge hit. "We have a problem."

Nicole blew out a long breath and pressed a hand to her naked breast. "No wonder Royce and Geek were detained."

"We have to get to D.C. and notify the President."

"They'll have posters up everywhere. I'm one of America's most wanted criminals by now. I won't get within twenty miles of the Capitol."

"We can. And we will." Dave's jaw tightened. "The man is killing our own soldiers. He has to be stopped."

"Yeah, but how? He's also the President's gatekeeper. We won't get past him to the President and who else will believe us? As it is, we'd have to get time alone with the President to show him the data. He won't believe it unless he sees it for himself."

"What about taking it to the FBI or CIA?"

"They've probably been given shoot-to-kill orders. Based on what happed with the Apache helicopter, by now we've been labeled terrorists."

"Come on. We have the data— we need to get moving with it." Dave handed her the clothes she'd discarded what seemed like hours ago but could only have been minutes. "Much as I'd rather stay here and make love with you again, the sooner we get this to Washington, the better."

When he turned to find his own clothing, a hand on his arm stopped him.

"You can't come with me." Nicole stared up into his eyes. "Anyone around me will be a target. You could be killed."

He gripped her arms and held her. "I know that. I also know that what he's doing is killing members of our U.S. military. It's not right and someone needs to stop it before any more of our soldiers die."

"But I don't want you to die for what I stole. I can do this alone. I don't need your or anyone else's help. You don't have to be involved."

He cupped the back of her head and bent to kiss her lips. "It's too late. I'm already too deep to let it go. I won't stand by and let you go it alone. Not when there's so much at stake."

"I almost wish I hadn't been inside Ryan Technologies' offices. That I hadn't gotten the data and decrypted it."

"And how many more of our soldiers would die because of corrupt men who call themselves Americans? I'm glad you found it and we have a chance to stop it before it goes any further."

Nicole held her clothes to her chest for a long moment, then nodded. "Okay, then. Let's do it."

"That's my girl." He kissed her and threw on his jeans, slipped his feet into his shoes and dragged his shirt over his head.

Nicole was dressed just as quickly. "The decrypted data is now saved to the flash drive. We don't really need the computers anymore."

Dave tore a strip of plastic off the trash bag and handed it to her. "Wrap it securely. We can't risk getting it wet if we get rained on or have to go for a swim."

Nicole rolled the flash drive in the plastic and tied it with the handles of the trash bag. When she was confident the flash drive would remain dry, she tucked it into her bra. "Ready?"

As Dave nodded, the sound of cans rattling reached them through the open window.

Dave blew out the candles and froze, listening.

The cans rattled again.

"We have company," he said quietly, his pulse speeding, adrenaline spiking. "Time to go."

The cabin had only one door. They'd have to exit using it and get around to the back before whoever was out there came within sight or shooting distance. They didn't have much time. A distraction was what they needed.

A loud bang ripped through the silence, followed by the rapid popping sound of weapons firing.

Nicole ran to the window.

A red glow rose from the woods, the color reflecting off the low-hanging clouds.

"What was that?" Nicole asked.

"Our cue." Dave grabbed her arm and shoved her

through the door and around to the back of the cabin. "Wait here."

He ran back around the front and returned in a moment. "Go."

She took off in the direction Dave indicated.

"Keep moving, to the south. We'll have to circle around and get back to the cove before they do."

They had the advantage of a straighter route. Dave prayed their unwanted company would stay too busy with the cabin and the next round of explosions to think clearly. Hopefully there weren't too many people guarding their transportation onto the island.

Staying as low as they could and sticking to the cover of the brush and trees, Dave and Nicole traveled along the ridgeline of the island to the south. When they were out of range and sight of the cabin or the main trail, they cut back to the east, running parallel to the trail leading down to the protected cove.

"They should be to the cabin by now." No sooner had he spoken than another explosion lit up the sky, glowing red from the top of the ridge like a smoky volcano.

"Flares?" Nicole asked.

"You bet."

When they got close enough, Dave halted. Nicole came up beside him and peered through the brush at what looked like an empty beach.

"Clear?" Nicole asked.

Dave shook his head. In the faint glow from the top of the hill, he could make out shadowy movement among the trees. A man dressed in black, wearing a helmet, flack vest and a military rifle—probably an M-4—stepped out into the open and stared up at the hill.

Nicole tapped Dave's shoulder and pointed to two black rubber boats.

Dave's heart lodged in his throat. "You seeing what I'm seeing?"

"If you're seeing a SEAL, yeah." She shook her head. "The man really doesn't want us to turn over that data, does he?"

"No."

"Well, let's get this ball rolling." She pulled her jacket off, tied her shirt in a knot, exposing her belly, and tugged her jeans low on her hips. "Either this works or I end up with a bullet to my head. Be ready, hotshot, And do your best not to hurt the poor boy."

"Wait."

"You got any better ideas?" She shook out her hair and let it fall over her shoulders and breasts.

She low-crawled into the open on the beach, just past the shadows of the trees before Dave could grab her back.

Dave almost went after her, but knew if he did, they'd be shot or captured. Waiting and watching for a chance to jump the guy was his best bet.

"Help me!" Nicole cried softly. "Please help me. I've been shot, I'm bleeding."

"Halt!" The navy SEAL dropped to the sand and pointed his weapon at Nicole. "Who goes there?"

"Please," she cried her voice weak, sounding desperate. "I'm bleeding."

The SEAL eased into the shadows and moved up the beach, the light from the flare probably playing hell with his night-vision goggles.

"Lady, just so you know… I'll shoot you if you try anything." He spoke low and insistently into his radio.

"I have a woman on the beach. Claims to be shot... Yes, sir. I'll wait for backup."

"I...can't...stop...the bleeding," Nicole held up her arm. "Please, help me." She dragged herself toward the SEAL, like someone mortally wounded. "Please."

"Stay where you are," the SEAL called out.

Nicole ignored him, sobbing. "I'm dying...please."

The closer she moved, the more Dave hated standing by, doing nothing. If he moved now, the SEAL would see his heat signature, thus giving away his position and compromising Nicole.

Dave held his breath, hoping the man didn't shoot her as she crawled closer.

She managed a coughing, choking sound and more sobs. "Please, help meee...." Her voice faded and she lay still, less than two yards from the SEAL.

Dave counted the seconds. Would the man take pity on Nicole and crawl over to her? He hoped he would and soon. It wouldn't take long for the rest of his team to get back to his position. They only had seconds before the SEAL team arrived and the game was over.

The SEAL finally crawled forward. "I have a knife and I'll rip your throat out if you're playing me."

Nicole lay still as death.

When the SEAL reached her, she erupted from the ground, pulled his arm up behind his back, shoved him face-first into the sand and straddled him. "Hurry!" she yelled.

Dave leaped from the underbrush.

The SEAL bucked beneath Nicole and threw her off. She landed on her back, hard. For a moment she lay there with her hand over her breast.

Dave reached the SEAL in time to kick the weapon

out of his hand before he could fire off a round. Knowing the man was in better condition and recently trained in hand-to-hand combat, Dave didn't stand a chance unless he subdued him quickly. Throwing himself on the man's back, he hooked his arm around his throat and held on. "I...don't...want...to hurt...you," he grunted, straining to stay on top of the man.

Nicole leaped to her feet, ripped the zip-ties from the SEALs web belt and threw herself on the man's legs. In seconds she had his ankles bound together. Without his legs to struggle with, the SEAL was a little easier to handle and weakening with the grip Dave had around his throat.

Nicole grabbed one of the man's arms and bent his thumb backward until he grunted in pain. "We're not here to kill you. We're on the same side."

"The hell you are. You're terrorists."

"You got bad intel. We're trying to save lives. The man who called for this attack is a traitor." Dave loosened his hold on the man's throat and grabbed the arm Nicole didn't have pinned to the ground. He yanked it up between the SEAL's shoulder blades.

Dave took the zip-tie from Nicole and wrapped it around his wrist, then pulled the hand Nicole held back and bound the two together. "Like we said, we're not here to kill anyone."

Nicole pulled the knife from the SEAL's scabbard on his leg and ran to one of the black rubber boats. She quickly jabbed holes in the sides.

Dave relieved her of the knife and ran to where they'd hidden their dingy and slashed holes in its sides, regret burning in his gut. All this destruction and people getting killed because of some greedy bastard in Washington.

He ran back to where Nicole was pushing the good black rubber boat out into the water. "Get in," he ordered.

She jumped over the side and hurried to the back of the boat and started the motor.

Dave leaped aboard as she swung the tiller arm around and aimed the boat away from the shoreline and out into the cove. Dave looked back over her shoulder. A flashlight blinked on from shore, its beam piercing the dark, searching for them.

"Can you make it go any faster, sweetheart? If we're still in range when that beam hits us, we're sitting ducks."

"I know. I'm giving it everything it's got."

The beam swept short of them again and off to the south, then back and again, the tip of the light bouncing off Nicole's blond hair.

"Get down!" Dave yelled.

Rifle fire echoed across the cove, the bullets splashing water into the boat, thankfully none piercing the rubber hull or either one of them. Just when Dave thought they wouldn't make it, they entered the open water.

Nicole turned the black boat to the north, skimming along beside the island they'd just left. She was powering toward the closest island, one larger than the one they'd just left. If they got lucky, it would be inhabited and they'd find a larger boat they could borrow to make it to the mainland of Washington State.

Nicole seemed to sense the urgency of making it to the next island as soon as possible. The SEALs hadn't landed on the island in rubber boats from the mainland. The boat that had transported them had to be nearby.

With the sky laden with clouds, the only light they had to guide them was the light shining from the next island. Dave kept watch on both sides, fully expecting the Navy to show up and haul them aboard. After the longest thirty minutes he'd ever lived through, they could just make out the shape of the island they'd been aiming for.

Dave took over from Nicole, circled the land mass and found a protected cove with a pier jutting out into the water. Tied to the pier was what looked like a thirty-eight-foot cigarette-style speedboat. Perfect for getting them to the mainland fast.

"What are the chances the owners left the keys in the ignition and the tanks are full?"

"A hundred to one," Nicole answered. "Let's hope it's our lucky day."

Dave climbed onto the dock, and slipped behind the steering wheel of the speedboat. "Baby, it's our lucky day."

Nicole stood on the dock, the flash drive safely tucked in her bra. "Music to my ears, Fish Boy." She dropped into the boat and sat beside Dave. "I hate stealing, but desperate times…" Nicole settled back in her seat and stared out the window, looking for other boats and land masses.

Dave drove the speedboat without the running lights. A full moon hid behind a long strip of clouds, allowing some of its light through, above and below. With only the control panel lit, he navigated toward the mainland, praying he wouldn't run into anything in their path.

An hour and a half later they approached land. After

thirty minutes of running parallel to the shoreline, they found a small port with a jetty and boat slips. Pulling into an empty slip, Dave shut down the engine and pulled the key from the ignition.

"Now the real fun begins."

"You have any ideas?" Nicole asked.

"If we can get to Tacoma, I have a friend who might help us out."

Nicole leaned against Dave in the front seat of the delivery truck that was taking them from the Port of Townsend all the way to Tacoma. She could barely keep her eyes open and let them drift shut several times.

The truck driver had been in the army and had been more than willing to give them a ride. He'd insisted on them calling him Jim from the moment they'd climbed into the cab of the truck. As soon as he'd set the truck in Drive, he'd started talking and didn't quit the entire way. He shared stories of his deployments to Iraq and Afghanistan and Dave listened, commiserated and responded to the man, leaving Nicole to catch up on her sleep.

When they stopped for gas, Nicole hit the head while Dave ducked into the station. When she emerged from the ladies' room, he was talking on a cell phone.

"We'll meet you there in less than an hour," he said. "And, Riley? Thanks." He clicked the off button and smiled.

"Who was that?" Nicole asked.

"An old friend from the army," Dave said.

"Whose phone?"

"Jim's."

"We're meeting this friend in an hour?"

"At the Tacoma Narrows airport."

Nicole shook her head. "We can't risk going through security."

"Relax. It's a small, general aviation airport. No one even has to know we're there. Riley will see to it that we get out unseen."

Nicole patted the plastic-wrapped flash drive, still safely tucked in her bra. They had a long way to go to get from one end of the country to the other. In a small airplane, it would take a lot longer than in a jetliner.

The thought of traveling almost three thousand miles by a plane the size of a crop duster made Nicole want to groan.

"Don't worry. Riley's only taking us as far as Spokane. She's got a friend with a private jet who needs a flight attendant for service from Spokane to Maryland. All you have to do is help serve drinks, meals and blankets to the passengers."

Nicole frowned. "What about you?"

"It's a private charter service. Riley arranged for me to be an extra passenger aboard, a business executive on my way to D.C. for a meeting with a lobbyist."

Nicole gave Dave a once-over. "You?" she snorted.

"We'll have an hour between landing in Spokane and flying out again. Riley's taking me shopping for clothes and a haircut. You'll have the opportunity to shower in the charter service's hangar."

"Gee, thanks."

"Ready?" Jim emerged from the station with a fresh cup of coffee and climbed into the truck. Nicole scrambled aboard, sliding across to the middle of the seat, Dave climbing in beside her.

The rest of the drive was accompanied by another long war story.

By the time they reached the little airport, Nicole was ready for silence or at least the loud roar of an airplane engine.

Jim drove away waving, happy to have had the company on the long drive south to Tacoma at zero-dark-thirty in the morning.

Standing at the entrance to the little airport, Nicole glanced around. "Are we early? Hell, it's still the middle of the night. Who in their right mind would be out this early?"

Dave stepped toward the building, a smile on his face. "Riley." A woman with deep red hair and a figure that didn't quit strode across the pavement toward them. She wore dark slacks, a black bomber jacket and a smile that lit up her face when she saw Dave.

"Dave, sweetie, how long has it been?"

Nicole's hackles rose.

"Three years, five months and two weeks, but who's counting?" He opened his arms and she fell into them, leaning up on her toes to kiss him full on the lips.

Chapter 15

Nicole clenched her fists at the kiss and the proprietary way Riley held on to Dave's arm.

And damn Dave. He smiled down at her as if she was a long-lost lover.

Grating her teeth, Nicole stood to the side feeling like a third wheel in a loving reunion story.

"I thought you'd fallen off the face of the earth," Riley said. "You didn't return any of my calls, texts or letters. Boy, have I missed you."

"I doubt that very seriously." He held her out to glance down at her. "You look like a million bucks. Life must be treating you well."

A stab of something mean-spirited struck Nicole straight through the heart and she wanted to reach out and punch someone in the face. It was a toss-up between the pretty redhead for kissing Dave and Dave for not clarifying just how pretty Riley was. She could have used a little warning on this meeting.

"Did you bring the items I asked for?"

Riley dug in the purse slung over her shoulder and handed him a packet. "I'll need those back as soon as possible."

"I promise I'll do my best."

The female glanced around Dave. "I've done my pre-flight. We can leave whenever you're ready."

"We're ready." Dave turned to Nicole. "Riley, this is Nicole."

Nicole grit her teeth and forced a smile as she extended her hand to grip Riley's, wishing all her hair would fall out or that she had yellow teeth, something, anything, that would make her instantly ugly.

Riley smiled with a genuinely nice, gleaming white smile, making Nicole feel mean and petty. "I'm really happy to meet you. It's nice to know Dave's dating again. We were all worried about him."

"We?"

"Dave didn't tell you?" She slapped Dave on the shoulder. "Dave and my older brother have been friends since high school. I was the tag-along little sister always getting in the way of their trio of friends. So much so I married the third man in the trio, Sam. It was a tough choice between him and Dave." She winked at Dave.

"Like hell it was. You always had eyes for Sam. I didn't stand a chance."

"He's right. Still, Dave's a sweetheart and if Sam wasn't in the picture, I might have considered him."

"And I would have politely declined. You're like my kid sister." He ruffled her hair and she slapped at him as though they'd performed this routine for years.

Nicole relaxed at their banter, feeling immediately better about the redhead. Although she was still miffed that Dave had failed to mention their pilot was a woman.

Her tension returned when she got a look at the plane they'd be flying in to Spokane. The single-prop Cessna 172 might as well be a crop duster to Nicole. She climbed aboard and sat in the back while Dave assumed the copilot's seat.

"Do you want to fly?" Riley asked Dave.

Nicole sat forward. Fly? The man knew how to fly an airplane?

Riley turned and caught her nervous expression. "I take it Dave didn't tell you he's a trained pilot, either, did he? He's even instrument-rated and has over a thousand hours. He taught me to fly when I was in high school. Heck, I wouldn't be flying my own plane if it wasn't for him."

"Sweetie's a regular saint." Nicole glared at the back of Dave's head. There were so many things she didn't know about Dave and apparently would never find out. Once they reached D.C. and delivered their package, he'd have no need to stick around.

He'd return to Cape Churn and his fishing excursions and forget all about the woman who'd made his existence hell for a few days of his life.

The thought was more sobering than flying across the mountains between Tacoma and Spokane in a crop duster.

As they taxied to the end of the short runway, Nicole found herself wishing she could be as casual and happy around Dave as Riley was. And she hoped that after all this was said and done, he'd find it in his heart to re-establish old friendships that meant a lot to him before the tragedy in Afghanistan that took his friend's life. The man had obviously not moved on.

The flight across the mountains was bumpy and frightening to Nicole. Not so much for Riley and Dave, who talked the entire way. They offered her a headset so that she could join in, but she refused, claiming she'd rather catch up on her sleep.

Unfortunately the dips and sudden drops due to wind shear had her holding on to her seat cushion and wishing they could hurry up and be there already. By the time they flew into the airport in Spokane, she was exhausted from the stress and ready to put her feet on the ground. Hell, she was ready to kiss the ground.

Dave climbed out first and held out his hand to help Nicole from the aircraft. "Are you okay?" He gazed into her eyes, his brows pulling together. "I guess it was pretty bumpy up there if you're not used to it."

"I'm fine." With Riley standing there, smiling happily and looking as fresh as someone who'd had seven decent hours of sleep, Nicole was damned if she'd utter one word of complaint. She was tougher than that.

Riley hooked her arm through Dave's. "If you'll follow me, I'll get Nicole set up with a shower and a uniform, then we can run into town for that haircut you so desperately need and a suit to fit the part. I know of a place to pick up shoes for Nicole so she doesn't have to wear muddy sneakers with the uniform."

Feeling a bit like a charity case, Nicole gave Riley her shoe size and dreamed of better times when she could wear her own clothes and shoes. She had excellent taste and nothing she'd worn lately made her feel quite as in charge as she preferred to feel.

An expensive outfit with the appropriate accessories

always made her feel as though she could conquer the world. Jeans and T-shirts put her off her game. Maybe that was why she'd been more dependent than usual on a certain charter fishing boat captain.

Riley was smiling at Dave again. "When you're back my way, you have to tell me what this was all about. Curiosity is practically killing me."

Nicole almost laughed. The truth of their mission had practically killed her and Dave several times. If they made it to D.C. in one piece she'd count that as a major miracle. If they made it in to see the President...well, she wouldn't count those chicks until the eggs were laid.

Riley continued talking as if she had three years of catching up to do in fifteen minutes. "I've flown this trip several times as a pilot and I'd fly this one, but they already have a pilot assigned. He's a very good pilot, so you can relax and be the CEO or whatever you want to be." Riley glanced back at Nicole. "The seats are full or I'd have gotten you one, as well. But since they're full, they needed the additional attendant, so you were in luck."

The private charter business had its own store with toiletries, new men's dress shirts, men's and women's underwear and even a few lacy bras for sale, probably for businessmen to purchase for their wives, girlfriends or lovers.

Nicole found one in a size close enough she could manage and a pair of matching lace underwear. It would be nice to be in clothes she hadn't worn for more than a day. She loaded her arms with the bra, panties, toiletries, a brush and a pair of flip-flops to wear until they came up with an alternative.

By the time Riley showed Nicole the locker room

and helped her find a uniform, the sun had risen and the clouds had burned off, leaving a bright, clear sky.

After a night of escape and evasion under the cover of darkness, Nicole felt exposed.

Riley wandered off to find a courtesy car to take Dave on his shopping and haircut expedition.

Dave snagged Nicole's hand and placed a paper bag in it. "Much as I love your hair, you're going to have to change it. You'll find hair dye in there."

Nicole nodded. "At the rate we're going, we can use all the help we can get. I can bleach it out."

When she started to turn away, he pulled her back into his arms. "I'll be back as soon as possible. If something happens and I'm not here, get on that plane without me."

She laughed, the sound falling flat. "Is this your way of ditching me?" Much as she hated to admit it, she felt safer in Dave's arms than anywhere else. For a woman who guarded her independence carefully, she'd come to depend on this man. "I'll understand if that's what you want to do." She'd hate it, but she'd understand.

"I'm with you on this one, all the way. But I can't get on the plane as an executive looking " he sniffed his shirt "—and smelling like this."

Nicole leaned into him, loving the way he smelled like the woods and the sea. "You're right. You do stink."

"Way to tell it like it is." He chuckled and tipped her chin. "Kiss me for luck. I hear the traffic in Spokane can be a pain."

"Not nearly as deadly as having an entire SEAL team shooting at you. And the traffic here is nothing compared to D.C." She was talking too much, avoiding that good-luck kiss, afraid it wouldn't be enough.

"Won't be long before we're there." Dave brushed a strand of her hair out of her face, tucking it behind her ear.

She leaned her cheek into his palm, closing her eyes. "With an entirely different set of challenges."

He brushed his lips across her forehead. "Ones that could get us arrested, imprisoned or shot."

Nicole opened her eyes and straightened. "As much as I'd like to have you with me, I wish you'd go back to Cape Churn and forget you ever offered to let me stay on your boat."

"Too late for that." He skimmed his lips across hers. "And I never really offered. I was outvoted."

"I'm sorry." She gave up pretending not to want it, and leaned up to kiss him, sliding her tongue across his bottom lip.

His arms tightened around her. "I'm not." Dave deepened the kiss, thrusting his tongue between her teeth to claim hers in a long, sensuous slide.

When he set her away from him, she struggled to straighten her wobbly knees.

Dave glanced over her head and nodded. "Riley's waving. I have to go."

"I'll be on that plane when it takes off." She touched his chest with the tip of her finger. "I expect you to be one of the passengers."

He captured her finger and brought it to his lips. "I'll be there." Then he jogged to the hangar exit and disappeared.

Nicole carried her new garments and the borrowed flight attendant outfit and entered the locker room.

After a thorough full-body scrubbing and washing her hair, she stepped out of the shower, dried off and brushed the tangles out of her hair. She dressed in the new panties and bra and opened the bag Dave had given her, pulling out a box of hair dye, her stomach dropping at the color on the model in the picture.

"What?" No way. She looked at the color name. Vivacious Red.

She'd go brown, black or even gray, but red? For a long moment she stared into the mirror, wishing this whole mess would just go away.

Swallowing her pride, she slipped her hands into the thin plastic gloves provided and went to work applying the Vivacious Red dye to her long blond hair. When she was done, she rinsed her hair in the sink and washed out the excess.

Without a blow dryer, she was forced to dry her hair beneath a hand dryer. When she had the long strands mostly dry, she pulled it away from her face and arranged it in a neat French braid, tucking the ends underneath. She settled the pillbox hat on her head and secured it with the combs sewed into the lining. Even with her hair pulled back away from her face, the color gave her an entirely different look. It wasn't bad. It might take her some time to get used to it, but it wasn't bad.

Satisfied that her hair was now safely disguised, she slipped into the soft gray flight attendant dress with its cute little Peter Pan collar and capped sleeves. The pencil skirt wouldn't give her much motion, but then how much motion would she need serving executives on a private charter plane?

Without adequate shoes, she couldn't leave the locker room. She searched some of the unlocked lockers hoping to find a pair of shoes should Dave and Riley fail to return in time to catch the flight.

A dark-haired woman entered the locker room and stripped out of her street clothes, put on a similar, light gray flight attendant uniform and pulled her hair back. Setting clips in her hair to hold it back from her face, she smiled at Nicole. "You must be the stand-in." The young woman held out her hand. "Stacy Grant."

"Nicki," Nicole said, taking the woman's hand. "With an *i*," she added.

"Well, 'Nicki with an *i*,' we have a full flight of pampered execs. I hope you're well rested. We'll be on our feet the entire time."

"How long a flight is it?"

"Six hours, give or take a few minutes, and depending on any delays landing at the airport in Maryland."

Nicole swallowed the moan threatening to rise up her throat. Her feet already ached at just the thought. She had to remind herself that six hours on her feet was better than six days traveling by road. In six hours she'd be so much closer to handing off the data and responsibility for it. And, hopefully, clearing Royce Fontaine, Geek and the rest of the SOS operatives.

Nicole pasted a smile on her face. "Can't wait."

"Oh, honey," Stacy clucked her tongue. "You *are* new."

"That's me," she said. "But I learn quickly."

Stacy glanced down at Nicole's feet. "That's a smart idea to wear flip-flops until right before we leave. Save your feet for as long as possible. Wish I'd thought of it." She straightened her dress, patted her hair and sighed. "I'll go check on the supplies and see if everything is in place. Join me when you get your shoes on."

"I will." Nicole smiled brightly, afraid her face would hurt more than her feet by the end of the day.

She followed Stacy to the door of the locker room and peeked out into the hangar. A man in a TSA uniform was speaking to another man in a pilot's uniform. He had a paper in his hand, pointing at it.

Nicole's heart skipped several beats. Was he there distributing a Wanted poster with her most recent photo plastered all over it?

She quietly closed the door and remained inside, pacing past the lockers and benches, counting the seconds and minutes until Dave returned. If the chief of staff was that concerned about finding her, he could have put out a massive Be On The Lookout message to all law-enforcement agencies. If that was the case, she might not get out of the hangar, much less onto the airplane.

As she paced, she checked her escape options. One emergency exit led out the back of the locker room, but it had a message painted on the door indicating that should it be opened it would set off an alarm and the TSA would come to investigate. Escaping quietly out that way was not an option. It could be a last resort only.

If she wanted out of the hangar, she'd either have to go out in the airplane or through the door from which she'd entered.

After allowing some time to pass, she peeked through the door again. The TSA agent was nowhere to be seen and neither was the pilot or Dave and Riley.

Several businessmen stood outside the airplane chatting as they waited to board.

If Dave didn't hurry, they'd be late and Nicole would be forced to go on board the aircraft wearing flip-flops. If that didn't attract attention to her, nothing would.

She backed away and went back to her pacing. On her tenth lap around the benches, the soft slap of her flip-flops hitting the concrete the only noise in the locker room, the door burst open and Riley ran in. "Oh, thank goodness. They're about to close the door to the aircraft. Here." She shoved a box at her. "Put these on and get on board."

Nicole stripped the shoes out of the box, slipped them on to her feet and thanked her lucky stars they were a perfect fit.

"Thank you, Riley," Nicole said on her way to the door. "It was nice meeting you."

"Same here. And, Nicole?" The redhead touched her arm. "Take care of my man, will you? He needs some TLC."

Nicole frowned. "He's not mine to take care of."

"I hope he is. He talked nonstop about you the entire time we were out running around." She smiled. "Go. And take care of yourself. You must be special if he's fallen for you."

Nicole left the locker room running for the airplane, her mind back in the locker room with the red-haired beauty.

Dave had fallen for her? Not a chance. The woman was mistaken. He wasn't in the market for a relationship. He'd told her so in no uncertain terms. And she'd told him the same.

Still, the thought that he'd talked about her left her feeling warm and fuzzy inside. And hot and achy in places farther south.

When Nicole climbed aboard the plane, Stacy slapped an apron into her hands. "Thank goodness. I thought you'd changed your mind and I'd be stuck serving all these people for the entire flight. If you'll start finding out what everyone wants to drink, I'll get the coffee brewing and start the warmer for breakfast. Oh, and just so you know, I have my eye on the hottie in row seven." She winked and got busy flipping switches and opening doors.

Nicole worked her way down the few rows of luxury seats, writing down on a napkin what each passenger wished to drink. She hadn't seen Dave board the plane and she was beginning to worry he'd missed the last call before they closed the door and started taxiing out to the runway.

When she reached the last row, a well-dressed man with dark, neatly trimmed hair slicked back like a Wall Street tycoon, wearing a black, tailored suit with a crisp white shirt and a bold red tie smirked at her.

Nicole nearly dropped the napkin she'd been writing on and gaped. "Dave?" she whispered.

He straightened his tie and said in his most formal tone, "I'll have coffee, black."

Dave nearly laughed out loud as Nicole's jaw dropped and her eyes widened. He and Riley had barely made it back in time for them to catch the flight, but the haircut, the suit and the rushing around to get it all done had been worth it.

Not only did he fit in with the rest of the execs onboard, but the fire in Nicole's eyes and the way her tongue swept across her bottom lip made him glad he'd dressed for the occasion.

Nicole clamped her mouth shut and nodded. "Yes, sir." Then she turned and walked back down the aisle, her bottom swaying nicely in the formfitting skirt. Just enough of her legs showed beneath the hem to make him want to corner her in the galley and kiss her thoroughly.

The woman was incredibly hot. Dressed in jeans or a flight attendant's uniform, she was classy. But he liked her best of all naked, her beautiful body stretched out against the sheets of his bed, her long blond hair fanned out across his pillow.

Okay, so now her hair was a bright red. He could get used to it. The woman beneath the fiery red was still Nicole and she would still be passionate and demanding and everything he ever wanted in a woman.

He swallowed hard and concentrated on not getting too excited. The flight would be long and tedious as it was, with little to no chance of stealing a kiss.

He and Riley had barely made it past a TSA agent at the door to the hangar. Riley had delayed him a precious minute going back to ask what he was doing. She'd returned with a flyer that was being distributed to all the agents at airports, bus stations, post offices and police stations across the nation. The picture on the flier was of Nicole, her long, straight blond hair hanging down around her shoulders. Beautiful as always. She was being advertised as a potential terrorist and was to be considered armed and dangerous.

Dave glanced at her now, with her dyed hair pulled back and tucked beneath a pillbox hat. Hopefully the outfit, the dye and hat would be enough of a disguise to keep agents of the TSA from recognizing her. She was too darned pretty not to be noticed.

The "armed and dangerous" part of the flier had him really worried. If they thought she might be a threat, they might shoot before they thought.

For the next six hours he didn't think they had much

to worry about. Riley had loaned him Sam's driver's license and credit cards. They were about the same height and had the same dark hair and brown eyes. She'd also given him her own driver's license and credit cards for Nicole to use should she need to get past security at the airport.

How they'd get past security at the White House was another obstacle entirely.

As he'd told Nicole, one step at a time. First, they needed to get to D.C.

He had to admit, his training in Special Forces hadn't prepared him for urban ops such as this. He'd done his share of training the trainers how to shoot, maneuver, organize for battle and camouflage. This was an entirely different kind of scenario. The one thing his training had done for him was to challenge him to think on his feet.

Six hours gave Dave time to think through possible scenarios, possible outcomes and everything that had led up to this point in time.

He'd gone from what he'd thought was a good life of ferrying bored businessmen out to catch fish by day and horrible nightmares at night to trying to save the nation. Now that he looked back, he'd been stuck in a rut of his own making, refusing to engage with people—and with life—any more than he had to, to make a living. He hadn't put down roots or championed any cause since leaving the military and it had taken its toll on him.

For the first time since Mike died, he felt as though he had purpose. And that purpose was to get Nicole to D.C. and in front of the President to stop a greedy bastard from providing weapons to the enemies of the U.S.

And maybe, by stopping the murder of hundreds of his brothers in arms, he could atone for letting Mike die. Mike would tell him that he'd saved him so that he could do great things. He'd believed in fate and would have said it hadn't been Dave's time to die. That was just the kind of guy Mike had been.

His eyes stung and the familiar knot of emotion clogged his throat. He closed his eyes and pretended he was asleep.

"Your coffee, sir," a familiar voice said softly next to him.

He glanced up into Nicole's clear blue eyes and accepted the cup. "Thank you." *For saving me from a living death. For showing me that my life has purpose.*

As if she sensed the depth of his gratitude, she laid a hand on his shoulder. "Let me know if I can do anything else for you."

She'd already done more than he could have imagined, by kicking his butt out of the sequestered life he'd made for himself. It was time he gave back and helped her bring the enemy down.

Chapter 16

As they neared the executive airport at Leesburg, Virginia, Nicole's pulse kicked up several notches. Having kept busy the entire flight, she'd barely had time to think past the next cup of coffee or spare blanket or pillow.

Thankful for the chance to work rather than worry, she now started her worrying. First thing she needed to do was to get in touch with a contact she'd made a few months ago when she'd been chasing down a corrupt politician who'd been killing off his opponents in the D.C. area. The police and FBI hadn't been able to pin the murders on the politician.

In her effort to pin the man to the murders, she'd gone undercover to locate his hired assassin. She'd found a man who went by the name of John Smith. He specialized in creating new identities for people who wanted to disappear, start over or hide in plain sight.

The man was cagey and had a habit of lashing out if he thought he might be caught and thrown in jail. When she'd dealt with him, she'd been up front that she was an agent and wasn't after him, but after the guy who'd murdered a senator, his wife and his little girl. She'd learned that John Smith was the father of a little girl and had used that knowledge to shame him into giving her a lead on the killer.

In return she'd promised not to turn him over to the authorities or to tell anyone where she'd gotten the lead. She also promised to take down the assassin so that he wouldn't be able to hurt any more children.

It had been more than a year and John had probably moved a couple times since she'd found him in the basement of a beauty salon, pumping out driver's licenses for all fifty states and passports for both foreign and U.S. identities. If she couldn't find him, she knew where she could find someone who did.

From her jump seat, buckled in to land, she glanced down the center aisle, willing Dave to lean out for just a moment.

When he did, Stacy, who was sitting next to her, wiggled her fingers and smiled at him. "I gave him my number. I hope he calls while I'm here on my layover in D.C. He's gorgeous."

Dave's gaze could have been on either Nicole or Stacy. Nicole preferred to think he was staring straight at her. The hint of a wink confirmed it.

The plane touched down and rolled up to the gate. Stacy waited for clearance and then opened the door, letting the steps down.

The businessmen filed off one at a time, carrying

briefcases or laptop organizer bags, thanking her and Stacy as they left.

Thankful the flight was over, Nicole was ready to get down to the business of getting the flash drive into the right hands.

When Dave left the plane he shook her hand, leaving a folded slip of paper in her palm.

Nicole shoved the paper into her skirt pocket and hurriedly helped Stacy clear the plane of trash and used blankets.

"That's all there is to it." Stacy held out her hand. "Thanks for helping out on the trip. You'd never know this was your first time. You handled it like a pro."

"Thanks, Stacy."

"Will you be on the return flight back tomorrow?"

"No. I have another gig."

"Oh, yeah? Where?"

"No time to explain. I have to go." Nicole smiled and hurried down the steps. Stacy stayed to talk briefly with the pilots.

Nicole scanned the facility, checking for men in uniform, TSA or police. So far the coast was clear.

Halfway to the exit door of the hangar they'd pulled the aircraft into, she pulled the paper from her pocket and unfolded it.

I'll pick you up at the door to the hangar in five minutes.

Nicole pushed through the exit door into the bright sun of the late afternoon. She blinked and glanced around. A Leesburg police car was parked beside the building, the officer in the front seat glancing down at his computer.

About to step back into the building and out of view of the officer before he looked up, Nicole noticed a plain pewter-gray sedan roll to a stop in front of her.

The window rolled down on the passenger side and Dave smiled out at her. "Get in."

Nicole yanked the door open and dropped into the seat just as the officer glanced up.

To avoid eye contact and full-on facial recognition, she leaned across the console. "Kiss me."

"Much as I'd love to lay one on you, shouldn't we be going?"

"That officer in the police car is staring straight at us, isn't he?" she said through clenched teeth and a smile.

"I believe you're right and I stand corrected. A kiss would be extremely appropriate right about now." He pressed his lips to hers.

What she would have thought would be a chaste meeting of the mouths extended into a breath-stealing lip-lock that curled her toes and reminded her how good he was at kissing.

When they broke apart, the officer's attention had returned to the computer in the seat beside him.

"Let's go before he feels obligated to look up again," Nicole suggested.

"I'm on it." He pressed the accelerator and drove out of the parking area and onto the highway. Soon they were battling the thousands of other drivers attempting to get home after a long day of work in the nation's capital.

"Take the next exit."

"That isn't the way in to the White House."

"We're not going directly to the White House."

"No?"

She shook her head. "Not yet. I don't want your friends to take the fall for letting us use their identities. We'll get some of our own."

"Okay, tell me where to go."

"See that secondhand store?"

"I do."

"Pull in. We need a new wardrobe."

"I kind of like this suit."

"You won't last two seconds in the neighborhood we're about to enter wearing that suit. Much as I like your new look, we'll have to dress down for the occasion."

Dave stopped at the secondhand store and entered with Nicole. After a quick perusal, they found jeans, a pair of boots that had barely been worn for Dave and a long-sleeved shirt that had a softly worn appearance for Nicole.

Nicole also found a kerchief, a pair of black, Goth shoes and a faux leather jacket that was too big for her. She paid for the items and asked if she could use the change room.

Dave selected a torn Harley-Davidson jacket that looked as if it had been dragged on the pavement for a hundred miles, a faded T-shirt with a silver howling wolf printed on the front and a black baseball cap with a silver skull and Harley-Davidson printed on the side. He pulled it onto his head. "Too much?"

"Go with it. That and the five-o'clock shadow makes you look tough."

They ducked into the change room and emerged in less than two minutes dressed in their disguises.

Nicole had released her hair from the braid and tied the kerchief around her head, the braid-induced waves in her hair making her look wild and unkempt.

He pulled her into his arms. "You look pretty hot."

She smiled, loving the contrast of Dave in the business suit and Dave in the well-worn biker outfit. "You don't look so bad yourself," she told him as they made their way back to their car.

Nicole drove from there, taking them off the main highways into the uglier, seedier part of town where the paint on the buildings was peeling, trash littered the roads, men loitered on street corners and children played without adult supervision.

Nicole pulled the car into an alley and shifted into Park. "Stay here." She reached for the door handle.

His hand stopped her. "Where are you going?"

"To get information."

"Why can't I come with you?"

She eyed him deliberately, running her gaze from his head to his feet. "I want information and you're…a bit intimidating."

"This is a rough neighborhood."

"I know. I've been here before." She laid her hand over his. "Be ready to go if I come back in a hurry." She got out and tucked her hands into the pockets of her jacket. Ducking her head low, she slouched onto the street, moving as though she had no place to be in a hurry.

A group of lanky teens sat on the steps leading up to a faded brownstone. Each wore baggy pants and hooded sweatshirts, some with the hoods pulled up. She glanced their way and nodded in what she hoped was gangster style and continued on.

One of the teens got up and fell into step behind her.

She kept walking, aware, but not alarmed. Until another teen fell into step with the first. Okay, two to one was a bit more daunting. When the third teen joined the other two, she knew she could be in trouble.

She picked up the pace, aiming for the door of a liquor store on the corner. If she made it there, she should be all right.

Her heart pounding, she focused on making her face show cool indifference. She knew gangs fed on fear.

"Hey, babe, new in the hood?"

She ignored him and continued walking.

As she came to the corner with the liquor store, one of the teens stepped in front of her. "Why don't you an' me go somewhere and get it on?"

She snorted. "You ain't got nothin' I want."

His buddies laughed and he turned red.

He puffed out his chest and sneered at her. "That's 'cause you ain't seen what I got."

"Move."

"Make me."

A burly man, as wide as he was tall, with hands the size of ham hocks grabbed the boy from behind and shoved him out of the way.

"Oh, come on, Rico. I was only messin' with her."

"Go home, go to school or get a job," Rico said.

Nicole ducked around the man and entered the liquor store, thankful for his interference.

The rotund Hispanic man followed her into the store and stepped up behind the counter. "What can I do you for?"

Nicole glanced out the window at the teens hovering outside.

Waving his hands, Rico shouted, "You boys get out of here before I call yer mamas."

The teens flipped him off, but moved away from the window.

Nicole waited until they were out of sight before she faced the man. "Rico, it's me." She pulled off the kerchief and stared into the man's eyes. "It's me, Nicole."

Rico's brows pulled together and he leaned close, as if trying to see her through her disguise.

She gave him a half smile. "You might remember me as a blonde."

His brows rose and a grin spread across his face. "Nicki. What are you doing back on this side of town? It's not safe for you here."

"I had to come. I'm in trouble and I need your help."

"Anything. I owe you for getting Antonio out of hot water." He crossed his arms over his chest like a genie ready to grant her wish.

If only it was that easy. "I need to find John Smith."

His arms dropped to his sides and his frown returned. "Anything but that."

"I have to find him. It's a matter of—"

"Life and death? That's what they all say."

"It really is. In the past twenty-four hours, I've been clear across the country, shot at and nearly killed a number of times."

His expression softened. "I could check to see if he wants to deal with you, but it'll take time."

Nicole was already shaking her head. "I don't have time. Others' lives are depending on me. I need a new identity. Now. I can't wait."

Rico's cigar-size fingers drummed the countertop,

his eyes narrowing as he considered her request. "You don't know where you heard this."

She raised her hand. "I promise, no one will know."

He wrote an address on the back of a discarded receipt. "He's been staying there for the past two weeks."

"Thanks, Rico. You're wonderful." She leaned across the counter and kissed the man on the cheek. "I owe you."

He shook his head. "No, we're even. Now go before my wife sees you kissing me. I'm more afraid of her than of John, you know."

Nicole smiled. "I know. Thanks."

As she headed for the door, Rico called out, "I like you blond better."

"Me, too," she replied softly.

As she stepped out of the liquor store, the pewter-gray sedan slid up to the curb and Dave leaned across to shove the passenger-side door open.

Nicole climbed in, the address clutched in her hand "Take a left at the next corner and drive five blocks. There should be a convenience store there. We need a throw-away phone. I need to get in touch with Kat. We might need some help getting into the White House. This is your last chance to back out. I won't think less of you if you do."

Dave pressed his foot to the brake, grabbed her hand and held it in his. "For the last time, I'm here to stay." He kissed her cheek and then drove away from the liquor store.

When she'd left him in the alley, Dave had climbed out of the sedan and walked to the corner. He'd leaned against the building and pulled his hat low over his eyes so any passerby couldn't tell he was following Nicole's every move.

He'd spotted the clutch of teens perched on the steps and smelled trouble before they'd even gotten up to follow Nicole. He had taken several steps toward the gang and would have taken more if the large liquor store owner hadn't come out when he had.

He could tell Nicole had gone into the store willingly, but he still hadn't liked that she was out of his sight. After waiting several minutes he'd gone back for the car, determined to park in front of the store and go in to check on her if she hadn't come out soon.

Nicole had stepped out as he'd reached for the gearshift.

He'd lost a year off his life in worry that she'd been hurt or killed inside that store.

Glad she was now safe, he drove to the convenience store and insisted on going inside and purchasing the phone himself.

He pointed at her and said, "Stay here and don't unlock the doors for anyone but me."

She frowned. "I can take care of myself."

"Please…" He stared at her for a long moment. "Just do it."

"Yes, sir."

He went inside, grabbed a throwaway phone off a rack and made his purchase with the dwindling amount of cash he had left in his wallet. Before long, he'd be out of money and he couldn't make a withdrawal from an automated teller machine without alerting the powers that be to his whereabouts.

He hoped Nicole's call to her friends would get

them some backup. They could use a little help right about now.

If the chief of staff was that heavily involved in the arms sales, who else might know about it? The vice president, secretary of state, speaker of the house? The only person they could hope to contact who could actually stop all this would be the President himself.

In less than two minutes Dave had returned to the car. Nicole unlocked the door and he slid in beside her.

He tossed the phone package her way and set the car in gear. "Where to?"

She gave him the directions he needed to get to John Smith's apartment and then dialed the phone number.

"Who are you calling?" Dave asked.

"Paul Jenkins."

"Should I know that name?"

"No. He's the brother of Kat Russell, another member of the SOS team. He might know how to get in touch with Kat. I hope she's still in D.C. with her husband, Sam."

Dave drove through the streets as the sun set over the capital. Streetlights blinked to life and the snarls of traffic eased up.

"Paul." Nicole let out a breath. "Tazer here."

Dave could barely think of Nicole as Tazer anymore. He'd learned her hardcore attitude had a lot more behind it than just a need to be tough. She'd been hurt. Played by someone who should have loved her instead of betrayed her.

"I know what's happening is wrong and I need to stop it." She glanced at Dave. "Do you know how I can get hold of Kat and Sam?" She paused to listen, nodding her head as she stared at the darkening streets in front of

them. "Yeah. I know the place... Thanks, Paul...I will."
She disconnected and tapped the cell phone against her
palm. "Change of plans. We should find Kat and Sam
first and put our heads together before I hit Smith up
for new identities." She leaned forward, studying the
street signs. "Head for K Street."

"K Street?" Dave asked. "Isn't that where all the
lobbyists work?"

"Yes, but it's also close to where the action is. Kat
and Sam have gone underground. Just go there. I know
where to find them."

Dave turned, a heavy feeling filling his gut. "You
sure about this?"

"Yes. If they haven't been discovered yet, their hide-
out is pretty safe."

"Famous last words," Dave muttered.

As they neared K Street in downtown D.C. the traffic had thinned considerably, yet there was still plenty
of lobbyists, politicians and support staff working late
and leaving for home after hours.

Once on K Street, Dave slowed. "Uh, remember
we're not exactly dressed for this neighborhood. We're
likely to draw attention."

"Just drive slowly until I tell you to turn." Nicole
leaned forward, her face illuminated by the streetlights, her gaze searching the buildings and storefronts.
"There!" She pointed toward a pizzeria with an alley beside it. "Drive down the alley. You'll see a garage at the
back of the alley. Park in front of it and wait in the car."

Dave pulled into the alley. Before he shifted into
Park in front of the garage, Nicole leaped out and, staying in the shadows of the buildings, hurried to a door
at the back of the pizzeria. She knocked twice and

waited, then knocked three times. Again, she waited and knocked once.

Dave could see her lips moving, but couldn't hear her voice. A moment later the door opened and she was yanked inside.

Dave sat forward, his hand on the door handle, ready to jump out and bust the door open.

Before he could do just that, the garage door in front of him lifted and a tall man with dark hair waved for him to enter.

Not feeling completely comfortable with a stranger urging him into a darkened garage, he shifted into gear and complied.

As soon as the car cleared the overhead door, it slid down, cloaking him in darkness for a moment before a light blinked on overhead and a face appeared in the window beside him.

Nicole opened the door for him. "Kat and Sam are here, but they're not staying for long. Kat's sources say there's a citywide manhunt on for me, her and any other SOS agents. Also, a photograph of you is floating around as a potential terrorist."

"Great." Getting around D.C. seemed even more of a challenge.

"Come on. We need to come up with a strategy and a place to hide until we can carry out the plan." Nicole glanced up at him. "How do you feel about wearing a mustache and beard?"

"Peachy. Just peachy."

Chapter 17

Nicole introduced Dave to Kat and Sam Russell as they pulled up seats around a card table set up in the back of the garage. Used as a storage space for extra chairs, large cans of tomato sauce and broken tables, the space was not the best, but it had a secret doorway leading into a hiding place with a bed and a dresser and cable television and internet. Sam had a laptop on the table in front of him, open and booted up.

Nicole couldn't believe they'd been cooped up so long and hadn't killed each other.

"How did you do it? I'd have been claustrophobic in the first ten minutes."

Sam waggled his brows. "We've had plenty to occupy us."

Kat's cheeks turned red and she elbowed Sam in the belly. "Yeah and all the pizza we could possibly eat."

Sam patted his flat belly. "So we could keep up our strength for all that occupied us."

Nicole's chest tightened at the way Sam and Kat teased each other, their love apparent in the way they exchanged glances and touched each other.

She envied them more than she'd ever admit. Without realizing it, her gaze shifted to Dave, sitting to her right. He still wore the biker clothing, looking as rough and sexy as he always did, if not more so. It didn't matter what he wore, his broad shoulders and narrow waist made everything look good on him.

Sam went on, "Working as an engineer in the wilds of Alaska, I thought I'd never hear these words come out of my mouth." He took a deep breath and announced, "I'm tired of pizza."

"You and me both." Kat sighed. "I'll be glad when I can have fresh lobster and elk steaks."

"Now you're talking." Sam hugged his wife. "It's too bad we weren't in Alaska when the crap hit the fan. It would have been easy to disappear up there and there would have been plenty of game to live off while things sorted themselves out down here in the lower forty-eight."

"Well, I believe we were here at the exact time and place for a reason," Kat said. "Tazer, Royce and Geek need our help. With everyone else on missions or laying low until the smoke clears, it's up to us to take care of the situation." She stood and walked to an old whiteboard probably used at one time to list the daily specials for the pizzeria. "We're intelligent people used to facing adverse situations. What have we got?"

Nicole waved the flash drive still wrapped in a piece of black plastic trash bag. "We have a corrupt chief of staff painting the SOS team as a bunch of terrorists to cover up the fact that he's the majority shareholder in a corporation selling arms to our enemy."

Kat gaped. "Seriously? That's what this is all about?"

Nicole pushed a hand through her hair. "I know it's hard to believe. The data on the flash drive is a list of the shareholders and their share percentage. It also contains copies of correspondence and emails exchanged between Brandon Ryan and Joseph Masterson, the President's chief of staff. The man owns 67 percent of a corporation responsible for the deaths of our soldiers in the Middle East."

"Bastard." Sam's lips thinned.

"Suggestions on how to bring him down?" Kat asked.

"Take the flash drive to the FBI and have them take it up with the chief of staff?" Sam offered.

Nicole shook her head. "No go. The director of the FBI is a golfing buddy of the chief of staff."

"NSA?" Kat suggested.

"Masterson used to lead the NSA. He's still got people loyal to him there. It could be our word against his. Or worse, they might cover up for him."

"So what you're telling me is that we can't trust anyone," Kat summed up.

Nicole nodded. "The only person who can override what the chief of staff has done is the President himself."

"And you have to get past the chief of staff to get to the President," Kat said.

Dave spoke up. "Would be nice to know what the President's schedule is for the next couple days."

"I might be able to help with that." Sam cracked his knuckles over the keyboard of his laptop and then entered a URL and pressed the touch pad. "Seems to me, the President is hosting a dinner tomorrow evening in the state dining room at the White House." Sam glanced up. "And we're in luck. It's a dinner in honor of the Women's Leadership Council. All we need to do is to find out who's going, make a couple of substitutions on the guest list and in the waitstaff, and we're in."

Nicole's heartbeat quickened. "Sam's right. This could be our best shot."

"Security is going to be tight. They'll be checking and double-checking the guest list as people arrive."

"Then we have to make sure we're on that list or that we *appear* to be on that list." Nicole leaned forward, warming to the idea.

"How so?" Dave asked.

"Kat and I are women. We replace two of the women scheduled to attend." Nicole's lips slipped into a smile. "I know of a makeup artist who used to work in Hollywood. She can make Richard Simmons look like Nicole Kidman."

Kat's eyes widened and a smile spread across her face. "If Dave and Sam can get in as waitstaff or as part of the security detail, we might have a chance of getting the President alone."

"Can we download the data onto a computer tablet small enough to fit in a purse but big enough the President will see his chief of staff's name on the list of shareholders?"

Sam glanced up from his laptop. "I'm pretty good with downloading data to a tablet. We use tablets out in the field all the time."

"This would all be so much easier if SOS headquarters was up and running," Kat lamented.

"Yeah, and if wishes were horses, we'd have fertilizer for a rose garden," Sam responded.

Nicole felt the first glimmer of hope since arriving in D.C. With Sam and Kat on their side, they stood a chance of getting past the chief of staff to gain an audience with the President.

"I'll contact my associate who gave me the decryption code to see if he can locate a list of the attendees and the seating chart," Nicole said. "The closer we can get to the President, the better."

"And once we know who we want to replace, we have to convince them not to go." Kat's eyes narrowed. "That might be tricky."

With the throwaway phone in her hands, Nicole walked to the other end of the garage to place a call to Zip using the special code they'd established.

He didn't answer the first time she tried. She went back to planning and waited an hour before trying again.

Just when she was about to give up, Zip answered. "Tell me this isn't Tazer and that you're not calling to ask for another favor. The last one cost me a move and the confidence of a couple of my long-standing clients."

"I'm sorry I got you in hot water, but this deal is turning out to be bigger than I'd originally thought."

"I take it the code worked." Zip's words were a statement, not a question.

Nicole smiled. The man was sure of himself and had a right to be. "It took three days to run, but it did the job."

"Must have run the entire gambit."

"It did. I'd almost given up hope."

"Oh, ye of so little faith." Zip laughed. "I have a reputation to uphold. And that's some of my best work."

"I know, and that's why I come to you when I need help." Nicole paused and then jumped in. "I need your help again. I hope this is the last time I have to ask for it."

"I'm not holding my breath."

"I wouldn't ask if it wasn't a matter of—"

"Life and death," Zip snorted. "Yeah, yeah. Tell me what you want so that I can laugh and hang up."

"I need the guest list and seating arrangement for tomorrow night's dinner honoring the Women's Leadership Council."

"The one the President is hosting at the White House?"

"Yes, sir."

"Is that all? You could have at least given me more of a challenge."

"How's this? I need the names of two of the female guests, their addresses, copies of their driver's licenses and passports and any documents the Secret Service might have issued to them for this event. I'll also need the same data on two of the staff at the White House who will be on duty during the event who are male and over six feet tall."

"Again, you could give me a more difficult challenge."

"I need it in the next two hours."

"I can't do it."

Nicole's hand tightened on the phone. This operation depended on them finding out as much as they could about the individuals they would be replacing. They'd need specifics for John Smith, the identity magician, to use to create the forms of identification that would be checked at the event. "Can't?" Nicole asked, her breath lodging in her throat.

"Not in two hours." He chuckled. "I'll only need an hour, if that much."

"You're killing me, Zip," Nicole breathed. "I owe you."

"Yeah, you do. I'll collect soon enough."

"Depositing it to the usual place?"

"If it hasn't been compromised." Zip paused, then added, "Tazer, just so you know…there's a price on your head."

"What?"

"The FBI is offering one hundred thousand dollars to anyone who'll bring you in alive."

Her stomach roiled and her hand shook. Not only did she have the good guys after her, every thug and bounty hunter in the country would be looking for her. The odds were stacking against her.

"Thanks for your help and for the heads up." She hit the end button and prayed Zip's phone was still secure and no one would trace the call to her location. Checking her watch, she noted they had an hour before they had what they needed to go to John for their new identities. That gave them one hour to study the layout of the White House entrances and ballroom. They'd only get one chance to make this happen. If they screwed up and got caught, they'd be buried in the deepest, darkest hole.

Apparently Joseph Masterson had that kind of clout, having used the forces at the President's disposal to launch his attack on the SOS agency. With the millions he must be making supplying arms to the enemy, he could afford to hire his own assassins to take care of his business.

Dave had been watching Nicole's back as she'd talked to her contact. Just before she'd hung up, she'd stiffened and her hand shook. What had she learned that had her upset enough to make her hand shake?

The woman was a rock who always had it together and never showed fear. A true professional. Dave had no doubt she was an excellent secret agent.

He'd begun to wonder what he had to offer in what amounted to an undercover spy mission in the Capitol. Their little band of misfits would be going in unarmed and surrounded by Secret Service agents who'd shoot first and ask questions later. Those trained bodyguards had a job to do to keep the President safe. The first sign of a threat and they'd have the commander in chief surrounded and whoever was threatening filled with bullets.

For the next hour the four of them made plans according to the floor diagram of the White House and the state dining room they'd found online. They'd also discussed how they'd hijack the ladies Kat and Nicole would be replacing.

Kat had a friend whose cousin worked for a car-for-hire business in the D.C. area. The service would send cars to the ladies' houses, pick them up, serve them champagne spiked with the equivalent of a truth serum drug that would allow them to have a good time, but block their memories of what had happened. They'd be driven all around D.C. until they got the word that the event was over. Then they'd be returned to their homes safe and sound, none the wiser.

At exactly one hour from the time Nicole had called her contact, she got on Sam's laptop and checked the drop site. All the information she'd asked for was there. With smooth efficiency, she downloaded it onto a clean flash drive Kat had in her supplies.

Nicole turned to Dave. "Do you want to sit this one out? Kat and I can handle this on our own."

His chest squeezed. "Aren't we a team?" He stood and held out his hand. "Didn't I get you off an island and all the way across the country?"

Her lips twitched. "You did."

"Doesn't that give me the right to finish this job?"

"I'm the one who's committed the crime. If I'm caught, I'll go to jail."

"Sweetheart…" He laced his fingers with hers. "Though I wasn't keen on harboring a fugitive to begin with, I've since come on board." He shook his head. "You're not getting rid of me yet."

"And here I thought you were only after truth and justice." She leaned into him, warming his front and making his groin tighten.

Sam and Kat smiled at them. "Don't mind us. We thought we were the only two lovebirds in the world."

Dave frowned. "Who said we were in love?" Love? He wasn't in love. He thought highly of Nicole and she was terrific in bed. But love?

"Yeah." Nicole slipped an arm around Dave's waist. "We're just really good as a team."

Kat snorted. "Team schmeam. Is that what you call it now?"

"Damn right." Dave swatted Nicole on her bottom. "Let's get moving. We have work to do."

Nicole glared at him. "I've clobbered dumber men for doing that."

"She has. I saw her face-plant a guy in a bar one time for brushing against her boob," Kat confirmed. "You have to be one brave man to try that."

"Time for face-planting later." Sam stood and clapped his hands. "Looks like we're all going. Take everything you'll need with you."

"We won't come back to the pizzeria. By now things are getting too sticky." Kat grimaced. "No pun intended."

"I might know of a place we can stay the night," Nicole said as they headed for the sedan.

Nicole and Dave claimed the front seats with Nicole driving.

Kat slid into the back, while Sam checked the alley, then opened the garage door.

Nicole backed out and Sam closed the garage door behind them. They headed out on K Street, once again headed for the not-so-upscale area of D.C.

Now that they had a plan, Dave was a little more optimistic. He had to trust that the secret agents, Nicole and Kat, had the experience of undercover ops and knew what they were doing. Things could go south really quickly if anyone got wind of what they were about to do.

Cape Churn and the life of a charter fishing boat captain seemed a long way away. Dave couldn't regret getting involved. What Masterson was doing was wrong. The men in his old unit and others were being killed due to a traitor in one of the highest political positions in the country. Dave was in it to see the man brought to justice.

If he was straight with himself, he would admit it wasn't just about the chief of staff and the weapons sales. One beautiful blonde-gone-redhead had a lot more to do with his decision to join forces with the members of the SOS to get this right.

He hoped they all lived to see Masterson brought down.

Nicole handled the driving like a pro. She knew her way around the streets, taking a zigzagging route to where she was going to make sure she wasn't being followed. By the time they arrived at the address she'd gotten from the liquor store owner, it was close to one o'clock in the morning.

Driving past the building, Nicole parked the vehicle in an alley a block away. "You all stay put while I wake John. I don't want him shooting at us or getting spooked and running."

Dave wasn't thrilled with her getting out in that particular neighborhood. Though it was the middle of the night, the die-hard partiers and sleazy characters were just leaving the local taverns and bars and wandering home. Some walked alone, others in groups.

After what had happened the previous evening, Dave wasn't taking any chances. He got out of the vehicle and followed Nicole to the street.

She turned and pressed a hand to his chest. "I thought I asked you to stay."

"You didn't ask. You told me to stay and, in case you haven't noticed, I'm not very good at following orders."

Nicole leaned into his chest. "Remind me to make you *want* to follow orders."

"Mmm." He captured her hand and pressed a kiss to her palm. "Sounds interesting."

She smiled up at him. "Guaranteed." With a quick peck on his lips, she turned to leave.

Dave hadn't let go of her hand and used it to pull her into his arms. "I'd feel better if I came with you."

"John would feel better if I showed up alone. He's already punchy."

"Understood. Not happy, but will keep an eye on you from here."

"Not that I've ever needed someone to take care of me, but…thanks." She walked away, hunched into her jacket, her hands in her belt loops, looking like any other loser schlepping around in the dark. When she reached the townhouse at the address she'd been given, she hurried down the steps to the basement apartment and knocked on the door.

Dave held his breath, hoping she'd been given the right address and that the identity guru would help them out. Once again, he was amazed by Nicole and her undaunted attitude and ability to go for what she wanted. Not many women had that much drive and determination or stomach for such dangerous missions.

When he returned to Cape Churn, he'd go back to his charter fishing business, without the constant danger and challenges he'd experienced in the past couple days. And since the first night with Nicole in the boat, he hadn't had another nightmare.

Maybe the slow pace and quiet life he'd been living hadn't been what he needed at all to get past the post-traumatic stress he'd been experiencing.

Perhaps he'd needed to feel challenged. Moving from being constantly on guard in the streets of Afghani villages to the unsettling quiet of the Oregon coast had been a major adjustment.

Nicole knocked again and waited. A few moments later the door jerked open and a man with a pasty-white face peeked out.

He couldn't hear their conversation from where he stood, but Dave could tell the man wasn't happy to be woken in the middle of the night.

After a long, fervent talk on Nicole's part, the man nodded and disappeared inside.

Nicole stayed where she was but raised her hand and waved Dave forward.

In turn, Dave went back to the car, knocked on the hood and tipped his head in the direction Nicole had gone. Sam and Kat got out and followed Dave to the basement entrance to John Smith's apartment.

Nicole had disappeared through the door by the time Dave returned with Sam and Kat. When he reached for the doorknob, it twisted easily in his hand and he pushed the door open into a tiny room with seven-foot ceilings. Papers, week-old pizza and boxes cluttered every surface except in front of the desk with a computer sitting on it. A webcam was perched on the corner of the monitor, pointing at a chair with a light blue sheet hung draped behind it as background. There were lights mounted on tripods on either side of the chair.

"Look, can we get a move on? I'd like to get to sleep, with what's left of the night," John grumbled. He wore a forest-green plaid bathrobe, his naked knees and bare feet as white as his face, and his thinning hair needed a cut and comb.

Nicole gave him the information Zip had provided and told him what she needed.

One at a time, the two men and the two women stepped in front of the camera. Using the DMV photos of the two ladies from the leadership council, John pieced together what he needed. Less than thirty minutes later he handed them driver's licenses, passports and credit cards with their adopted names. Kat and Nicole would have to apply sufficient makeup and the correct hairstyles to match their photos and pass off as the ladies they would be replacing. Likely the Secret Service would not only have a list but one with photos.

Done with his work, John Smith herded them toward the door. "Leave before someone finds you here."

Kat and Sam exited first. Dave followed, with Nicole bringing up the rear. She turned at the last minute and said something to John as she left. A stern frown dented her forehead, her voice low and urgent.

John's mouth pinched into a tight line and he nodded.

Nicole turned toward Dave. "I thought you'd be in the car by now."

"Just waiting on my partner." He held the door for her. "What was that all about?" Dave asked after the door closed behind her.

"I just told him to keep our visit to himself or he'd be the next one I face-planted on the floor."

"Can he be trusted?"

"Sometimes."

"Then let's get out of here."

"I'll second that." She jogged to where they'd left the car.

Dave glanced down the street left and right for any other vehicles before stepping into the alley.

Once again, Nicole took the wheel, zipping in and

out of the city streets, checking her rearview mirror every few seconds.

Dave checked the side mirror as often, an adrenaline rush rising inside him. He had that alertness that came when he felt danger creeping up on him from all sides.

"Where to?" Sam asked.

"The Jekyll and Hide," Nicole answered.

"The costume store in downtown D.C.?" Kat asked.

Nicole nodded. "That's the one."

"It's the middle of the night."

"I know the owner. She lives over the store and she's the one who'll be doing our makeup and outfits for the President's dinner tomorrow night."

The closer they got to downtown D.C. the more exposed Dave felt. "Are you sure this is a good idea?" The streets were clear, with very few cars to blend in among.

A Metropolitan Police Department vehicle passed them, heading in the opposite direction.

In the side mirror, Dave saw the taillights on the police car glow bright red as it stopped in the middle of the street.

"You see that?" he asked Nicole.

Nicole's gaze was on the rearview mirror. "I did."

She took a right at the next street, making it an easy, natural movement.

The police car performed a U-turn in the middle of the street.

As soon as the buildings on the sides blocked the police officer's view of their vehicle, Nicole slammed her foot to the accelerator and raced down the street to the next one and made a left turn.

"Tazer, honey," Kat said. "I think he might have seen

us take that left. I could see the hood of his car as we made the turn."

"Damn." Nicole gripped the steering wheel and turned into an alley, raced to the end and turned right on the next street. Zigzagging through streets and alleys, she found an alley with a couple of large trash containers and pulled in between them, parking the car and turning off the lights.

"I can just see the street at the end of the alley between the brick wall of the building and the trash container," Dave said.

Sam twisted around his seat. "I have a view of the other end of the alley."

A light shone at Dave's end and a car eased past. A spotlight shone into the alley, its beam rocking back and forth.

"Just don't hit the brake lights," Kat warned.

"Don't worry, I took my foot clear away from the brake," Nicole assured her.

"How far are we from the Jekyll and Hide?" Sam asked.

"About five blocks." Nicole reached for the key. "I think we've waited long enough. Let's go before MPD comes around the other end."

"Let's ditch the car and walk from here," Dave suggested.

"Good idea," Kat said. "If they suspect us for anything, the next time we might not be so lucky."

"Wait a minute or two more until we know that guy is well past us." After what felt like a very long time to Dave, Nicole reached for the door handle. "Okay. Let's go before he comes around the other end."

The four of them piled out of the car and moved toward the end of the alley where they'd last seen the patrol car.

On his feet, Dave felt more in control and able to react. He reached the corner of the building first and poked his head out enough to see both directions. "Clear."

The action put him right back in Afghanistan, moving through the residential areas, searching for insurgents. Only this time the streets were paved, the buildings were red brick and the night air was cool against his face, not radiating the residual heat of a desert summer.

"Tell you what," Sam said, "Kat and I will meet you there in fifteen minutes."

"He's right," Kat agreed. "Two people would draw enough attention. Four screams 'to be stopped and questioned.'"

Alone with Nicole for the first time in a couple hours, Dave tugged her hand and brought her close to his side as they started down the street, keeping within the shadows. When they encountered vehicles, they ducked behind bushes, trees or buildings.

Dave loved how quickly Nicole moved and how she seemed able to blend in with her surroundings.

"You know, when this is all over, remind me to buy you a beer," Nicole said.

"You don't owe me anything. Though a beer sounds good." Especially if Nicole came with it.

"You think we'll have half a chance to get close to the President?"

"We have to," Dave said.

She glanced up at him. "I believe you've bought into

this whole idea of taking down a high-powered politician."

"I don't have much patience for traitors, liars and self-serving bastards when good men and women are dying at their hands." He'd been faced with a similar situation when Mike had died taking a grenade to save those kids. He'd be damned if he let another man in a position of power sentence American soldiers or innocent children to death because of greed.

Nicole leaned on his arm. "Tomorrow will be difficult. We can only hope we can get close to the President."

"We can and we will," Dave said.

Chapter 18

Very familiar with the area, Nicole led Dave to Jekyll and Hide, arriving two minutes before Sam and Kat. She was glad they'd gotten there first so that she had time to wake the owner, Leslie Saunders.

The entrance to the upstairs apartment was at the back of the building, thankfully out of sight of the street. After knocking on the door several times, Nicole waited, finally hearing footsteps on the other side. There was a pause as Leslie peered through the peephole then removed the chain locks and dead bolts.

"Nicole, what are you doing here so late?"

"We need help."

"Please come in." Leslie stood back, welcoming them into her upstairs three-bedroom apartment, which was roomier than they'd expected and just what they needed.

Nicole paused on the threshold. "I have two more

with me." She turned as Kat and Sam appeared at the bottom of the steps.

"By all means. Any friend of Nicole's, and all that." Leslie urged them to come inside, as well. Wearing a delicate Oriental robe in light blue silk, her long, curly, platinum-blond hair bounced around her shoulders as she moved through the kitchen. In minutes she'd set up the coffeemaker, pulled crackers out of the pantry and cheese from the refrigerator.

The guys ate and downed coffee while Nicole picked at the crackers and cheese.

As they settled around her dining table, Leslie laid a hand on Nicole's arm. "It's been a long time since I've seen you."

"I know." Nicole's mouth twisted in a wry smile. "I've been out of touch, and I hope to fix that."

Leslie glanced at the clock over the stove. "Given the hour, I take it this isn't a friendly visit. What do you need help with?"

Nicole stared straight into Leslie's eyes, deciding to be blunt and truthful. The woman deserved to know. "We're on the run from every law-enforcement agency this country has to offer."

Leslie smiled. "You're kidding, right?" She glanced at the others' faces and frowned slightly. "Why? You haven't murdered anyone, have you?"

Nicole chuckled. "No, but I've been shot at more times than I care to admit in the past couple of days."

Leslie shook her head, her brow furrowing. "I don't understand. I know you, Nicole. You love this country more than anyone. You wouldn't do something that bad."

"Someone is determined to bring me down before I expose him."

"Who?" Leslie asked.

"I hope to reveal all tomorrow. Until then, you have to trust me—it's bad. I know it's a lot to ask, but we need a place to hide out for the night. We will understand if you'd rather not get mixed up with us. We can walk out that door and never let anyone know we stopped here."

"No way." Leslie grabbed her hands. "I trust you. You're one of the good guys. This man who's after you, you'll get him, won't you?"

Kat laid a hand on Leslie's shoulder. "We're going to do the best we can."

Leslie nodded. "Good." Her gaze shifted around the room. "Anything I can do to help besides putting you up for the night? And I mean anything, although I have to warn you, I'm no good with a gun."

Nicole laughed. "Actually there is something you can do, and it doesn't require your sharpshooter skills. However it does require your former Hollywood makeup artist skills."

Leslie's eyes widened and a smile spread across her face. "Now, *that* I can help you with."

Nicole told her what they needed and the time they'd need to be ready before they left for the President's dinner party.

"I'll collect all the supplies I need and we can get started in the morning." Leslie looked around at the four of them. "In the meantime, you all look like you could do with some rest."

"We could. It's late and none of us has had much sleep."

"Sam and Kat, come with me." She led them to the larger of two guest bedrooms, showed them the shared bathroom in the hallway and gave them fresh towels.

Nicole waited for her friend to finish with Sam and Kat. She wanted to spend the rest of the night with Dave. Call her selfish and stupid, but that's what she wanted and hoped he wanted it, too. The next day would be hard enough and she wasn't feeling very confident that it would all work out for the best. Any one of them could end up shot or incarcerated for sneaking into a dinner with the President disguised as one of the guests vetted by the Secret Service.

Leslie emerged into the living room. "Nicole, I can put you in the other guest bedroom and Dave can sleep on the couch."

Dave stepped up beside Nicole and slipped a hand around her waist. "I'll be with Nicole."

Warmth stole over her and she swayed into the strength of Dave's body.

Leslie looked to her for confirmation.

Her cheeks heating, Nicole nodded. "He's with me."

Leslie ducked her head, hiding her smile. "By all means. Come with me and I'll show you your room." She led the way.

Up until that point, Nicole had kept her private life private. By allowing Dave to declare they were sleeping in the same room, she'd opened herself up to examination by others, not just her own self-assessment.

Rather than being uncomfortable, Nicole realized she didn't give a damn who knew she was sleeping with Dave.

Leslie handed her a towel and showed her the bathroom. She hurried into her room and came back out carrying a fresh pair of panties and a frilly baby-doll nightgown. "Since you don't have any clothes with you, I thought you might appreciate clean lingerie." She winked at Dave. "Sorry, I don't have anything that'll fit you."

"That's okay," Dave said. "I sleep in the nude."

Nicole could have kicked him. Okay, so they'd be sleeping together. Anyone would assume at some point, they'd be naked, but to announce it? Her cheeks heated, but she squared her shoulders and looked Leslie in the eye, pretending she wasn't shocked by Dave's words.

Her face a bright pink, Leslie stepped back. "Well then, I'll leave you two to it. Good night."

"Thanks, Leslie," Nicole said. "You're a good friend."

The other woman touched Nicole's arm. "I'm just glad to see you again, and want to help in any way I can." Leslie slipped into her room and shut the door behind her.

Sam and Kat's door was closed, leaving Nicole and Dave in the hallway.

Suddenly shy, Nicole clutched the skimpy items to her chest. "I'll get the first shower." She dove for the bathroom, but before she could close the door, Dave pushed in behind her and closed the door.

"For a tough woman, you're running like you're afraid of something." He backed her up against the counter and slipped a hand around the back of her neck. "Are you afraid of me?" Dave bent, his lips hovering close to her ear, his breath tickling her throat.

She tipped her chin up, her shoulders straightening. "Of course I'm not afraid of you, or any other man."

When she tilted her chin, it exposed more of her neck

to the man and he took advantage of her move, swooping in to press a feather-soft kiss to the pulse beating at the base of her throat.

Nicole rested her hands against his shirt. "For a man about to corner the President and who might be going to jail tomorrow, you're taking your time now."

"Damn right I am. I want to prolong the pleasure." He unzipped the hoodie she wore and pushed it off her shoulders. "How do you do it?" He lifted the hem of her shirt and tugged it up her torso.

"Do what?" Nicole raised her arms and the shirt came off.

"Make looking like a bum a fashion statement."

She laughed. "Shut up and kiss me."

"Ah, now that's the Tazer I know and I—" He bent to press a kiss to her collarbone.

Nicole didn't realize she held her breath waiting for him to finish his sentence until he sucked her nipple into his mouth. She figured he'd caught himself before saying it. The L-word

Nicole's throat tightened and her eyes stung when she admitted to herself that she'd wanted him to finish the word. Wanted to hear him say he loved her.

She had fallen for the charter fishing boat captain. After only a few days with him, she'd done it again. Fallen for someone completely wrong for her. Only this man wasn't the lying, cheating bastard Rodney had been.

Dave was a tortured former soldier, who'd give his life to save others. Though he'd been reluctant to get involved, once he'd known the stakes, he'd jumped in with both feet, risking his life, his freedom and his reputation to help her. Damn it, Dave was a good man.

A deep sadness rippled across her. He'd started to say love, but stopped himself, because he wouldn't lie. The man didn't love her. Sure he enjoyed having sex with her, but love? No. She was too bossy and too afraid of commitment to be right for him. She'd always be on a mission, away from home. No relationship could last in those circumstances.

What about Kat and Sam? Or Creed and Emma? a little devil on her shoulder reminded her. *And there was Nova and Molly, too.*

Even if a relationship could work, Dave wasn't interested in one. All along, he'd been as adamant as she was about this ending when the chief of staff was revealed. He'd go back to the West Coast and she'd go on to her next assignment.

This meant that even if by some quirk of fate they accomplished their mission and the President was shown the evidence marking the traitor working by his side, this could be the last time she and Dave would make love.

Whether or not he loved her, Nicole wasn't giving up her chance to be with him one more time.

She shoved his jacket off his shoulders and ripped his shirt up over his head, and then trailed a line of kisses across his chin and down his throat.

"Hey, slow down." He chuckled and backed away to turn the water on in the shower. "We have all night."

"That's just it. We have tonight." She kicked off her shoes, unbuttoned her jeans and pushed them down over her hips, stumbling backward in her impatience.

He caught her and steadied her against his body. "You're going to hurt yourself."

"No, I'm going to hurt you if you don't get naked and

make love to me now." She flicked the button loose on his jeans and dragged them down his legs.

He kicked his shoes and pants to the side and followed her into the shower, pulling the curtain closed behind them. "So now it's making love? I thought it was *just sex*." He lifted her, wrapped her legs around his waist and pressed her back to the cool tiles of the shower stall. He held her up, his member barely nudging her entrance. "So, which is it?"

Nicole tried to ease down and take him inside, her body aching for him to fill her. "It doesn't matter," she said, her voice catching. She struggled to control the emotion rising up her throat. "I want you. From the looks and feel of it, you want me. We have the night. Let's not waste it."

He held her a moment longer, then shook his head. "You're a force to be reckoned with, Nicole."

"Shut up and make love to me."

"*I'll* give the orders from here on out."

"Fine, as long as you get down to business."

"There you go again, giving orders." He crushed his lips to hers.

He stole her breath away in a wild kiss that made her head spin and her body ache for more. When he let her up for air, she said, "See? If you'd just—"

"Shut up and feel," he said before his lips covered hers, cutting her off.

When he raised his head, Nicole tried again. "But I w—"

He turned with her still wrapped around his waist and ducked them both beneath the shower spray while letting her slide down over him.

"—want you," she sighed against his lips. Her arms

circled his neck and she threaded her fingers through his hair.

With water dripping down their bodies, he thrust into her again and again. She rested her hands on his shoulders, pressing against his rock-hard muscles to rise up, coming back down each time he drove deep inside her.

His body tensed and he thrust once more then withdrew and set her on her feet.

Nicole soaped her hands and ran them over his skin, reveling in the steely strength of his shoulders, arms, abs and thighs. Her hands stopped at his shaft, sliding the length with a soapy trail of bubbles.

He soaped her neck, her shoulders and slid down to lather her breasts, tweaking her nipples. He turned her to face the water and ran his hands over her back and down to her buttocks and stopped. "Enough," he growled.

"Hey, don't stop now." She leaned into him, her hands reaching behind her to capture his tight backside. "You can't stop. We've only just started."

He kissed the side of her neck. "To be continued." He slapped her bottom. "If you hurry."

Nicole rinsed the soap from her hair and body, stepped out of the shower and wrapped the towel around her. "What are you waiting for?"

"Kind of pushy, aren't you?" He stepped out and dried off, taking his sweet time.

Nicole tapped her bare toe, ready to get into bed and take up where they'd left off. "Could you go any slower?"

He finished toweling off, tossed the towel over the shower curtain rod and fished a condom from his wallet.

Nicole took it from his hands and slid it over his

member, her fingers lingering at the base, holding him, reveling in the power of his manhood.

Then Dave scooped her into his arms and carried her across the hall and into the bedroom they'd been assigned.

"Are you crazy? You're naked!"

"Really? What was your first clue?" He chuckled.

Nicole glanced back over her shoulder at the hallway, fully expecting Sam, Kat or Leslie to poke their heads out their doors to see what was going on.

Dave kicked the door shut, dropped her legs and let her slide down his body to her feet, then he yanked the towel off her. "That's more like it."

She stood in front of him naked, shivering with excitement and strangely sad.

Before she could say anything, he lifted her again and carried her to the bed. When she thought he'd toss her caveman-style, he set her down gently in the middle of the mattress and spread out beside her, leaning up on one elbow, staring down into her eyes.

She trailed her fingers over his chest. "I thought you were in a hurry."

"Not anymore. I want to make this night last." He leaned down and kissed her, sliding his tongue across the seam of her lips until she opened for him.

The kiss was gentle, tender and moved her more than anything else he'd done. It was as if he was saying goodbye.

When the thought struck her, it reinforced the fact that she didn't want what was going on between them to end. Nicole curled her hand behind his head and deepened the kiss, pulling him down over her. She couldn't get close enough to fill the hole that he'd leave in her heart when they went their separate ways.

Dave dragged his lips along the curve of her jaw, down the long line of her throat and lower to the swell of her breast.

Nicole curled her calf around the back of his thigh, urging him to take her.

He resisted, gently tasting her pebbling nipples, rolling them on his tongue and between his teeth, bringing her along for the ride as he ignited every nerve ending from her lips on down.

Dave didn't stop there, his hands skimming down her belly to the apex of her thighs. His lips following the same path until he parted her folds and dove in, tonguing her there until her fists bunched in the sheets and she raised her hips. Her body tensed, the sensations pulling her as tight as a bowstring.

One more flick of his tongue sent her shooting to the stars. "Dave!" she cried out.

"I'm here."

"Come…come with me." She entwined her fingers in his hair and tugged, urging him up her body until he slid into her in one long, hard drive.

Then the slow, gentle strokes grew more urgent, his control slipping until he rammed into her like a rutting beast.

She threw back her head, jammed her feet into the mattress and gave back, thrust for thrust.

The bed shook, the springs squealed and once or twice the headboard thumped against the wall.

Nicole reached her second climax as he reached his, her body rigid, his shaft throbbing inside her.

When they fell back to the mattress, she curled into

his side, her hand draped over his chest, the rapid beat of his heart thumping against her fingertips.

Wanting to stay awake throughout the night, she lay there, listening to him breathe, running her fingers over his skin, reading his body like a blind woman reads Braille. She wanted to memorize his touch, his smell, his voice. Though she tried to stay awake, before long her eyes drifted closed and she slept.

Dave lay awake until Nicole fell asleep. Their lovemaking had been more than he could have dreamed of and he hated that it was coming to an end. He couldn't be with her when he had too many issues of his own. But he didn't want to let her go... Soon he fell asleep, as well.

He didn't wake until the sun shone through the window into his face.

Nicole still lay in his arms.

He bent to kiss her gently, then slipped out of the bed. His clothes were still in the bathroom across the hall. He checked for early risers and when he determined the coast was clear, crossed the hall naked and entered the bathroom.

After a quick shower, he dressed in the biker clothes and combed his hair with his fingers.

Sam was exiting his room when Dave left the bathroom. "We have work to do this morning," he said.

Dave nodded. "We have to find the men we're replacing and get into the White House."

Nicole, wrapped in the big towel, peeked out the door to the bedroom she'd shared with him. "What's going on?"

"Sam and I are headed out," Dave said.

Nicole shoved a hand through her hair. "How will I know you got in?"

Dave smiled. "Same way I'll know how you got there."

Nicole tucked the corner of the towel in over her breast. "Be careful."

"Two things before I go." Dave pulled her into his arms and kissed her.

She melted against him, sliding her hands around his neck to hold him closer.

When he released her mouth, she blinked, gazing up into his eyes. "That was one?" she whispered.

"No. I downloaded the data to Kat's computer tablet. I'll sneak it into the White House somehow."

"That's one?" Nicole stared at his lips, hers slightly swollen from the previous night's kisses.

He smiled. "Yes. The second item is when this is all done and you get that information to the President, if we're not killed and if we're not tossed in jail, would you consider going out with me on a date?" He couldn't help himself, he had to ask. He couldn't let what they'd shared end. Not yet.

She laughed. "That's a lot of ifs."

"I'm an optimistic kinda guy."

Her lips twisted. "A relationship with me is doomed to fail."

"I'm not such a catch, either." He kissed her again, then looked into her eyes. "You didn't answer my question."

"If I'm not hauled away in a straitjacket, if I'm not sent to live out my life in a maximum security prison, and if I'm still sane when this is all over..." She smiled. "I'll go out with you on a date."

He nodded. "You're on." Dave looked over her shoulder at Sam. "We have a job to do. Let's make it happen."

"I'm ready."

Sam kissed Kat goodbye.

Dave thanked Leslie for her hospitality and left the apartment, his heart heavy, knowing the task ahead would be dangerous. He prayed he would see Nicole, as planned, later that evening in the White House state dining room. After all they'd been through together, this couldn't be the end.

Chapter 19

Nicole and Kat had done their homework on the ladies they would be impersonating at the President's dinner. They'd spent the day getting to know their life histories, their group of friends and downloading photos of their hairstyles and clothing preferences.

Leslie pulled out the tools of the great Hollywood makeup artists: paintbrushes, putty knives, colored pencils, shadows and liners. She caped Nicole and Kat and, using the photographs as her guide, applied light brown or gray lines with eyebrow pencils, giving them crow's feet around their eyes and deepening the lines on their foreheads. She toned down the healthy color of their skin, making them look just a little older.

As the owner of the most prestigious costume house in the city, she had every kind and color of wig imaginable. She worked the hairstyles to match the photographs.

Once she was done, she turned Nicole and Kat around to face the large mirror hanging on wall.

"Ladies, meet Kimberly Haskell and Nancy Fischer."

Nicole stared at the woman in the mirror as if she were looking at someone other than herself. She had soft brown hair that hung down to her shoulders in large, loose curls. Leslie had made her face look rounder, her nose narrower and her upper lip thin.

She'd given Kat highlighted, sandy-blond, shoulder-length hair that went well with her blue eyes and made her eyes tilt slightly like in Kimberly's picture.

"Holy crap, Leslie," Kat exclaimed. "Is that me?"

"No," Leslie replied. "That woman in the mirror is Kimberly Haskell. For tonight, Kat Russell does not exist."

Nicole stared at the picture taped to the mirror and then at the reflection. "You're amazing, Leslie." Hope swelled in her chest. "We might actually have a shot at getting in."

"I certainly hope so." Leslie straightened. "You two are some of my best work. I'd hate for it to go to waste."

Nicole rose from the chair and hugged her. "Thank you so much."

"Honey, we're not done yet. We have to dress you appropriately for dinner at the White House."

Nicole glanced down at her watch, her heart skipping several beats. "It won't be long before the drivers leave to pick up the real Kimberly Haskell and Nancy Fischer. I hope the plan to occupy them goes off without a hitch."

Kat and Nicole remained upstairs in the apartment

while Leslie went down the stairs to her store, currently being manned by one of her assistants. She returned within minutes with two long, gorgeous gowns draped over her arm. One was a slim-cut shimmering pearl pink with a sweetheart neckline and capped sleeves. A large rhinestone broach sparkled at the center of the neckline.

The other gown was a light mink-brown taffeta, sleeveless with a deep-cut V-neckline.

Leslie helped Nicole into the pink gown while Kat slipped into the brown.

"Five minutes until the car is due to arrive," Kat announced. "We need shoes and purses."

Leslie laid two pairs of heels at their feet. "I guessed on the size. I'm pretty good at it."

Nicole slipped her feet into the heels, surprised at how perfectly they fit. She slid her freshly made driver's license and passport into the matching clutch and looked one last time at her full-length reflection.

Kat stood beside her, looking like the mirror image of the photograph of Kimberly Haskell. She squeezed Nicole's arm. "This will be easy. Nothing can be as hard as running the Iditarod with a killer on your heels."

Nicole laughed. "You got that right." She held out her arm. "Ready to gain an audience with the President?"

"Dave has the data?"

With a nod, Nicole patted the broach between her breasts. "I've got the flash drive as backup."

"You don't think they'll frisk you or run a wand over you?"

"I'm counting on it. Hopefully the broach will disguise the presence of the flash drive."

A honk sounded outside the windows.

"Your chariot has arrived," Leslie said. She kissed Nicole's cheek. "I expect you to come back and tell me all about it."

"If not," Kat said, "tune in to the national news. You might see your creations hauled out of the White House."

"No way. This is going to work." Nicole gripped her clutch, squared her shoulders and headed for the door. "Come on, there's a devious son of bitch we need to take down."

Kat chuckled, following her out onto the landing. "I like your attitude."

Dave and Sam had managed to slip past security at the servants' entrance to the White House by arriving with the designated high-end caterer providing the additional waitstaff for the event. He and Sam had showed up early that morning to help set up the dining room. Dave had slipped the computer tablet into a box of food supplies before it was carried into the building.

Dressed in black suits, white shirts and skinny ties, their hair slicked back and neat, they hurried to place the charger plates, napkins and utensils exactly as instructed.

By noon, they were excused to leave while the bomb-sniffing dogs made a pass through the dining room and the rest of the building to ensure the safety of the guests that would be arriving later that evening.

Dave and Sam moved to stay out of the way of the dog handlers when they came through. Dave recovered the computer tablet from the box he'd stashed it in and found a new hiding place for it among the gold-colored napkins in the linen closet.

"Now all we have to do is work and wait," he whispered to Sam.

When the dog handlers declared the room clear, the waitstaff returned to complete the setup.

As the hour neared, Dave was busy filling glasses with water and popping corks on the wine bottles. He and Sam, along with the entire staff, were briefed on their duties and responsibilities.

For a man who'd never eaten at a place setting with more than one fork, it was baffling to Dave. The splendor was overwhelming and everything had to be placed exactly.

He couldn't wait to get back to Cape Churn where mac-and-cheese was acceptable cuisine, eaten on a paper plate with a single plastic fork.

While concentrating on blending in, he wondered how things were going for Nicole and Kat in their preparations to enter the front door.

Every strange sound made him flinch as he prepared for the event of one of them being caught with their fake identities. Tension was high and faking being calm was wearing on his nerves. And he'd thought fighting the Taliban in Afghanistan was nerve-racking.

As the hired car drove toward the White House, Nicole received word on her throwaway phone that their doubles had been collected and the wine had set in.

Feeling a little more at ease, she went over the information she could remember about Nancy Fischer. By arriving as fashionably late as possible, she hoped to avoid uncomfortable chitchat with Nancy or Kimberly's acquaintances. From the copy of the seating chart Zip had obtained, none of the names at the tables where Nancy and Kimberly were assigned were identified as close friends. But that didn't mean they hadn't met before.

All too soon, the limousine pulled up to the front of the White House and an attendant opened the door for them.

Nicole stepped out and turned to Kat, smiling. "Ready?"

Kat returned the smile with a sophisticated one of her own. "Yes, indeed I am."

Together they entered the White House on the State Level into the beautifully decorated entrance hall where other invited guests had gathered.

Their first hurdle was in the form of a Secret Service agent with a formal guest list, checking IDs against the printed photos and names in his book.

Nicole handed him her driver's license and waited, glancing around as if to find familiar faces. She glanced at the agent's hand moving down the list then sliding across on the line with Nancy's photo. He glanced up at her face, checked her ID again then paused. Nerves were getting the better of her. "Kimberly, darling, is it true the Schwarzeneggers will be here tonight?"

Kat fell in with her playacting. "I don't know. Clooney was here at the last state dinner. I wish we'd been there for that one. He's so handsome."

The agent's eyes narrowed and he glanced at Nicole again, then at the photo on the page. Finally he handed her the ID. "You're clear, Ms. Fischer."

Kat handed her ID to the agent and smiled. "That's such an awful picture of me. Why do photos have to be so bad at the DMV? Wouldn't it be nice if they'd let us bring our own?"

"Oh, look!" Nicole raised up on her toes. "Isn't that John?"

Kat pivoted beside her. "I believe you're right."

The agent handed back her ID and said, "You're clear, Ms. Haskell."

"Thank you, young man." Kat snatched the card from the man and hurried after Nicole. "If we hurry, we can catch him before the President arrives. I want to ask after his mother."

Once they'd cleared security, Nicole could breathe again. She leaned close to Kat, smiling at the crowd as she whispered, "I'd prefer to stay out of sight as long as possible in case we bump into someone we're supposed to know."

"I'm with you, Nancy. Lead the way."

Nicole already knew what table she and Kat would be sitting at. It was one table over from the President and near the front of the room.

Pausing near a statue and a potted plant, Nicole scanned the entrance hall. "Have you seen the men yet?"

"No. I'm sure they won't be here. They're probably in the dining room helping set up. But it looks like the President is about to arrive."

The Marine Band drummers and buglers played a round of ruffles and flourishes to get the attention of all the guests.

Everyone turned to watch the President, First Lady and the special guest of honor, the prime minister of India, descend the grand staircase. As they reached the bottom, the band broke into a rousing rendition of "Hail to the Chief."

The President and First Lady smiled and nodded at

the crowd, then turned as the U.S. flag was presented by the marine corps color guard while the band played the "Star-Spangled Banner." The national anthem of India was played next as India's national flag was presented.

Soon after, the reception line was established and each of the guests was introduced to the President and the First Lady who, in turn, introduced the guest to the prime minister.

One by one the crowd moved through until Nicole and Kat were next to be introduced.

Nicole wanted more than anything to grab the President then and there and tell him what she'd come to say. She could feel the words forming on her lips and she was on the verge of blurting them out. In her peripheral vision, she spotted the chief of staff, Joseph Masterson, standing in the line of dignitaries farther along. When she turned to confirm, she could swear he was staring straight at her, his eyes narrowed.

Rage shot up in her veins, heating her cheeks and making her blood boil. Masterson stood there among highly decorated soldiers and sailors and the color guard representatives from every branch of the U.S. military, shaking hands and smiling as if he belonged, and was a part of making the country great.

Then she couldn't think about the lying traitor because she was being introduced to the President.

"Mr. President, this is Ms. Nancy Fischer of the Women's Leadership Council."

"Ms. Fisher, let me introduce you to…" The President turned to the Indian prime minister and the rest was a blur as she was handed down the line of dignitaries.

When she came to the chief of staff, she fumbled

with her clutch, anything to have an excuse not to shake hands with the bastard.

Masterson's lips firmed briefly, but he recovered and Nicole moved on down the line.

When they'd completed shaking hands, all Nicole wanted to do was to grab a bottle of hand sanitizer. What a bunch of hooey. She obviously wasn't cut out for pomp and circumstance. Or was it that she couldn't stand being in the same room as a man responsible for the deaths of his own country's men? For all the tall ceilings and spacious setting, the room seemed to grow warmer by the minute.

"Holy hell, Tazer." Kat caught up to her. "I thought you were going to blurt out why you'd come in front of the President and everyone."

"Isn't that what we're going to do?" she said.

Kat's lips thinned as she stared back toward the reception line. "It was all I could do not to slug Masterson in the face."

Nicole smiled, some of the tension leaving her, determination stiffening her spine. "We'll get him."

Once every guest had been introduced, the President and the First Lady led the Indian prime minister down Cross Hall to the state dining room, closely followed by a gaggle of Secret Service agents.

The guests followed, keeping a distance from the presidential entourage.

By the time they entered the state dining room and found their table, Nicole was ready for it all to be over. She struggled to keep from marching over to the president and demanding he arrest his chief of staff.

Masterson sat at the President's table on the President's left. The Indian Prime Minister sat on the opposite side of the President.

Nicole and Kat sat one table over, with a wide gap between the tables.

"There they are," Kat whispered in her ear as she stood behind her assigned seat and waited for the Commander in Chief to take his seat, signaling to the rest of the guests that they could take theirs, as well.

Across the room, Dave and Sam stood against the wall with the other waitstaff, blending in, waiting for the dinner to start.

The President, the First Lady and the prime minister took their seats and the rest of the guests followed their lead.

Unobtrusively as possible, the four-course meal was served, the waitstaff slipping in like shadows, depositing beautifully prepared entrées in front of them.

As appetizing as the food was, Nicole couldn't manage to eat more than a bite or two, her gaze straying to the President, wondering when Dave would make his move to slip the computer tablet in front of the man.

The more she studied the bodyguards and Secret Service men positioned nearby, she couldn't imagine Dave getting close enough to actually hand off the tablet without being dragged out before completing the task.

The meal progressed and a speaker rose to the podium introducing himself as a member of the prime minister's scientific community who was there to announce the joint venture between India and the United States to design and build the next craft capable of flying to the moon and back.

An overhead projector displayed the concept on a

screen behind the speaker as the man gave a brief description.

The audience clapped as the next course was slid onto the table in front of the guests.

Nicole glanced up in time to see Dave make his move. Her heart lodged in her throat as he weaved between the tables, headed for the President's table, a tray balanced on his shoulder.

She touched Kimberly's arm and whispered, "Here we go."

Dave broke protocol and instead of heading to the table he'd been assigned made a beeline for the President's table. It was now or never. First he had to create a diversion to distract the chief of staff.

When he got close enough, he quickly bent over the chief of staff and knocked over his wineglass, spilling it into Masterson's lap.

The man jumped up from his chair. "What the heck? Get me something to clean this mess up."

Sam appeared at the chief's side with a hand towel and dabbed at the man's suit jacket, turning him away from the President.

"My apologies, sir," Dave mumbled. The Secret Service agents rushed forward. Before they could reach them and while Masterson was occupied, Dave slipped the computer tablet into the President's lap and whispered into the man's ear. "Look at this data, Mr. President. Your chief of staff is a traitor."

Before he could verify the President got the message, a waiter came rushing forward with another Secret Service agent. "He is not the assigned waiter to the President. I am."

A flurry of movement erupted around them and Dave was jerked away from the President and shoved between the tables toward the exit. As he and Sam were hustled off, a hushed excitement filled the room.

Some of the ladies gasped and stood. Men rose to see what was going on.

Dave tried to look back to see if the President had reviewed the data. It was then he saw the chief of staff snatch the computer tablet from the President's lap.

Nicole was sitting close enough to the disturbance to hear Masterson say, "Obviously the man is deranged. I don't know how he got past our security screening." He took the tablet from the President. "I'll get this out of here. For all we know, it might explode."

Nicole's heart plummeted as she watched her chances of bringing this man to justice fly out the window. She stood and pressed a hand to Kat's brow. "Kim, darling, you look pale. Are you feeling all right?"

Kat stood and swayed. "No, I don't. Could you see me to the ladies' room?"

Nicole led her toward the podium as if she would swing around the room and find her way out the other side. On the way, she was jostled by Secret Service agents and bodyguards hurrying to surround the President, First Lady and the prime minister of India.

Nicole took an elbow to the side of her head and felt her wig shift. Pressing her hand to the disguise, she pushed forward.

With the guests' attention on Dave and the President, Kat made her move, pretending to fall against the speaker's stand.

The man left his position to help her.

Nicole slipped behind the podium while the speaker dropped down to check on the downed woman.

Kat lay on the ground, an arm over her forehead, glancing up at Nicole standing behind the podium. "Uh, Nancy, honey, I believe your wig slipped."

Nicole slapped a hand to her head to adjust, but it was too late. Joseph Masterson had circled behind them and stood within a few feet of Nicole. He had three Secret Service agents with him and he pointed at her. "Arrest that woman. She's the one on the Wanted posters that have been circulating all around the country. She's a known terrorist suspected of planning an attack on the President of the United States."

The people standing closest to them gasped and backed away. A woman screamed and some scrambled from their seats, heading toward the exits.

More agents rushed forward, surrounding Nicole. They grabbed her arms and pulled them behind her back, zip-tying her wrists together.

"I'm not a terrorist," she called out. "I'm a citizen of the United States of America, and I'm here to tell you there's a traitor among you."

"Get her out of here," Masterson urged the agents holding her.

"I can prove it," she said as they hauled her toward the exit. "Look at the screen. It says it all. Chief of Staff Masterson is selling arms to our enemies. Weapons that are killing our soldiers and our allies' soldiers."

"She's lying," Masterson said. "Get her out of here."

"No, wait." The President stepped forward, his body-guards close beside him. "What is this you have on the screen?" He pointed to the overhead where a list displayed types of weapons and quantities and the recipients of each.

Nicole struggled against the hands holding her. "It's the manifests of weapons being sold to the Taliban by Ryan Technologies."

The screen changed and the shareholders' names were displayed with the percent of ownership plain for all to see.

Nicole nodded toward the data. "Joseph Masterson owns 67 percent of Ryan Technologies."

"Mr. President." Masterson stepped between the President and Nicole. "Are you going to listen to her, a known terrorist, or me, your chief of staff?"

"Masterson has been making the decisions at Ryan Technologies based on the emails he's been sending back and forth to Brandon Ryan." Nicole stood straight, shoulders thrown back, ready to do battle. "He's a traitor."

"She's lying," Masterson repeated.

"Ask him where he's keeping Royce Fontaine," Nicole shouted. "Ask him on what grounds he's holding him."

Masterson turned toward the bodyguards. "Take her away. She's disturbed the guests enough."

The hands on her arms tightened, but the men holding her waited for a command from their President.

"No." The President raised his hand. "I want to hear what this woman has to say." He turned to his guest. "Please excuse me while I speak with these two women in private.

"Secure the device from the computer," the President ordered. An agent removed the flash drive from the computer and handed it to the President.

Then Nicole and Kat were escorted to a room down the long hallway where they were told to wait until the President joined them.

Out of sight of the flash drive, Nicole worried it would be destroyed or lost. After all they'd gone through to attain the data and get it to D.C., she imagined the worst.

"He's taking a long time," Nicole worried aloud.

"Trust him to do the right thing," Kat assured her.

"They got the guys out before the President could stop them. I hope they're not in danger."

Kat nodded. "Me, too. It's hard to find a man like Sam. I'd hate to live without him."

Nicole's thoughts went to Dave. Images of him behind the steering wheel of the *Reel Dive* flashed through her mind. The sun in his long hair, a smile on his face, him helping his clients bait their lines and how he'd held her in the cabin on the island.

Every moment she'd experienced with Dave flitted through her memories, making her want to run out of the room to find him. He had to be all right. Surely the chief of staff hadn't taken them somewhere to be disposed of.

By the time the President entered the room, Nicole was ready to get it over with and find Dave.

The Secret Service agents frisked Nicole and Kat and then the President waved them away. "Wait outside."

The men left the room and it was just Nicole and Kat, alone with the President.

"Tell me what's going on. It appears I've been kept out of the loop. What's this about Royce? The SOS is mine to command. I would have known if they had been tampered with."

"Unless your chief of staff did the tampering and kept it from you." Nicole told the President all that had happened and that the information he needed to put Masterson away could be found on the flash drive.

"Do I want to know how you obtained this information?" he asked.

Nicole straightened her shoulders. "Sir, the SOS does what it takes to protect this country and the men and women who serve it."

The President's lips quirked at the edges. "That's right. I'll have Royce and the others released as soon as possible."

"And, sir, the men who tried to give you the tablet earlier. They're not part of the SOS." Nicole smiled as she continued. "Though they should be. They were helping me get to you with the information."

The President nodded. "Don't worry, I'll take care of them, as well. I must say I'm shocked and disappointed at my chief's betrayal. However, the show must go on, and I have guests waiting. Now, will you join me for the rest of an important and highly interrupted state dinner?"

Nicole smiled. "If you don't mind, sir, I'd prefer to see to the others of our party and get some rest."

He turned to Kat. "And you, Ms. Russell?"

"I'm with Tazer. We're pretty beat. Hiding in plain sight is exhausting."

"I'll have my men call off the manhunt for the terrorist Nicole Steele. Seems she's on our side." The President straightened and gave Nicole and Kat a salute. "Thank you for your service." Then he left the room, immediately surrounded by Secret Service agents.

Nicole hugged Kat. "We did it."

A moment later a man entered the room dressed in a black suit like all the other Secret Service agents. "If you'll follow me, I'll take you out to your car."

"Not without Dave and Sam."

"The gentlemen to whom you're referring are waiting for you outside the White House."

"Why didn't you say so in the first place?" Nicole hurried through the door.

Kat followed, chuckling. "In a hurry, Tazer?"

"Damn right." She couldn't wait to see that Dave was all right. As she neared the exit, her feet slowed. They'd resolved the threat to the nation. Royce and Geek would be freed and the SOS would continue to exist. She'd still have a job to do.

Where would that leave her and Dave?

When she stepped outside the White House into the cool night air, Dave stood in his black suit, looking so handsome it made her throat constrict.

Kat ran into Sam's arms and he swung her around, yelling, "We did it!"

Nicole stood on the steps, staring down at Dave, wondering what he was thinking, if he was glad that the operation was over and was counting the minutes until he could get back to his life in Oregon.

Then he opened his arms, a gentle smile spreading across his face.

Nicole ran down the steps and fell into those strong arms. She'd never felt so content than in that moment. But still, she didn't know where they stood.

"See? I told you it would be okay." Dave held her close, then bent to kiss her. "I've been wanting to do that since I saw you enter the state dining room."

"Now, how would that look for the waitstaff to be

kissing one of the President's guests?" She laughed shakily, having been more afraid than she'd ever been. "I have to admit, I much prefer being the hunter, not the hunted."

He pushed the wig hair out of her face. "Or the fisherman, not the fish?"

"Something like that." She rested a hand on his chest, feeling the beat of his heart beneath her fingers. And it was beating as fast as hers. "So, Fish Boy, where to from here? Are you headed back to Oregon?"

"That depends on you." He brushed his lips across hers. "I kind of like having you around."

Her heart swelled, but she was afraid to let herself get too excited. "And if my job is here?"

"I'm not sure how that'll work, I like Cape Churn. It's grown on me."

"Long-distance relationships are risky." She fiddled with the button on his jacket.

"A relationship with a man with my issues could be even riskier. I'm not any good for you, Nicole."

"You're kidding me, right? After all you did to get me to D.C. alive and you think you're not good for me? I've never known any man willing to go to the lengths you did for me and for your country. You're a better man than you know, Dave Logsdon."

"You tell him!" Kat said.

"Besides, isn't it my decision what I think is good for me?" Nicole threw hesitation and self-doubt to the wind, choosing to go for broke. She leaned up on her toes and kissed him. "Are you willing to walk away from this?" She kissed him again. "Are you willing to give up making love with me onboard the *Freedom's Price* or in a cabin on an island?" Another kiss followed the first but he held still, his hand on her waist, but not pulling her closer.

"I thought you said it was just sex."

"Not for me," she said. "I only said that because I didn't want to admit what was happening."

"And what was that?"

"I was falling in love with a man who turned out to be my hero." She pressed her lips to his once more then stepped out of his arms. "So what's it gonna be? Am I going to get that date you promised, or are you going to prove me wrong and walk away? Which I might add would not be very heroic."

Dave stood for a second longer, making Nicole's heart skip several beats before a smile curled his lips and he swept her up into his arms. "We have a date." He kissed her soundly. "And we'll have another one after that. Then we can work on the logistics of a long-distance relationship." He winked. "Yeah, you heard me right, I said relationship."

Nicole wrapped her arms around his neck and pressed her forehead to his. "And what made you change your mind about relationships, big guy?"

"I never thought I'd meet a woman strong enough to put up with me until I met you. A woman who believes in championing a good cause, whether it's to fix a broken soldier or to nab a traitor." He tipped his head back. "And what made you change your mind, Ms. I Don't Do Relationships?"

"I finally met a man who believed in me and something bigger than himself, his country."

"If you two are done making a spectacle of yourselves in front of the White House, maybe we could find hotel where we can get out of these dresses."

"She's got the right idea." Dave squeezed Nicole. "I wouldn't mind getting out of this penguin suit." He carried her toward the waiting vehicle and set her on the seat. "Let's get out of here."

Sam and Kat followed. The driver stood beside the limousine, holding open the door. As Nicole and Kat slid across the seats, the driver asked, "Where to?"

As one, the four of them said, "The nearest hotel with king-size beds."

Nicole leaned against Dave, her heart swelling so big she thought it would explode in her chest. She'd met her match, found a hero and had hope for the future with a man like no other. She truly was blessed.

* * * * *

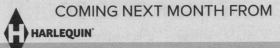

REQUEST YOUR FREE BOOKS!
2 FREE NOVELS PLUS 2 FREE GIFTS!

✦ HARLEQUIN®

ROMANTIC suspense

Sparked by danger, fueled by passion

YES! Please send me 2 FREE Harlequin® Romantic Suspense novels and my 2 FREE gifts (gifts are worth about $10). After receiving them, if I don't wish to receive any more books, I can return the shipping statement marked "cancel." If I don't cancel, I will receive 4 brand-new novels every month and be billed just $4.74 per book in the U.S. or $5.24 per book in Canada. That's a savings of at least 14% off the cover price! It's quite a bargain! Shipping and handling is just 50¢ per book in the U.S. and 75¢ per book in Canada.* I understand that accepting the 2 free books and gifts places me under no obligation to buy anything. I can always return a shipment and cancel at any time. Even if I never buy another book, the two free books and gifts are mine to keep forever.

240/340 HDN F45N

Name _____ (PLEASE PRINT) _____

Address _____ Apt. # _____

City _____ State/Prov. _____ Zip/Postal Code _____

Signature (if under 18, a parent or guardian must sign) _____

Mail to the Harlequin® Reader Service:
IN U.S.A.: P.O. Box 1867, Buffalo, NY 14240-1867
IN CANADA: P.O. Box 609, Fort Erie, Ontario L2A 5X3

Want to try two free books from another line?
Call 1-800-873-8635 or visit www.ReaderService.com.

* Terms and prices subject to change without notice. Prices do not include applicable taxes. Sales tax applicable in N.Y. Canadian residents will be charged applicable taxes. Offer not valid in Quebec. This offer is limited to one order per household. Not valid for current subscribers to Harlequin Romantic Suspense books. All orders subject to credit approval. Credit or debit balances in a customer's account(s) may be offset by any other outstanding balance owed by or to the customer. Please allow 4 to 6 weeks for delivery. Offer available while quantities last.

Your Privacy—The Harlequin® Reader Service is committed to protecting your privacy. Our Privacy Policy is available online at www.ReaderService.com or upon request from the Harlequin Reader Service.

We make a portion of our mailing list available to reputable third parties that offer products we believe may interest you. If you prefer that we not exchange your name with third parties, or if you wish to clarify or modify your communication preferences, please visit us at www.ReaderService.com/consumerschoice or write to us at Harlequin Reader Service Preference Service, P.O. Box 9062, Buffalo, NY 14269. Include your complete name and address.

HRS13R

SPECIAL EXCERPT FROM

HARLEQUIN®

ROMANTIC suspense

When Josh Patterson, Marine Corps sniper, is sent on an
op to rescue a woman kidnapped from her charity nursing
work deep in the Amazon jungle, he gets more than he
was prepared for in the brave Aly Landon.

Read on for a sneak peek of

JAGUAR NIGHT

by Lindsay McKenna, part of the
COURSE OF ACTION: THE RESCUE
anthology coming September 2014 from
Harlequin® Romantic Suspense.

Glancing at her, he saw that she had gone even more ashen.
She kept touching her neck. Damn. He turned, kneeling
down. Taking her hand away, he rasped, "Let me." She nodded, allowing him to examine the larynx area of her throat.
When he pressed a little too much, she winced. But she
didn't pull away. Aly trusted him. He dropped his hands to
his knees, studying her.

"You've got some cartilage damage to your larynx. It has
to be hurting you."

Aly nodded, feeling stricken. "I'm slowing us down. I'm
having trouble breathing because that area's swollen."

"You're doing damn good, Aly. Stop cutting yourself
down."

She frowned. "Are they still coming?"

"They will. Being in the stream for an hour will buy us some good time." He glanced down at her soaked leather boots. "How are your feet holding up?"

"Okay."

He cupped her uninjured cheek, smiling into her eyes. "Who taught you never to speak up for yourself, Angel?"

Josh closed his eyes. Aly was a trouper, and she did have heart. A huge, giving heart with no thought or regard for herself or her own suffering. He leaned down, pressing a kiss to her brow, and whispered, "We're going to get out of this," he rasped, tucking some strands behind her ear.

He watched Aly's eyes slowly open, saw the tiredness in them coupled with desire. Josh had no idea what the hell was going on between them except that it was. Now he had a personal reason to get Aly to safety. Because, general's daughter be damned, he wanted to know this courageous woman a lot better.

Don't miss
COURSE OF ACTION: THE RESCUE
by Lindsay McKenna and Merline Lovelace,
coming September 2014 from
Harlequin® Romantic Suspense.

Copyright © 2014 by Eileen Nauman and Merline Lovelace

HRSEXP0814

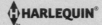

ROMANTIC suspense

UNDERCOVER IN COPPER LAKE
by Marilyn Pappano

A past he'd rather forget, a future he secretly longs for...

DEA informant Sean Holigan never imagined he'd return
to Copper Lake and revisit the ghosts of his past. But bad
memories aren't the only thing waiting for him. With their
mother in jail, Sean's nieces are in the care of their foster
mother, Sophy Marchand. Years and miles haven't erased
Sean's high school memories of the young, studious
Sophy, but she certainly has grown up. Beautiful and
benevolent, Sophy represents a life, and love, Sean longs
for—and one of three lives he must protect. Targeted by
ruthless killers, Sophy and the girls depend on Sean...
almost as badly as he depends on them.

Look for UNDERCOVER IN COPPER LAKE
by Marilyn Pappano in September 2014.

Available wherever books and ebooks are sold.

Heart-racing romance, high-stakes suspense!

www.Harlequin.com

HRS27886